WALKING THE RAZOR

ORLANDO A. SANCHEZ

Published by: Bitten Peaches Publishing

Cover Art: Deranged Doctor Design www.derangeddoctordesign.com

ABOUT THE STORY

The brightest light casts the darkest shadow.

Would you kill to save a life?

In order to save those closest to him, Tristan has stepped closer to darkness.

In order to save Tristan, Simon must do the impossible.

When Monty uses blood magic, he enters a schism—which puts him, and everyone close to him, in mortal danger. His use of blood magic has alerted the Black Orchid, a mage sect tasked with apprehending and eliminating dark mages.

Now, Simon, with help from Monty's closest allies and family, must find a way to stop him from going over to the darkness. If they fail, Monty will surrender to darkness, the Black Orchid will attempt to eliminate him, and Evers will be one step closer to her goal: the destruction of magic.

No one said it was ever easy in the Montague & Strong Detective Agency.

"Come on! Do you want to live forever?"
-Daniel Daly
First Sergeant of the 73rd Machine Gun Company

"When you light a candle, you also cast a shadow."
-Ursula K. Le Guin

ONE

I stepped out of the conference room and into a green flash.

Grim Whisper was in my hand a split second later.

"Put that thing away, boy, before someone gets hurt—starting with you."

It was Dex. An angry-sounding Dex.

I holstered my weapon and realized Dex wasn't alone, which would've been bad enough. Two figures were standing next to him. I squinted as my eyes adjusted to the aftereffects of the teleportation circle Dex used.

It was TK and LD.

Dex was dressed in his mage casual look: gray dress shirt, blue jeans, and work boots. Actually, I was surprised he was dressed at all. LD was dressed similarly, opting for a black T-shirt instead of the more formal dress shirt. Only TK looked out of place. She was wearing black combat armor and appeared ready to take on a group of enemies. For her, this was mage casual.

LD gave me a quick look of sympathy that said, *Brace*

yourself while TK glared at me as if I had broken into Fordey and stolen an artifact of value. It wasn't a good look. On the glare-o-meter, not even a Clint Glint could withstand TK's withering gaze.

"You didn't think to call us?" TK said, her voice slicing through the air like a scalpel through skin. "You actually thought it best to tackle this situation on your own?"

I looked at LD, who shook his head.

"Monty said not to call you?" I answered, knowing it was the wrong answer. "It was his idea. He said it would protect you."

"Protect us?" TK replied, and I took a step back. Her two words expressed anger, disappointment, and more anger. She was pissed. "He can barely protect himself. Especially now."

"Are you daft, boy?" Dex said, placing a gentle crushing hand on my shoulder, making me wince. "We should have been the first on the scene. Now you have to deal with"—Dex glanced at Jessikah—"the Black Orchid."

He said the sect name like a curse.

"Whoa," I said, raising my hands. "I didn't call her. She just showed up."

"They usually do," TK said, narrowing her eyes at me. "Like mold or an unwanted growth. We'll deal with her in a moment. What did you do?"

"I didn't do anything," I said, suddenly defensive. "Monty used blood magic...I couldn't stop him from casting again, and then..."

"I wasn't referring to that," TK answered. "Your energy signature is a mess, more so than the last time I saw you. What did you do?"

"I don't know."

"Ach, boy," Dex said, glancing at me. "She's right. You're a proper mess."

"Thanks, I'll deal with it."

"Not on your own you won't," TK said. "We'll deal with it. But first, your guest."

Dex stepped around me and looked at Jessikah closely.

"Farsight Division?" he asked, then pointed at the large black cat. "A Daughter of Bast? Well, at least they're taking this seriously. How many seconds?"

Jessikah stood frozen in place, her expression one of shock. The cool, collected Black Orchid agent had left the building. In her place stood an awestruck mage rookie. To her credit, she regained her composure almost immediately.

"Three seconds," Jessikah answered. "I've just begun at Farsight."

"Three seconds?" Dex scoffed. "You're a novice." He glanced at TK and LD. "This is sending a lamb to slaughter. Forget what I said about taking this seriously. Who did you cross, girl?"

"Excuse me?" Jessikah asked. "I don't understand."

"Of course you don't," Dex growled, the anger coming off of him in not-so-subtle waves. "That's why they sent you."

"She must have pissed someone off," LD said, looking at Jessikah. "Are you sure you're Farsight?"

"Yes sir," Jessikah said. For a second, I thought she was going to salute. "Farsight Division, and a Daughter of Bast."

"Good for you," Dex answered. "You can leave now. This is a family matter, and you are *not* family. We'll take it from here."

"I'm afraid I can't do that, sir," Jessikah answered, demonstrating how much she enjoyed living dangerously. "My superiors—"

"Can go suck an egg," Dex finished. "Who was it? Which Elder from the Orchid sent you?"

"All of them, sir."

"Ach, they must still be upset," Dex said, throwing up a hand and shaking his head. "Mages with their fragile egos and petty grudges. The war is a distant memory. That was decades ago."

"Not to them, sir," Jessikah answered. "They still remember."

"Of course they do," TK said. "It's difficult to forget, much less forgive, a humiliation."

"No matter," Dex spoke up gruffly, with another wave of his hand. "Your services are no longer required, Miss...?"

"Jessikah, sir. Jessikah Onuris."

"Onuris?" TK said, with a slight look of surprise. "You're Gregor's child?"

"He's my father, yes," Jessikah said. "You are TK and LD from Fordey Boutique. The Orchid speaks highly of you."

"Only those who don't know us," LD said with a smile. "I'm sure your Elders say otherwise."

"They do," Jessikah said, looking away. "They call you dangerous, rogue mages, a threat to every sect, and...worse things."

LD smiled and nodded.

"That sounds about right," LD said. "They're breathing today to insult us because of how dangerous we are, and the things we did...for them."

"Gregor was a formidable mage," TK said, examining

Jessikah. "Not overly skilled, but a diligent student. He excelled by outworking his peers."

"You...you taught my father?"

"Of course not," TK replied with a slight smile. "I taught the person who taught your father."

"Doesn't matter who she is," Dex said with a growl. "Her services are no longer needed. Go back and tell them Dexter Montague said so."

Jessikah reached into her pocket and pulled out a black envelope. She handed it to Dex, who took it with one eyebrow raised.

"What's this?" Dex asked, warily examining the envelope.

"They told me to give this to you when you 'made your appearance' to stop me."

Dex grumbled something under his breath and opened the envelope. Standing beside him, I managed to get a look at the letter. The paper was a light gray color and the flowing script was in blood red ink. The top of the letter was adorned by the same image of a black orchid that I had noticed on the rear of Jessikah's card. They took their branding seriously it seemed.

To the esteemed Dexter Montague,

If you are reading this letter, you have no doubt attempted to dissuade our mage from performing her duties as an agent of the Black Orchid.

This is a formal missive to notify you that we are operating within our jurisdiction. Your nephew, Tristan Montague, has been under observation for some time now. The casting of void vortices inside a populated city, not to mention the devastation he and his partner visited upon London, has not gone unnoticed.

The Penumbra Consortium is actively using back channels to have him erased, declaring him to be a menace to humanity and to all historical structures of import. Understanding your propensity for the disregard of rules, regulations, or any semblance of order, we are certain the Penumbra Consortium and their petition cause you little to no concern.

We are not the Penumbra Consortium.

With this understanding, we are prepared to take the following steps and inform you:

If our agent, Jessikah Onuris of the Farsight Division, is hindered in her investigation of one Tristan Montague by you, or any of the rogue mages who comprise the group known as "The Ten" we will consider it a violation of sect law.

To that end, we will enforce the dissolution of the Golden Circle sect—as is our right—if we feel such a violation has occurred. To convey this in plain speech, keep your nose out of this one, Dexter, or it will be broken and bloodied. We will do what must be done. If you interfere in any way, shape, or form, we will remove the Golden Circle from existence, with extreme prejudice and overwhelming force.

With the utmost sincerity and resolve,

The Black Orchid Elders

I saw Dex get angrier by the second as he read the letter again, before handing it to TK.

"Those bloody shites!" Dex yelled, as Peaches whined and moved closer to my leg. He stared at the now startled and visibly scared Jessikah, who bravely stood her ground. "They dare threaten me? My nephew? The Golden Circle?"

To be fair, Dex was scary even when he was happy. He always had an undercurrent of danger and insanity, mixed into a package of magexuberance.

In his current state, he had stepped way beyond scary,

and planted both feet firmly in petrifyingly frightening territory. The power coming off of him was palpable as his energy signature rose.

I could see why the Morrigan would be attracted. He was nearing her level of fearsome.

"This will be a problem," TK said, looking up at LD from the letter she held. "It would be a good idea if Dex got some air while we explored the details."

"Good plan," LD said quickly. "Let's go see if we can get you something strong to drink over at the Rump."

LD escorted a grumbling Dex outside.

TK turned and focused all of her attention on Jessikah. From her expression at that moment, Jessikah was beginning to understand the setup. She looked ready to bolt, but to her credit, foolish as it was, she remained where she stood.

"It's unprecedented that the Black Orchid would send you," TK said, when LD and Dex had left the office. "You're not nearly qualified enough to deal with the intricacies of this particular situation. How many cases have you handled?"

"This is my second one, ma'am."

"Don't ma'am me...ever," TK replied with a raised eyebrow. "What happened on your first case?"

"I...I miscalculated my timeskip," Jessikah said. "Many Orchid agents were injured...because of me."

"Did anyone die?" TK asked. "Did you cause any deaths?"

"What?" Jessikah said, surprised. "No, ma"—Jessikah caught herself in time—"no deaths. I wasn't officially Farsight at the time."

"After the mishap, they placed you in Farsight?"

"Yes. They said I could better hone my abilities in Farsight."

"A death sentence," TK answered. "Did they make the appointment official? They inducted you into the Farsight Division?"

"I'm Farsight," Jessikah said with some defiance. "They said the dark mage, Tristan Montague, needed to be apprehended, and they sent me."

"Do you know who Tristan Montague is?"

"I've read the dossier," Jessikah said. I realized she was in way over her head. "He seems...formidable, but I think I can apprehend him."

"Apprehend him?" TK asked. "The older mage you met earlier is his uncle, Dexter Montague."

"I'm aware."

TK narrowed her eyes slightly. Jessikah was venturing into dangerous, painful territory.

"Did you read *his* dossier?"

"There wasn't a dossier on Dexter Montague."

"Didn't you wonder why that was?" TK asked. "It didn't concern you that the sect tasked with policing all the other sects lacked information on a mage of his... reputation?"

"I found it odd, yes. When I asked, they told me—"

"He wasn't relevant to the case," TK finished. "Correct? In fact, the dossier on Tristan was thin to the point of being practically useless, yes?"

Jessikah looked genuinely surprised.

"I did find it somewhat lacking, yes."

TK shook her head slowly.

"You are being used, Miss Onuris," TK said. "I'm

certain other Black Orchid agents are tasked with this case...other *more experienced* agents."

"If they sent me," Jessikah said, "they must think I'm qualified."

"They don't expect you to return from this case, I'm afraid. You will have encountered the dangerous dark mage and been killed in the line of duty. At least that's what the report will say."

"Killed?" Jessikah replied. "Why would they...?"

"Like my husband said, you've angered someone who would like you out of the way...or worse," TK said. "Do you have any enemies in the Black Orchid?"

"Enemies?" Jessikah asked, confused. "I was top of my class at Farsight and I'm a Daughter of Bast. Why would I have enemies?"

"Why indeed," TK said. "I'm sure everyone loves you. Daughters of Bast are quite known for their wide circle of friends and the admiration of their peers."

"I didn't have any friends," Jessikah answered slowly. "Once I became a Daughter of Bast..."

"You were isolated and trained mostly on your own. I know. Being Farsight and a Daughter of Bast doomed you from the onset. I'm actually surprised you're still alive."

"They told me I was rare."

"The Black Orchid used to retire mages like you in childhood," TK said. "Gregor did an excellent job of hiding your abilities."

"How did you know?"

"In the past, your combination of abilities was considered too dangerous," TK said. "The only way you could have made it to adulthood was a runic mask. It was only a matter of time before your abilities revealed themselves."

"My classmates looked up to me," Jessikah answered. "When the farsight happened, they were all scared. The elders said I needed to be kept apart. It was for my safety."

TK smiled.

It was the kind of smile that made sharks nervous.

"Of course they did. Three seconds is novice level in the Farsight Division," TK answered evenly. "Can you explain how they expect you to apprehend a mage of Tristan's caliber and bring him back?"

"I'm supposed to conduct an erasure if the mage is uncooperative," Jessikah answered, "or combative."

"Or die in the process."

LD walked in a second later.

"We have a situation," LD said. "Dex is gone."

"Bloody hell," TK said. "He'll be in a foul mood."

"Already is."

"Finding him will prove difficult, if not impossible."

"It gets better."

"How many Black Orchid?" TK asked. "Did you leave them alive?"

"That wicked brain of yours is why I asked you to be mine."

"Your twisted mind is why I said yes," TK replied. "How many?"

"Dex was not pleased to see them," LD answered. "Three at the Rump, possibly more. This seems personal."

"At the Rump?" TK asked. "They must be doing a proximity search first."

"Overheard some of their conversation before Dex went...well...*Dex,* and nearly blasted them all *inside* the Rump. They're using this one"—he pointed to Jessikah—"to bird-dog Tristan."

“Makes sense,” TK said, looking at Jessikah. “Miss Onuris, you have a choice to make.”

“A choice?” Jessikah replied, confused. “What choice?”

“Help us find Tristan, or die where you stand. Choose.”

Green energy crackled around TK’s hands.

TWO

"What do you mean?" Jessikah asked, taking a step back. "Die where I stand?"

"I'd pick option one if I were you," I said. "She's not kidding."

"I lack a proper sense of humor," TK replied. "To date, only LD understands it."

"My gift," LD said with a mock bow. "Let's not atomize the novice, dear. They tossed her to the wolves. Besides, she's Farsight—she could come in handy."

"Three seconds is"—TK glanced at Jessikah—"not entirely useful."

"Neither is blasting her to bits," I said. "Wouldn't that just piss off the Black Orchid?"

"You're operating under the presumption that I care about what the Black Orchid thinks...I don't. Let alone that the Black Orchid actually cares about Miss Onuris's welfare. It doesn't."

"Disintegration is a little harsh though," I said. "She didn't know they set her up."

"That's why I gave her a choice," TK said, still looking at Jessikah. "Miss Onuris?"

"I'd like to stay alive," Jessikah said slowly, realizing she was outclassed. "I'll help you find Tristan."

"You will not engage Tristan when we do," TK said. "He's not in a normal state of mind and may decide to obliterate you. Understood?"

"Obliterate me?" Jessikah asked. "Is he really that powerful?"

TK narrowed her eyes at Jessikah.

"He's undergone a schism," TK answered. "Are you aware of this?"

"I was instructed to stop a dark mage," Jessikah answered. "No one mentioned a schism."

I stared at her. She was either hated or dangerous. Possibly both.

"Monty was powerful before this happened," I said. "Scary powerful. Now..."

"He's more powerful than you," TK answered after a few seconds. "You would be eliminated before you were aware of the danger."

"My farsight..." Jessikah started.

"Would allow you an entire three seconds to accept your fate," TK finished. "Nothing would prevent your death...even with your farsight."

"Why would they send me?" Jessikah said, her voice suddenly angry. "If they knew he was that powerful?"

Jessikah's cat purred next to her.

"No, I don't think so," she said, looking down at the cat, then back at us. "Sorry, this is Inkling—Ink for short. He and I can communicate. I know, it's weird."

"Not really," I said, pointing at my hellhound. "That's

Peaches. We can communicate too, although most of our conversations revolve around meat, how hungry he is, and how I don't feed him enough."

"Will he be okay around Ink?" Jessikah said, looking at my hellhound. "He looks...I want to say, impressive."

"But you really mean dangerous, I know. He's the friendliest hellhound I know."

"Do you know many hellhounds?"

"Just his dad," I said, rubbing Peaches behind the ears, "who is not friendly at all."

"Ink isn't exactly keen on strangers. Takes a while for him to warm up to people and...hellhounds."

"I'll make sure Peaches doesn't try to snack on him," I said, looking at my hellhound, who pretended to be ignoring the entire conversation. "Do not eat the cat. No eating Ink."

<She said I'm impressive. Did you hear that?>

<I did, and you are. Especially the amounts of meat you can devour.>

<I'm a growing hellhound.>

<Try not to scare her or her cat.>

<She is not scared. Her animal is ignoring us.>

<I know you're always hungry; make sure you don't accidentally munch on the cat.>

<I don't want to eat the cat. He is too thin, and he is not a cat.>

<Not a cat? What is he?>

<If that is a cat, then I am a dog.>

<That's not an answer.>

<The cat is...more. More than a cat.>

<Well, that's perfectly clear. Thanks.>

<You're welcome. Can you ask the scary lady to make some meat?>

<She seems upset right now. Maybe later?>

<I'm so hungry. I haven't eaten in a long time.>

<You ate about an hour ago.>

<Like I said, a long time. Ask her. I'm sure she would do it.>

<You need to understand what 'delayed gratification' means.>

<Is that when you get meat, and I eat it right away?>

<The exact opposite. It's when you learn to wait.>

<Where is the angry man?>

<Monty is going through a rough moment right now. He's not here.>

<If he ate more meat, he wouldn't have rough moments.>

"You can speak to him...mentally?" Jessikah asked, staring at me. "That's quite advanced, but you're not a mage. What are you?"

"Difficult," TK answered. "The Black Orchid sent you after Tristan to eliminate you. They couldn't take action against you directly in the sect, but out here in the field, on a dangerous case...you become collateral damage."

"Two birds, one blast," LD said. "They take down Tristan, and she just happens to die in the process. Neat—evil as hell—but neat."

"Precisely," TK said, looking at Jessikah. "Do you understand the position you are in?"

"Not really," Jessikah answered. "But I do know they sent me out here to die, and I'd prefer staying alive.."

"For now, that's enough," TK said, turning to me. "We need to track Tristan. Where did the schism occur?"

"Kali's place," I said. "Her dimension."

"No," TK said. "That's unlikely. Kali would never permit that kind of casting to occur in her realm. It's possible that's where it manifested, but not where it occurred."

"That is where he went dark and scary," I said. "Mostly scary."

"Where were you before you headed to Kali's?" LD asked. "The place where he cast the blood magic?"

"We were dealing with my energy signature going sideways," I said. "Kali seemed like the best and only solution. Once we were there, we were dealing with a few Rakshasas. He cast to help me, and then went all Darth Monty on me. I told him not to cast."

"It's not your fault," TK said. "Don't take blame that doesn't belong to you."

"I'm his shield-bearer."

"Which means he still has free will," TK said. "Continue...you were dealing with Rakshasas?"

"They attacked us," I said, remembering the details. "Seems they're Kali's security force, at least on her plane. These were stronger than any I had encountered before."

"Rakshasas, nasty buggers," LD said with a nod. "That was the activation, not the catalyst. What did Tristan do before that? Think back."

I thought back to the sequence of events before entering Kali's plane. Monty had been unconscious for most of the time at the temple in Jersey. Everything had happened at Haven.

"Monty was trying to protect us from the entropic sphere at Haven," I said. "Specifically Roxanne. She was on the skywalk when he cast...the skywalk. Evers said she had laid a trap for him there. We have to go to the skywalk."

"An entropic sphere?" TK asked. "That is a particularly dangerous cast."

"Evers?" LD asked. "Did you say Evers?"

"I thought she perished," TK said. "This complicates things significantly."

"She's a bit out there," I said. "Some kind of chronomancer?"

"A dangerous, accomplished chronomancer," LD said. "She was, or is, a war mage."

"If Evers is involved, Talin can't be far behind," TK said.

"Talin?" I asked, confused. "Who's Talin?"

"Dark mage," LD answered. "Dangerous, deadly, and demented."

"Don't forget delusional," TK added. "He and Evers want to eradicate all magic."

"Is that even possible?" I asked. "How do you eradicate energy?"

"You don't," LD answered. "Hasn't stopped him from trying. Talin has an insane mage body count. The man is a serious threat."

"Why hasn't he been stopped?"

"Certain authorities have prevented his capture on two occasions," TK said, glancing at Jessikah. "He's gone underground."

"He'll resurface if Evers is in play," LD said. "This is not good. Dealing with Evers is bad enough."

"We need to get to Haven," TK said, her voice tight. "Roxanne should have more information for us."

"I'll pass," I said, looking at the large, green teleportation circle TK formed. "It will be better for me, digestively."

LD shook his head.

"Time is of the essence," TK said, her voice low. "Please step into the circle."

"Won't my current energy signature mess with the circle?" I asked, trying to get out of the teleport method of transportation. "I don't want to end up at Haven a scrambled mess."

"You're already a scrambled mess," LD said, putting a hand on my shoulder. "TK isn't Dex, but she's close. You'll be fine."

TK made a sausage and placed it in the center of the teleportation circle, enticing my traitorous hellhound promptly into it as he inhaled the meat.

"No," I said, putting my life in danger. "I'm not going with you, and neither is my hellhound."

I stared at Peaches and pointed to the floor next to me. He finished inhaling the sausage before padding over to my side—a clear indicator of where his priorities lay.

"I beg your pardon?" TK said, surprised. "I must have misheard. Did you say you were not stepping into the circle?"

"That's exactly what I said," I answered. "I'm not going to Haven."

"Did you suffer a traumatic brain injury?" TK asked. "If not, you're about to."

"First, teleportation sucks," I said. "My body doesn't like it, never has."

"That has more to do—"

"I know," I snapped, further risking my life. "I need to reconcile with my 'bonds' and untangle whatever mess I have going on. Got it. Doesn't change the fact that it screws with my body in horrible ways."

"Listen," LD said, trying to be the voice of reason. "I

know Tristan going dark isn't easy to take, but you need to come with us. If Talin is out there, you're in danger."

"No," I repeated firmly. "You're looking for clues. I'm looking for Monty. I need to get to him before Evers, Talin, or those other Black Orchid do."

"We want the same thing, Simon," TK said. "We want Tristan back...whole."

"What am I going to do at Haven?" I asked. "I don't read runes. Roxanne is there, and she can help you with whatever runic trap was on the skywalk. Besides, she's not going to be happy to see me right now."

"He has a point," LD said, looking at TK. "She'll hold him partially responsible for Tristan casting when he wasn't supposed to."

"Where are you going to go?" TK asked, each word a threat of pain. "Tristan doesn't exactly want to be found at the moment. He expressed as much the last time you saw him, I'm sure."

"I'm going to go see Ezra," I said. "I have questions only he can answer."

TK nodded.

"Very well," she said. "I understand."

"You do?" LD and I said simultaneously.

"Of course," TK replied, stepping into the circle. "You feel you must take some kind of action. I would hazard that, as his *shieldbearer,* you should have acted sooner, preferably before he went dark."

"Considering that I'm not the mage here," I answered, measuring my words carefully to prevent disintegration by an angrier TK, "I would say that those who *are* mages should have seen this coming and done something about it. Just a thought."

"We're doing something now, before it gets worse," TK said, her words soft as titanium. "I'm not your mother; you don't need my permission. Do what you must, and try not to get killed."

LD shook his head and chuckled.

"You, hombre, like to live dangerously," he said, glancing at Jessikah before stepping into the circle. "You coming, Farsight?"

Jessikah shook her head.

"I think I'll stay with Mr. Strong," Jessikah said after a pause. "He didn't threaten to kill me where I stand."

"This is why you need to be nice," LD said, looking at TK who began to gesture. "Now she's scared of you."

"I would say that's the appropriate and correct response," TK said, glancing at Jessikah. "It will keep her alive."

"Fear shouldn't be the go-to response," I said. "How will you get answers?"

"Fear has a way of providing the answers I need."

"You want her scared of you?" I asked. "That doesn't make sense."

"She *should* be scared of me," TK said. "I am a real and present threat to her. Fear will make her careful and keep her alive—two excellent qualities to possess, considering her present situation."

"You're going to have the Black Orchid after you, Farsight," LD said. "They'll try to take you out and make it look like an accident. Watch your six. A little fear is a good thing."

TK nodded. "For the record," TK said, with a final gesture which caused the circle to glow, "I *was* being civil.

I don't do nice...now or ever. It's not like I blasted her into oblivion, which was a viable option."

"True," LD said, looking at me and stepping back into the circle. "We'll be at Haven for a while, then we'll meet up with you. If you see Tristan, be careful. Don't try to convince him to come to the light side. He's not thinking straight right now."

"I know," I said, remembering his words. "He threatened to end my immortal existence."

"Try not to find out if that's possible," TK said. "Do not engage him. Once we decipher the trap Evers used, we will find you."

"Be careful," LD said, before they disappeared in a green flash.

"Who is Ezra?" Jessikah asked. "Why do you need to see him so badly?"

"Ezra is hard to explain," I said. "Are you sure you want to come with? I'm not going to let you attack Monty."

"I have no intention of attacking Tristan."

"Good. I'd hate to have to shoot you."

"It's not like you could really stop me," Jessikah said. "You're not a mage."

"It amazes me every time I hear that," I said, staring at her. "It's usually right before I have to put a mage down."

We left the office in silence and headed for the stairs.

THREE

We took the stairs down to the garage, surprisingly avoiding my landlady until the lowest level. I didn't want to have to explain why Monty was "away" or on an "extended vacation" until further notice. For once, her radar must have been down as we navigated the stairs.

Or so I thought.

Standing next to the Dark Goat, in all her frozen splendor, was a displeased-looking Olga. Somehow, she always knew when I was about to leave or enter the Moscow. At this point, I was beginning to wonder if she had some kind of tracker on me.

"What is that?" Jessikah pointed to the Dark Goat as we approached. "It feels—"

"Later," I said under my breath. "I have to deal with this."

"Stronk," Olga said, arms crossed, glaring ice daggers at me. "Where is *prepodavatel*? Where is teacher?"

Olga was dressed in a bespoke, dark-blue pantsuit, made by some designer even I didn't recognize. It meant she was probably wearing the equivalent of a small country's GDP. Her sky-blue eyes glowed softly with latent energy, and her nearly white-blonde hair was pulled back into a severe bun, which only made her look more imposing.

"Monty is away on mage business," I said, keeping my voice calm. "He should be back in a week or so."

Olga narrowed her eyes at me.

"You lie poorly, Stronk," Olga said, glaring at me before glancing at Jessikah. "Who is this?"

"This is a...friend," I said. "She is going to help me work a case."

"She is detective?"

"Something like that," I said, placing a hand on the Dark Goat and unlocking it with the clang of a hammer on anvil. "Is everything okay?"

"No," Olga said. "Everything not okay."

"What happened?" I asked, suddenly concerned. The last time we'd had an issue, the Moscow was slowly being encased in ice. "Where is Cece?"

"That is problem."

"Is Cece in trouble?"

"Cecelia is big trouble."

It was vague, but we were heading in the right direction. Olga would not be rushed.

"Tell me what happened," I said slowly. "Is it like last time?"

"No, no," Olga waved my words away. "She is learnink, but still dangerous."

"Is she freezing the building?"

"Cecelia needs class to control ice," Olga said, upset.

"Ice everywhere. Her *teacher* needs to teach. Buildink is not frozen, but ice everywhere...everywhere, Stronk."

I breathed out a sigh of relief. The last thing I needed was an out-of-control ice mage freezing everything, especially when her teacher was currently MIA.

"As soon as I speak to Monty, I'll make sure he knows."

"This one," Olga said, looking at Jessikah, "is police?"

"Not really," I said. "She's more like..."

"*Chernaya Orkhideya*," Olga finished. "Black Orchid...yes?"

Jessikah looked at Olga with an expression of mild surprise.

"Da," Jessikah answered with a slight nod. "*Ochen priyatno*. A pleasure."

"You are the KGB of mages," Olga said, her words laced with venom. "You are here as his guest." She pointed at me with her chin. "Do not bring trouble to my home. If you do, I will blame him, but punish you. *Ponimayesh*?"

"I understand," Jessikah replied. "Thank you."

Jessikah opened the passenger side and sat quickly in the Dark Goat, closing the door and ending any further conversation.

Olga looked at me for a few, long seconds.

"Black Orchid is dangerous, Stronk. Not good...ever," she said, shaking her head and looking off to the side. "They only destroy and kill. This one,"—she glanced down at where Jessikah was sitting—"will bring you problems. *Rezh*—cut from her, before too late."

"Working on it," I said, opening the suicide door for my hellhound, Sprawly McSprawl. "Inside."

Peaches bounded in and took up the entire backseat with a masterful extension of fore and back legs. Then the ham gave Olga the biggest of puppy-dog eyes, complete with a hellhound grin of terror. Olga's expression softened and she rubbed his head behind the ears.

"Persiki is growing," she said, as she kept rubbing his head. "If Black Orchid misbehaves, you bite hard, Persiki."

Peaches chuffed and pushed his head farther into her hand, milking the rubs for all he was worth.

"Good boy," she said, turning to look at me as she hardened her expression again. It hovered somewhere between frozen tundra and glacial frost. "Stronk"—I was beginning to think she enjoyed mangling my name—"find teacher, bring home to teach. Soon."

"I will," I said, getting behind the wheel. "Tell Cece not to use any of her ability until Monty gets back."

Olga nodded as I backed out of the parking space and drove out of the garage.

<You are shameless.>

<She rubs my head nice. I like the ice lady. She is like the cold girl. The cold girl is my friend.>

<I know. You'll get to spend some time over there soon. Right after we find Monty.>

<Is he lost?>

<Can you smell him?>

Peaches sniffed the air and gave off a low rumble.

<I can't smell him. You still smell bad, but the angry man has no smell.>

<Thanks, I'll work on fixing my smell.>

<If you ate more meat, your smell would be better.>

<Doubt it, but thanks.>

"She's intense," Jessikah said once we left the Moscow. "Who is she?"

"She owns the building," I said. "She seemed to know you, or at least she knew about your sect."

"The KGB of mages," Jessikah said, repeating Olga's words. "Not exactly the most popular sect, no."

"No one likes IA or MPs, but someone has to police those with power and responsibility," I said. "Means you won't be popular or liked, but you knew this."

"She does know it's the FSB now, right?" Jessikah asked. "The KGB has been gone for years."

"Would you like to explain that to her?"

"No, thanks," Jessikah replied quickly. "She wants to call the Black Orchid the KGB of mages, she's entitled to her opinion."

"Good call," I said. "Olga is..."

"Dangerous," Jessikah finished.

"Complicated," I said. "Let's just say I'd rather not have to face her in combat...ever."

"That's a good call," Jessikah added, before looking down at the purring Ink. "I'll tell him, but I'm sure he knows."

"I know what?"

"Ink says your energy signature is depraved."

"Excuse me?" I asked. "My energy signature is what?"

"Oh, sorry," Jessikah said, holding up a hand. "Sometimes things get lost in translation. I'm still new to this communication. He says your energy signature is on a degrade. It's...compost?"

"My energy signature is compost?" I asked, confused. "What kind of medication is Ink on? And maybe you should consider lowering the dose."

Ink growled at Jessikah.

"Oh, I apologize. He means it's decomposing," she

said, then looked shocked. "Decomposing? Your energy signature is decomposing?"

"Something like that," I said. "Decomposing sounds a little extreme. Better than depraved compost, but not by much."

"I've never heard of an energy signature decomposing," Jessikah said. "For that to happen, you should be..."

"Dead," I said. "I know. I'm a mystery."

"What *are* you?" she asked, staring at me. "You're not a mage, but you're bonded to a hellhound. You clearly move in our world, but you don't possess any abilities?"

"I'm complicated, too," I said. "What is a farsight?"

"Do you usually answer a question with a question?"

"Only when I want to avoid giving an answer," I said, swerving to avoid traffic. "Does farsight mean you can see into the distance...like you have eagle vision or something? Is that what your sect trains?"

Jessikah laughed and placed a hand on Inkling as she looked out of the window.

"Not really, no," she answered with a short laugh. "Farsight means I can see probabilities."

"Probabilities?" I asked. "You can see the future?"

"No," she said. "Seeing probabilities means I can see possible outcomes of any situation. I can see three seconds forward from any fixed point in time."

"Basically, you can see three seconds into the future," I said.

"The key is from a fixed point," Jessikah answered, still rubbing Ink. "It's more of a curse than a gift right now."

"That must come in handy in a fight," I said. "No one can sneak up on you."

"Not really," Jessikah answered, still looking out of the

window. "A fight is not a fixed point. It's fluid, in flux, constantly changing and shifting, moment to moment. Three seconds of farsight isn't much help in a fight—everything is moving too quickly."

"So, not seeing into the future?"

"Farsight allows me to see probabilities," Jessikah explained. "Not certainties. When I use it, I can see what *could* happen, not what *will* happen."

"Like a chess master anticipating moves?"

"Except I can only see three moves ahead."

"Still pretty good," I said. "Seeing three moves ahead is excellent."

"Some of the great chess masters can see fifteen moves ahead on several branches of plays. A farsight master can see up to twenty seconds ahead on multiple branches. I'm still a novice, and a poor one at that."

"Is that what happened on your first case?" I asked. "You looked at the wrong branch?"

"Do you always ask such personal questions?"

"Yes," I said with a nod. "Especially if we are going to be facing angry Black Orchids who want to kill you—and by default, me—along with some heavy-hitting, dark mages that want Monty to go full dark."

"Or dead," she added. "They may just want him gone."

"Evers isn't exactly what I would call stable," I said, "and this Talin sounds like he's up there on the batshit scale with wanting to get rid of magic."

"You have an interesting circle of acquaintances," she answered, glancing in my direction. "Why are we going to see this Ezra? Who is he?"

"Ezra is short for Azrael," I said. "Azrael, as in the..."

"The Angel of Death?" she scoffed. "*That* Azrael?"

“These days he just goes by Death...capital D.”

“You’re serious?” she asked in disbelief. “We’re going to go meet Death?”

“I think you’ll like him,” I said. “He makes a mean pastrami sandwich.”

“A pastrami sandwich?”

“The best in the city,” I said. “Hold on.”

I jumped onto the Westside Highway and headed downtown to loop around the lower half of the city. It was the fastest way to Ezra’s.

FOUR

We arrived near Ezra's twenty minutes later.

I parked the Dark Goat about a block away from Ezra's. Peaches bounded out as I opened his door. The Dark Goat rocked on its suspension, swaying side to side slowly.

I was seriously going to have to put him on a diet or get a Dark Goat truck. Hades never told me how large hellhounds grew, but if Cerberus was any indicator, Peaches would outgrow the Dark Goat at some point. Hopefully not too soon.

<The place!>

<Keep it calm. I'm sure Ezra will give you extra meat today... if you behave.>

<I always behave like a hellhound.>

<That's what worries me. Try not to get too excited. You'll scare Jessikah.>

<I will practice my furry gratificating.>

<It's deferred...never mind. Just try to stay calm.>

He tried to sit still, practically vibrating off the ground in excitement.

"Your hellhound seems happy," Jessikah said, giving Peaches a wide berth as she exited the Dark Goat. "He knows this place?"

"It's one of his favorite places," I said. "Give me a sec, I need to secure the Dark Goat."

"Won't it get towed?" she asked, looking around. "This is a busy street. I can't believe you're going to—"A loud anvil clang, followed by an orange wave of energy racing across its surface, indicated the Dark Goat was locked. A few seconds later, the full effect of Cecil's runes could be felt. "Oh, I see. Who runed this car? What did you do to anger them so?"

"This is a SuNaTran vehicle," I said. "I'm pretty sure it's tow-proof. It's been runed to prevent theft, among other things."

"Or proximity for that matter," Jessikah said, stepping away from the locked Dark Goat. "It feels..."

"Menacing?"

"I was going to say...evil," she said, taking another step back. "But we could go with menacing, sure."

"I think Cecil is punishing us, but Monty disagrees. He says..." The words gave me pause. "Monty says, Cecil just wants to figure out how to destroy the Beast."

"This is not the Beast?" Jessikah asked, pointing to the Dark Goat. "It feels like an angry beast."

"No, this is the Dark Goat," I said, rubbing a hand gently over the hood. "She's mean, and impossible to kill, but she's not evil. The Beast...well, that one *may* be evil. I don't think we need to worry about it, though. That's Grey Sneaker's problem."

"Do you mean Grey Stryder?"

"You've heard of him?" I asked. "Owns a place downtown...a real dive."

"Yes, he is known to the Black Orchid, as is his sword," Jessikah answered. "He is a mage of considerable power. Several years ago, he unleashed a cast that killed a fellow mage. The Black Orchid has had him under observation ever since."

"What kind of cast?"

"An entropic dissolution," Jessikah answered, her voice grim. "A few levels above the void vortices Tristan unleashed on the city not long ago. Frankly, I don't know how he's still alive...that cast should have killed him, along with his partner."

"He's worse than a roach and harder to kill," I answered, not sharing that Grey was only alive because of his sword—or at least that's what Monty had shared with me. "Is it possible he's stronger than the Black Orchid knows?"

"Not likely," Jessikah said. "We keep track of all mages of interest. While there are many variables, it's unlikely our data is incorrect. He is powerful and dangerous. The sword he wields possesses an unknown source of power. Once a mage lands on our watch list, he or she is under observation indefinitely."

"You realize how creepy that sounds?" I asked. "Can you blame Olga for calling your sect the KGB of mages?"

"I know it sounds bad," Jessikah replied. "But we do plenty of good. We've prevented many dark mages from attacking places of power, including your city."

"Really," I said, raising an eyebrow as I thought about the nastiness Monty and I had dealt with in the past, without ever running into a bad case of BO. "I only have one issue with self-appointed keepers of justice."

"We weren't self-appointed. All of the sects agreed to create the Black Orchid as a check and balance against the other sects."

"Who watches the watchers?" I asked. "Who checks the Black Orchid when they step out of line?"

"The Black Orchid would never step out..."

She became silent as the realization of her suicide mission dawned on her.

"Exactly," I said. "All of the sects are dangerous. Even the ones tasked with watching the others. Especially those, because they can easily believe their own press."

"I don't understand. What do you mean believe their own press?"

"The Black Orchid may have started out honorable and with good intentions," I started. "Somewhere along the millennia, something got twisted, something broke."

"What are you saying?"

"How can you not see it?" I said. "They sent you out here to *die*. Either Monty was supposed to blast you to little orchid bits, or one of your own sect will take you out. One of the mages who has more than two cases under their belt."

"I'm not denying it," she said, her voice full of denial... and anger. "It's just that..."

"It's hard to process," I said. "I know. You better speed up the processing phase if you want to keep breathing" Before she could say anything, I looked up at the deli entrance. "This is it."

"Death lives in a deli?" Jessikah said, looking at the storefront of Ezra's place. "You're kidding, right?"

"I don't think you can use the term 'lives' with Ezra," I said. "He resides here, but the real question is: Where is here?"

"What?" Jessikah said, confused. "What does that even mean?"

"Sorry," I said, holding up a hand in surrender. "I spend so much time around mages, I'm beginning to sound like one."

"I'm a mage and I still didn't understand what you said."

"Right," I said, looking at Ezra's. "This place is a place Ezra chooses to inhabit. It looks like a regular deli until you cross the threshold, and then we shift planes to wherever Ezra wants it to be. That clearer?"

"Not by much, but I think I get it," Jessikah answered. "This is an interstitial pocket dimension existing outside of time and space, but controlled by an entity named Ezra. Created to look like a...deli? Of all things?"

"There you go," I said. "You sound like you just left one of Ziller's classes."

"You know who Ziller is?" Jessikah asked, surprised. "His work is required reading."

"He sounds worse in person, trust me."

"You've *met* him?"

"I still have the headaches to prove it," I said. "It wasn't all fun."

"Amazing," she said. "There are mages who go their entire lives without meeting him."

"I'm sure the ones who do wish they hadn't," I said, heading toward Ezra's, and noticed something was missing. "Where's your cat?"

Jessikah shrugged.

"He does that sometimes," she said. "He'll be back. Doesn't your familiar go off on his own?"

"He's my bondmate, not a familiar, and no...he doesn't."

"Bondmate? Really?" Jessikah said, glancing from Peaches to me. "He doesn't go off on his own at times?"

"He goes where I go," I said, looking at my still-vibrating hellhound. "Sometimes even *when* I go. He never leaves my side."

"Ink isn't my bondmate," Jessikah said, "but he's there when I need him...always."

"You don't know where he is?"

"No, but he'll be back. He always comes back."

"Must be a cat thing," I said, remembering TK's cat-being, Dinger. "Once we cross the threshold, we'll be in Ezra's. It's a little different in terms of customers. I can't believe I'm saying this: try not to cause trouble or destroy anything."

"Why would I cause trouble?"

"Olga knew you were Black Orchid," I said. "Stands to reason some of the customers in here will sniff you out as well."

"Sniff me out?" she asked, smelling the air around her. "I smell?"

"Wow, you really are new, aren't you?" I asked. "They will tell you're Black Orchid."

"It shouldn't be an issue if they aren't up to anything nefarious."

"You can't possibly be that naive," I said. "Did you really just use 'nefarious'?"

"Now my vocabulary is under scrutiny?"

"Just dial it back a bit," I said. "You can't be a mage cop in here. Unless you want to end up smushed by Ezra."

"Are you saying this place is a den of criminals?"

Jessikah stepped back to examine the deli entrance with narrowed eyes.

"It's a neutral location," I said. "Ezra will not tolerate you to apprehending or detaining anyone in there, so don't try it."

"I sincerely doubt this supposed angel of death or his deli customers can hinder me in the execution of my duties as a member of the Black Orchid."

"Do you even have jurisdiction here?"

"The Black Orchid has jurisdiction everywhere."

"I get the impression that some of the customers in Ezra's aren't exactly fans of your sect," I said. "Probably all of them. Keep your jurisdiction in your pocket. If you attract attention, you'll alert the other Black Orchid—remember those? The ones who probably want to reduce you to little orchid petals?"

"Good point," she said with a nod. "I'll make sure to keep a low profile."

"Sure," I said, giving her the once-over. Her energy signature stood out like beacon in the dark. "Can you dial down the energy? You're blazing all over the place."

"Sorry," she said, taking a breath. "That sometimes happens when I'm nervous."

"How *new* are you?"

"I've been a Farsight Mage for ten years and a Daughter of Bast for twice as long," she said, pushing out her chin defiantly. "What of it?"

"Ten years a mage?" I said. "Officially?"

"Yes. Black Orchids take much longer than the other

sects to advance," Jessikah answered. "We have to master several disciplines before we can become ranked mages."

"What rank are you?"

"I'm not," she said, looking away for a moment. "Daughters of Bast are not allowed to be ranked."

I could sense she was upset by the topic and let it go...for now.

"Rank isn't everything," I said. "Especially out here on the street."

"It is in the Black Orchid," she said after a moment of silence. "I'll get my signature under control. Give me a moment."

"Good plan," I said. "I'd prefer not to cause an incident in Ezra's. This is Peaches' favorite pastrami place. Meat is right up there with breathing, for hellhounds. That makes Ezra's extremely important. The last thing I need, or want, is an upset hellhound."

"Understood," she said, closing her eyes and taking a deep breath. After a few seconds, I could barely sense her energy signature. "Better?"

"Much. Once we cross the threshold, we'll shift over. Let's go."

FIVE

The runes on the threshold blazed with orange energy as we crossed it and stepped into Ezra's. I stood in the doorway for a few seconds, letting the tingle of energy wash over me as I scanned the floor. I didn't want any surprises, even though I doubted anyone would try something inside Ezra's.

Ezra was particular about maintaining the peace in his spaces. I still remembered the meeting with Ken in the deli's basement. The amount of power Ezra commanded staggered the imagination. Aside from the incredible amount of runic defenses in place, he was able to shut everything down with barely any visible effort.

Not something I wanted to go through again.

The energy of the deli shifted slightly when we entered. By now, most of the customers were used to seeing Peaches and me come in. The pause was caused by Jessikah, or rather what she represented.

It was a barely discernible hiccup in the ambient energy of the deli, almost as if the entire place just held its collective breath. It was subtle, but I sensed it. Paying attention to fluctuations like that had saved my life on more than one occasion, especially after meeting Monty.

I looked in the corner, saw Ezra poring over a book, and started moving in his direction. Several sets of eyes were fixed on Jessikah as we crossed the floor. It wasn't until they saw where we were headed did that they began to look away.

Some of the observers kept their gazes on us indirectly, using the reflective surfaces situated around the interior. I was aware of the tactic, using it often myself. Knowing about it didn't mean I was at ease. Some of the eyes belonged to heavy-hitters with angry expressions focused on Jessikah. It was one of those hatred-by-association situations. I doubted any of them knew Jessikah personally, but I was certain they knew of the Black Orchid.

"Have they never seen a member of the Black Orchid?" Jessikah said under her breath, as we made our way to Ezra's table. "I'm not here to accost them."

"I think the stares are because they *have* seen the Black Orchid in action before," I said, focusing on Ezra. "Just keep moving. No one would dare oppose Ezra in this place...or any other, I would imagine."

She gave me a brief nod and kept walking.

Ezra was sitting at his usual table. I looked around but didn't see Mori. She must've been in the back, or out on whatever business it was she was responsible for when Ezra was in the deli. I made a mental note to ask Ezra what Death's PA did when she was out. Did she scout out the potential deceased? Look out for hot spots? Hang around cemeteries? It was a puzzle. If Monty were here, I'd have asked him.

Ezra, as was his custom, had an enormous book on the table before him. The seats around him were empty. He wore his usual pair of half-moon glasses, and peered at me over the lenses for a few seconds, before slowly closing the book. He beckoned to us with a hand, and then pointed to the chairs.

Ezra was dressed in his regular white shirt, with black vest and pants, and his rune-covered yarmulke, which gave off a faint violet glow. I glanced down at the tome; it was easily a foot thick, which placed it squarely in tome territory. To my surprise, the title was legible. It read: *Ziller's Principles on Advanced Paradoxes and Entanglements of Interstitial Dimensions.* Looked like he was doing some light reading.

It was easy to confuse Ezra with an elderly scholar, or a professor of some kind, and not the personification of Death—until he let you feel a minuscule amount of his massive, fear-inducing energy signature.

He was releasing some of that energy right now, probably in response to Jessikah's arrival and the reception she received. It was basically a subtle, *Back off or I will completely obliterate you,* message of warning. The deli exhaled and went back to its normal flow of energy after that.

No one challenged Ezra for long...and lived.

Once we were closer, he motioned for one of the many servers crisscrossing the tables.

"Come, sit," he said, "It's almost time for lunch."

"Ezra, it's still morning," I said, pulling out a chair and sitting down. "We can eat—"

"A healthy pastrami on rye for you," Ezra said, cutting me off, "and a special salad for you, miss."

"Thank you," Jessikah said. "I'm not really that hungry."

"But you will eat," Ezra answered. "Then we talk."

"Right," I said. "The usual."

"Correct," Ezra answered, pushing up his glasses. "Now, let me look at you. You're wasting away. Are you eating? How was Kali?"

I had stopped being surprised by his questions long ago. Ezra just seemed to *know* things without having to be told. I guess that was one of the perks of being Death.

"Kali was extra grumpy," I said. "Not very helpful."

"She's always been a bit cranky," Ezra admitted. "I keep telling her to get out more."

"She smashed me into a stone wall and nearly disintegrated me," I said. "It wasn't pleasant."

"I'm certain you deserved it," Ezra answered. "She's not impetuous. At the very least, you're still here to tell the tale. She must have been in a good mood."

"My energy signature..."

"Is all jumbled," Ezra finished, shaking a hand in the air. "No one can fix that but you, Simon. You know this. Stop looking for help outside when it's inside."

"I understand, but..."

"But nothing," Ezra continued, staring at me. "You *must* deal with this, or it *will* deal with you."

"That would be great if I knew what 'this' was," I said. "As it stands, I'm still looking..."

"Simon," Ezra said, "you have everything you need. Think inside the box."

"That's the second time I've heard that."

"Then maybe you should pay attention, eh?"

"Sorry. Where are my manners? Ezra," I said, looking at a slightly stunned Jessikah. "This is—"

"Jessikah Onuris, Farsight Mage and a Daughter of Bast," Ezra finished, with a slight nod. "Welcome. You must forgive Simon. His mind is otherwise preoccupied."

Jessikah sat with a perplexed expression.

"How did you...?" she asked, then looked at me. "You met Kali...the Kali? Did you tell him about me?"

She reminded me of myself, when I'd first met Monty and found myself thrust into a world beyond anything I could imagine. Shocking doesn't begin to describe it.

"Didn't need to," I said. "As far as I know, he pretty much knows everything I'm about to say."

"I'm not omniscient, Simon," Ezra said. "Just well informed."

Peaches gave off a small whine from under the table, and Ezra held up a finger before I answered. He waved a hand, forming a large titanium bowl inscribed with a large letter P on the side. It was filled with pastrami—too much in my opinion, even for Peaches.

"You don't think that's a little much?" I said, looking at the overflowing pastrami. "Even for a bottomless hell-hound? He's going to get immense."

"Anton briefed me on your plan to put a growing hell-hound on a diet," Ezra said, scolding me as he shook his head. "*All* the pastrami in this place is healthy pastrami. I added an extra portion because he needs it. If you starve him, he will become irritable; that's never good when it comes to hellhounds. Especially the puppies."

My vibrating hellhound fixated on the bowl, before gracing me with his puppy-dog eyes. I nodded and he proceeded to inhale the contents of the bowl with a velocity that hurt my brain to watch. I wondered where all the meat went. When he was done, he turned in a circle several times and plopped down under the table with a satisfied chuff. The snoring started a few seconds later.

"*Starve* him?" I said, glancing under the table. "He can barely fit in the Dark Goat."

"He's a puppy?" Jessikah asked. "I would hate to see what he's like when he's fully grown."

"They *can* be a handful," Ezra said, waving our words away and adjusting his glasses, "but we aren't here to discuss hellhound care. You're here because you want to know about Tristan facing his *yetzer hara*."

"His yetzer what?" I asked, confused. "If that means going all Darth Monty...then yes, his yetzer thing."

"His shadow self," Ezra translated. "You want to know what you can do, now that he is embracing his darkness."

SIX

"Is that what it's called?" I asked. "Embracing your darkness? Are you saying he's not fully dark yet? More importantly, can I get him to break this embrace? He's making a large amount of people twitchy...powerful people, who would prefer to see him dead rather than dark."

"If anyone can do it," Ezra said, "it would be *you*—his shieldbearer. Do you know how?"

"I don't even know *where* he is," I answered, frustrated. "How would I know how to get him back?"

"He has to want to come back," Ezra said. "The allure of darkness...is powerful."

"I know he may be close, but he isn't dark completely. Not yet."

"Tristan Montague has gone dark," Jessikah said, firmly. "The elders of my sect sent me here to stop him."

"The elders of your sect sent you here to perish," Ezra said gently. "Surely you understand that by now?"

"She's getting it...slowly," I said, giving Jessikah a hard look. "What is a yetzer hara?"

One of the servers—not Anton—arrived with a large tray of food. The smell overpowered my senses, suddenly making me ravenous. For a second, I thought I was going to pull a Peaches and drool all over the table.

The server placed an enormous pastrami sandwich before me with deft expertise. The sandwich, which was at least two pounds of pastrami, with the illusion of some slices of bread, defied the laws of physics. It teetered on the brink of collapse, only held in place by large toothpicks. Jessikah's salad threatened to spill out of her plate and looked delicious. The meal was capped off with two industrial-sized egg creams.

Jessikah looked down at her plate and slowly shook her head.

"There is no way I could..." she started, stopping when I gave her a look.

"Thank you, Ezra," I said, barely managing to get my hands around half of the sandwich. "This looks and smells delicious."

"Thank you," Jessikah said, picking up her fork, still unsure where to begin. "This looks absolutely excellent."

"Good, good," Ezra said. "You two eat, and I'll explain."

I took a large bite of the sandwich, barely diminishing its size. My taste buds did a happy dance as I chewed. Ezra's was the best. I could totally understand why Peaches loved this place.

Jessikah took a few tentative forkfuls before joining me in appreciation for the food, with a small groan of her own.

"This is so good," she said after a few more forkfuls. "I've never had anything this good."

Ezra nodded, evidently satisfied that we were enjoying the food.

"Is there a way I can stop Monty from falling deeper into this yetzer thing?"

"The yetzer hara, or shadow self, isn't something he's falling into," Ezra said. "It's still Tristan. Everyone possesses a shadow self...everyone."

"Even you?" I asked. "I mean, how could you possess one?"

"Let me correct," Ezra said with a small smile. "Everyone who is mostly human possesses a shadow self."

"Are you saying I can't stop him from going dark?"

"Why do you want to?" Ezra asked. "What does it mean to go dark?"

It was still too early to be hit by Zilleresque questions. My brain hadn't been fully caffeinated, but I knew those two questions were important.

"He will become evil," Jessikah said, with a certainty rooted in myopic conditioning. It was her Black Orchid training talking. "Any mage that goes dark eventually surrenders to evil and needs to be neutralized...before it's too late."

"I expect that answer from the Black Orchid," Ezra said, then turned to me. "What say you, Simon?"

I gave it some thought. Monty and I had come across plenty of powerful, dark beings; some of them were mages, some of them were more than human. Not all of them were evil. Dangerous and scary as hell, yes, but not inherently evil.

"Darkness doesn't equal evil any more than light equals good."

"It has been my experience that at some point in every

life, a radical choice is given and a radical choice is made," Ezra said, tapping his nose lightly. "One that alters the course of that life."

"A 'fork in the road' kind of thing?"

"That's a simple way to see it. Think more along the lines of a pivotal choice that impacts a timeline," Ezra answered, tapping the book beside him. "You can't stop the flow of time, merely divert it...like a river."

"Rivers can be dammed," I said, thinking I was clever. "We can stop the flow of a river."

"Rivers are diverted. A dam without maintenance is called rubble."

"So we can't stop time, just like we can't stop rivers?" I asked. "Merely divert or alter the course?"

"Eventually, rivers return to their natural course," Ezra answered. "The same with time; you only have the illusion you can stop time."

"Does that mean Monty *has* to go through this?"

"Right now, he is standing in the schism, this fork you mentioned—walking the razor," Ezra said, holding out a hand perpendicular to the table, as if about to shake hands. "If he slips"—he turned his hand palm down—"he could slip into full darkness. Does that mean he becomes evil?"

"Yes," Jessikah said quickly. "Slipping into darkness will only result in his becoming evil. He will surrender to his base nature and destroy everything and everyone around him."

Ezra gave her a gentle smile as I stared at her in disbelief.

"The brashness of youth is only exceeded by its limited perspective on the deeper aspects of life," he said. "Not everything is so neat and tidy as good and evil, or light and dark. Despite what the elders at the Black Orchid believe. This world is full of gray, which, if you want to help Tristan, is where you need to go…to Grey."

Jessikah looked confused. I was really starting to worry about my exposure to mages, because I understood what Ezra was trying to share with her, and where he was sending us.

"Don't you have some 'stay away from darkness' rune I could use?" I asked, really not wanting to go see Grey. "Something in an easy-to-use form, like a hammer. Then I could just tap Monty on the forehead with it."

"No," Ezra said with a small chuckle. "You need to see Grey." He pointed at Jessikah as he stood. "This one needs to meet a dark mage who isn't trying to kill her, and you need to find out where Tristan has gone. He can help."

"He means Grey Stryder?" Jessikah asked. "I'm not authorized to…"

Ezra and I both looked at her.

"Sorry," she mumbled, and continued her salad. "Habits."

"Will Grey know where Tristan is?" I asked, dreading the visit. "Maybe I could just call him?"

"He will know where to point you," Ezra said, grabbing his book. "He may even be able to help with your confusion."

"Confusion?" I said, confused. "I'm not confused."

"Of course you aren't," Ezra said as he shuffled off. "Please enjoy the meal. Give my regards to Grey, and tell him he needs to pay me a visit."

"I'm sure he'll love to hear that."

Ezra headed off to the kitchen with a wave.

"Am I supposed to finish this entire forest?" Jessikah asked, looking down at her plate. "It feels as if there's no end to it."

"It'll sustain you," I said, after taking another bite of my sandwich. "We may not get another chance at food this delicious for some time. Especially if we're going to go see Grey."

"Why? Does Grey live in a wasteland where food is difficult to locate?"

"No," I said. "I have a feeling Ezra wants us to go see Grey for...reasons."

"Reasons?" she asked. "That makes no sense."

"Welcome to my world," I said, removing the bread from my sandwich and placing it on the table. "I moved into the state of confusion long ago. You get used to it. Right now, we need to go see Grey."

"What are you doing?" she asked when she saw me dismantle my sandwich. "Is that how you eat your food? By deconstructing it?"

"I'm cheating," I said, taking my plate and placing it down near my ever-vigilant hellhound, who proceeded to disappear the remaining pastrami. "Sorry, he doesn't eat salads."

She glared at me as I produced an empty plate a few seconds later. She pushed her plate forward, shaking her head.

"This is impossible," she said. "Does he always serve you this much?"

I nodded.

"Let's go," I said, getting up. Peaches shook his body, nearly tipping the table over as he joined me. "Eyes front.

Don't engage the natives. They saw us at Ezra's table, which should keep them calm...for now."

"Is he really *the* Death?" Jessikah asked under her breath. "He just seemed like a pleasant, but quirky, old man."

"He is...until he isn't."

"Pardon?" she said, as we headed to the door. "You didn't answer my question."

"He's Death, capital D," I said. "Why don't you ask him to show you next time?"

She shuddered in response.

"No, thank you. I think I prefer the old-man disguise."

"Most do," I said, opening the door. "Let's go see Grey."

SEVEN

We arrived at the Dark Goat only to be met by a reception party of three.

They were looking particularly scowly and self-important, sizing us up—well, Jessikah, actually, like something out of a strange version of West Side Story. Any second now, I half expected them to break into song and dance with a rendition of "When you're a mage, you're a mage to the end."

I chuckled to myself at the image, which only made Jessikah glance at me, probably questioning my sanity. She quickly turned back to focus on the reception party.

They were low-level mages, judging from the energy signatures, and were giving Jessikah some hard stares, barely acknowledging my presence. I almost felt insulted. Not even my hellhound got a second glance. Peaches always got a second glance. Sometimes even a third.

They were either clueless or suicidal. No one ignored a hellhound...for long.

These three were doing their best to be imposing.

They were dressed in typical mageiform: black suits with the black ensemble to go with it. The only difference was that I was used to Monty's runed, bespoke, Zegna suits, and these three clearly shopped at Benny's Bargain Basement.

I looked for the leader of the group. There was always one who acted as spokesperson and defacto point man. This one stood in the middle of the trio, arms crossed and legs slightly apart. I gave him a cool look and raised an eyebrow in my best Spock imitation, before Peaches gently nudged my leg. This time he actually managed to just nudge my leg, not dislocate my hip. I still had to take a step to the side, to regain my balance.

<*You need to work on those nudges.*>

<*I've been practicing.*>

<*On what? Buildings?*>

<*Can I bite them? They look angry.*>

<*I think they want to talk to Jessikah. Let's hear them out.*>

<*The cat-lady is scared. Should I bite them first, then let her talk to them?*>

<*Let's hold off on the biting for now. If they do something stupid like attack, stop them.*>

I glanced at Jessikah.

She was doing a good job at maintaining a calm exterior, but her energy signature was all over the place. She *was* scared. I glanced over at the three mages.

They were smarter than they looked. They knew better than to attempt an attack inside Ezra's. Seemed they enjoyed breathing. They were standing close, but not too close, to the Dark Goat and waiting for us. Well...mostly waiting for Jessikah.

They must have seen us exit the Dark Goat when we

arrived. They only slightly miscalculated. Anyone else would have sensed the menace from the Dark Goat and thought twice about confronting its driver. Somehow, they missed it or didn't care. I was leaning to the suicidal side of the equation with these three.

"Friends of yours?" I asked as we approached. "They look upset."

"I don't have friends," Jessikah replied. "I'm a Black Orchid. Friends would only make me vulnerable."

"It's good to have friends," I said. "Even *I* have friends, and I'm mostly antisocial."

"I never had the opportunity nor inclination to make any. My sect, the Black Orchid, actively discouraged it."

There was something in her voice, a mixture of bitterness and sadness rooted in regret. Her response was something I, too, had believed long ago. Living that way only led to being angry, lonely, and alone. Not a good place for anyone to be, especially for a mage wielding destructive amounts of energy.

"Friends will also save your ass when you're in a tight spot," I said, thinking about how many times Monty had prevented my disintegration by irate beings. "Even if they're the reason you're in a tight spot to begin with."

"Friends are a liability," she answered, stepping forward. "I was taught to eliminate all liabilities from my life."

I opened my jacket, making sure I had access to Grim Whisper. I didn't think it would escalate to the point that I would need it, but I *was* dealing with mages. Things always escalated. If the Three Stooges wanted to attack, they would have by now. They were probably just as scared as Jessikah.

"Got it," I said with a nod, taking a step back. "All yours then. You may want to open with diplomacy. Seems to never work for me or Monty, but there's always a first time."

She glanced back at me again with a look of, *You can't be seriously suggesting diplomacy* before approaching the three.

"Can I help you?" Jessikah asked the three mages, as she took a few more steps forward. "Do you need assistance?"

"You can't help me, you Black Orchid bitch," the leader said. "My brother was erased because of you Black Orchids."

Things were escalating quickly. It seemed like the diplomacy was going in typical mage style...south, and fast. At least no one was trying to kill anyone yet, which was always a win.

"I'm afraid I had nothing to do with that," Jessikah answered apologetically. "If he was erased, I'm certain he was engaged in an illicit activity that merited an erasure."

Ouch. Wrong answer.

"Are you saying my brother deserved to be erased? Is that what you're saying?"

"Was I not being clear?" Jessikah asked. "An erasure is usually the result of a mage taking action that jeopardizes the life of others...*in extremis*."

The Latin was a nice touch, but I was convinced diplomacy was a failed strategy when mages were involved. Even though what she was saying was technically correct, it wasn't what these three wanted to hear.

They just wanted an excuse to fight.

I let my hand drift to Grim Whisper's holster. I didn't want to risk forming Ebonsoul, especially with my energy signature acting wonky. This situation needed diffusing before someone got hurt.

<Why don't you let them know you're watching, boy?>

<Should I speak? That might hurt the cat-lady.>

<Just a low growl should do. Something to let them know she's not alone.>

<Are their eyes broken? Don't they see you?>

<Sometimes when people are angry, they can only see what they want to see. Right now, they see Jessikah as a target, someone to blame. Let's remind them that attacking her would be painful... for them.>

Peaches let out a low rumble.

The two mages on either side of the leader looked past Jessikah and focused on Peaches. Both of them took a small step back.

"Richard...?" the mage on the left said, tapping the leader's shoulder as he pointed to Grim Whisper. "Maybe we should do this another time? He's got a gun."

"So what, Tony?" Richard snapped, narrowing his eyes at me. "We're mages. I don't know what he is, but he isn't a mage. Just some freak with a big dog."

"That dog looks weird," the mage on the right chimed in. "He's kind of large...and ferocious-looking."

I looked down to see Peaches trying to be 'friendly' with an enormous hellhound smile.

<What are you doing?>

<I'm smiling so they don't attack the cat-lady.>

<I don't think that's helping.>

<Frank says be nice first, until you can't be nice anymore. Then tear them apart.>

For once, Frank and I agreed on something.

<If they do attack, don't hurt them too much.>

<Bite, but don't chew?>

<That should work. They don't seem too dangerous.>

<The loud one smells scared. Should I bite him now?>

<Not yet. The cat-la—Jessikah is going to try and calm them down.>

"Stop being such chickenshits," Richard said, brushing Tony's hand away. "He's not even a threat." Richard pointed at me. "You're scared of a guy with a dog? What's wrong with you? Mage the hell up. We're doing this."

"I don't know," Tony said, shaking his head. "He feels weird, and that's not a regular dog."

Now, I really felt insulted. They knew I was there...but I was being intentionally *dismissed.* If this kept up, my feelings might actually be bruised or something.

Still I waited. This wasn't my fight...yet.

I wasn't going to let them beat on Jessikah, but I needed to know if she could handle herself. I had a feeling that Evers and Talin were going to be significantly more dangerous than three low-level mage punks trying to establish how badass they were. I didn't even want to think about facing a semi-dark Monty. I chuckled to myself again. A semi-dark Monty sounded like something I would say to a barista. It was becoming increasingly apparent that my energy signature was screwing with my thought processes.

"Would you like to file a formal complaint?" Jessikah asked, really attempting the diplomacy route and failing spectacularly. "If you give me your name, I'm sure I could—"

"File this," Richard said, forming an orb of bright yellow flame and unleashing it. "Burn, bitch."

EIGHT

Before I could draw Grim Whisper, Jessikah moved.

I was surprised at her velocity. She flicked the burning orb away with one hand, diverting its trajectory...right at me. I jumped to the side, avoiding the orb as it crashed into the wall behind me, destroying some of the bricks.

"I'd prefer not being collateral damage today, thanks," I said. "Can you handle them, or do you need help?"

"It's being handled," Jessikah said, without turning. "Please stay back. For your own safety."

"That wasn't much of an orb," I muttered to myself, examining the minimal damage, as Peaches padded forward. "Wait. She's got this."

Peaches stopped with a low growl, causing the mages on either side of Richard to take a step back.

"Attacking a Black Orchid agent is a punishable offense according to statute 3.141592, Section P, subsection I," Jessikah said, forming an orb of dark red energy. "I'm willing to let you off with a warning—this time. Will you cease and desist from your current course of action?"

I'd never heard of the statute, but it made sense. If the Black Orchid was some sort of mage police, attacking them would have consequences. Painful ones.

Richard formed another orb...larger this time.

"Richard," I said, letting my hand rest on Grim Whisper, "don't be stupid. She doesn't want to hurt you, but if you keep flinging your balls of flame around"—I glanced at the destruction of the wall behind me—"*lame* balls of flame I might add, I will shoot you and your friends."

"Don't worry, freak," Richard answered with another sneer. "I'll take care of you and your mutant dog right after I'm done with her."

I looked from my hellhound to the minimal damage Richard's orb had caused to the wall, and shook my head.

"Did you not have breakfast this morning?" I asked, thumbing over my shoulder to the wall and moving forward. "I hope you have more firepower than that."

"Enough to deal with a freak like you and your mutant mutt."

Jessikah raised a hand to me and I stood down.

"Just so you know," I said, moving back, "I'm not appreciating the insults."

"Please let me handle this," she said, without turning away from Richard. "Is this your final response?"

Richard nodded.

"You die today, Orchid," Richard answered with a sneer. "We're going to make sure of it."

By this point, Richard had lost his bookends. They had moved so far back, Richard was basically standing alone against Jessikah. She cocked her head to one side.

I made sure my mala-bead bracelet was free and accessible. His orbs didn't seem to have the power to do serious damage, but that didn't mean I wanted to get peppered by them either.

"I don't think your friends agree with you," Jessikah answered. "Seems like you're on your own."

Richard glanced to his sides and cursed under his breath.

"You cowards," he said, forming another flame orb. "She's nothing. I'm going to make sure you two hurt when I'm done here."

They took off at speed.

<*Can I chase them?*>

<*No. We deal with the leader.*>

Richard was a bully. I was seriously considering just shooting him and calling it a day, but Jessikah wanted to deal with him. I knew better than to step on a mage's fragile ego.

Without taking her eyes off him, Jessikah responded with a short nod.

"You'll be too busy dealing with your own pain to inflict any on anyone else," she said. "Last chance to surrender."

Richard answered by throwing his orbs at her, but she was already moving. After her last move, I anticipated she'd be hard to hit, and I pressed the main bead on my mala bracelet, activating my shield. I made sure Peaches was next to me.

One of the orbs bounced off the shield and caromed into a parked car, causing a dent. The other orb sailed past, missing us completely. Anemic and inaccurate—this mage needed to go back to mage school, or wherever it was they trained. Even my magic missile wasn't that weak.

Jessikah unleashed her orb.

From the moment she formed it, I knew it was stronger than Richard's. It wasn't quite at Monty's level, which only reinforced the fact that sending her after Monty was a one-way mission.

Her orb slammed into Richard, punching him in the chest. He was airborne a second later. The look of surprise lasted until he crashed into the concrete, where it was quickly replaced by a grimace of pain. He landed hard and cursed. I saw him slowly make his way to his feet before I shot him, once.

Jessikah whirled on me with a look of surprise and anger.

"You shot him?" she asked, walking over to where Richard lay. "Did you...?"

"It's the middle of the morning on 1st Avenue, and you planned on what?" I asked, realizing I was the last person who should be calling her on this. "Having a mage duel in the middle of the day on a crowded city street? That would be discreet. I'm sure *no one* would notice."

"I, uh, didn't think of that," Jessikah answered, looking down at the now writhing Richard. "That was reckless, though. You could have killed him."

"Do I come across as some cold-blooded killer to you?" I asked, staring at her and seeing the answer in her face. "Never mind. I didn't kill him."

"What is that smell?" she said, stepping back from Richard. "Did he soil himself?"

Peaches chuffed and padded away.

<I'm not biting him now.>

<No need, boy.>

"Persuader rounds," I said, tapping Grim Whisper as I

holstered it. "They take the fight out of mages, along with anything currently in their bowels."

"What are persuader rounds?" she said, covering her face and stepping back even farther as Richard moaned in pain and gastrointestinal distress. "That smell is horrid."

"Persuader rounds are designed to scramble neural networks," I said. "For mages, it means no more spell-casting for a good ten-to-twenty minutes."

"It suppresses runic energy?" she asked, narrowing her eyes at me.

"In addition to making the target lose control of all bodily functions," I replied, pulling out my phone. "That's the stench you smell. Richard here was a little shit. I just helped him reveal his true nature."

"That's...quite effective," Jessikah said. "Undignified, but effective."

"It's hard to focus on killing someone when your bowels no longer listen to you and expel, well, everything," I said. "I use Persuaders when lethal force is not the answer, contrary to popular belief."

"You are the known associate of a dark mage," Jessikah answered. "What was I supposed to think? The amount of destruction you and your partner have caused in the past is staggering. Even by mage standards."

"There were extenuating circumstances," I said, raising a finger. "Give me a moment. We need to have your friend here picked up."

"He is *not* my friend," Jessikah answered, covering her nose. "Disgusting."

The call connected.

"I was just about to call you," Ramirez's gruff voice answered. "Where are you?"

"I'm down the block from the deli," I said. "I need a pick up."

Everyone knew about Ezra's, especially the NYTF. They made sure to give it plenty of latitude—considering who Ezra was—but they kept an eye on it...from a distance.

The New York Task Force, or NYTF, was a quasi-military police force, created to deal with any supernatural event occurring in New York City. Ezra's Deli more than qualified as supernatural.

"Have you been near City Hall in the last few days?" Ramirez asked. He was fishing. "Anywhere near City Hall park?"

"I haven't even been in town for the last few days."

"Do you have someone that can back up your story?" he asked. "Someone besides the mage?"

"Since when do I have to verify my whereabouts?" I asked, somewhat bothered. This was unlike him. "What's going on? This is me you're talking to, Angel."

"That's exactly why I'm asking," he said with a long sigh. "I got the brass all over my ass on this, and I thought maybe there was a simple solution...like you, the mage, and your cute puppy of destruction."

"What happened?"

"Apparently someone decided City Hall Park needed a massive makeover," Ramirez answered after a few seconds. "There's a crater where the park once was. Had all the looks of your detective agency's work."

"It wasn't us," I said. "Why would we blow it up?"

"Same question I ask every time I'm standing in rubble, courtesy of the Montague & Strong Detective

Agency," Ramirez said. "Why would they blow this place up?"

"Not fair," I countered. "You know it's usually in self-defense."

"Is that what we're calling wholesale destruction these days? Self-defense?"

Ramirez had a point, and we were catching some heat for the destruction in the city. It probably had something to do with the targets being destroyed, more than the destruction itself.

"Still," I said, "why do you assume it was us?"

"Are you kidding?" Ramirez answered with a short laugh. "Every day I wake up and I marvel at the fact that you two haven't reduced my city to a crater."

"Hilarious, Angel, really."

"I knew it wasn't you two," Ramirez added. "This job was actually neat, surgical even. No runic backlash or residue, just plenty of old-fashioned C4 used by someone who knew what they were doing."

"What was destroyed?"

"Mostly the park, but the brass is raising a stink about some landmark sculpture that's been on the site forever," Ramirez answered. "Irreplaceable, I've been informed, along with priceless. That's what made me think of you. I know how you like to preserve the city's historical landmarks with explosive renovations."

"You're in rare form today," I said, ignoring the last remark. "I need a pick up."

"For you?"

"No, some mage rookie tried to attack me," I said, trying to keep Jessikah under the radar. The last thing I needed was the NYTF investigating a Black Orchid mage.

It would create all kinds of the wrong questions. "He must have had me confused for someone else. I persuaded him to stop his attack."

"You used Persuaders?"

"Would you have preferred I actually used something lethal?" I asked. "Entropy rounds?"

"Those are banned," Ramirez said, his voice grim. "You better be fighting for your life if you're using those."

"I know," I said, trying to calm him down. He got growly when the law was being bent, or in my case, twisted into a pretzel. "Look, this is messy, but at least he's alive."

"Just one?" Ramirez asked with a sigh. "Tell me it's just one."

"Just one. He had a pair of friends, but they were smart and ghosted him when it got serious," I said, looking down at the still writhing Richard. The effects would last for at least another ten minutes. A lifetime for poor Richard. "Get one of the EMT*E*s down here to pick him up. Give him a three day vacation with a warning. Should straighten him out."

EMT*E* stood for EMT *Elite*. The NYTF used these paramedics whenever they encountered some kind of supernatural disaster, or when Monty was allowed to run rampant—which, according to them, was pretty much the same thing.

"I'll send Frank around. His bus is in the area," Ramirez said, and I could almost hear the grin. "I'm sure he'll enjoy this run."

"He's going to kill me," I said with a groan. "Can't you send someone else?"

"Next time, think twice before you make a mess on my

streets. I'll give the victim three and a warning. Is he a threat?"

"Maybe in a few decades," I answered. "But not really. Just a mage with an oversized ego."

"Got it, typical mage," he said with another chuckle, before becoming serious. "If you hear anything about what caused the City Hall Park crater, let me know, Strong."

"Will do," I said, my voice pensive. "Have you tried the Dark Council?"

"They're giving me the usual line of not having rogue elements in their ranks that would be causing such...what was it, oh yeah, 'wanton destruction of property.' They actually suggested I call you."

"I'm sure they did," I said. "If I hear anything, I'll let you know."

I ended the call and pocketed my phone.

"Who was that?" Jessikah asked, as we stepped to the Dark Goat. "What was that about a crater?"

"Director Ramirez of the NYTF," I said. "They're like the Black Orchid without mages. They deal with all of the supernatural activities in the city, from the non-supernatural side. Looks like someone blew up City Hall Park."

"And he assumed it was you?" she asked. "Why would he do that?"

"We've been known to be in the vicinity of some major explosions in the past," I said. "Not that we are always the cause, mind you."

"Extenuating circumstances causing staggering destruction?" she asked. "I'm sure it's just an extreme case of prolonged self-defense."

"Anyway, he's going to hold Richard here for three days

and let him off with a warning," I said, pulling out Grim Whisper. "Unless you prefer I end his existence now?"

"What? No!"

I holstered Grim Whisper with a smile.

"Just checking," I said with a grin. "You know how us cold-blooded killers can be."

She shook her head as I unlocked the Dark Goat.

"Are we just going to leave him there?"

"Yes, the EMTEs will be here soon," I said, hearing a siren in the distance. "You don't want to be here when they arrive. Too many questions. Too much attention."

"Shouldn't we...I don't know...move him? Maybe place him in your vehicle until they get here?"

I stared at her for a few seconds.

"A few things," I said, looking at Richard and then at her. "He tried to fry you. That makes him unfriendly."

"But, surely..."

"No, the EMTEs will pick him up and clean him off before dropping him at the NYTF HQ for his short vacation."

"He seems to be quite distressed."

"Persuaders are one of the gentler options, trust me."

"It just seems inhumane to..."

"There is *no way* he is getting in the Dark Goat like that."

"Very well," she said with a final nod. "It is your vehicle."

She got into the Dark Goat. I opened the suicide door and Peaches bounded in with a small leap, rocking the Dark Goat. I slid in behind the wheel, feeling the familiar ants-on-my-skin sensation and started the engine. I had a few questions, but I wanted to make sure we were some distance from Ezra's before I asked her.

"I almost pity him," she said as she strapped her seat belt. "He was clearly out of his element."

I was thinking the same thing about her, but we would discuss that after meeting Grey.

"Let's go talk to a dark mage."

NINE

The Dive was located about ten minutes away from Ezra's by Dark Goat.

I needed to prep Jessikah before we got there. She had no idea of what dark mages were, or how they should be treated. Grey was a dark mage, but he was no slouch. Even Monty respected his ability and power.

The fact that he'd recently added a dangerous sword—the counterpart to Ebonsoul—to his arsenal only made him more dangerous. Add all that to the fact that The Dive was Grey's batcave and an unofficial neutral location, and we were walking into a situation where we needed to tread lightly.

I couldn't have her going all official Black Orchid on Grey and trying to arrest him on the grounds of being dark and grouchy. That wouldn't end well for anyone...especially us.

I pulled out my phone and pressed the button that connected it to the Dark Goat speaker system. Another button press began the call. After a few rings, the call connected.

"The Dive...Be discreet or be delicious," the voice said, reminding me of Dahvina and her T-shirts. "How can I help you?"

"Hello, is Grey there?"

"Who's asking?" the voice replied, warily. "Whatever you're selling, we're not buying."

I knew it was him.

The lizard.

The one trying to corrupt my innocent and guileless hellhound.

Frank.

"Oh, *I'm* not selling anything...*lizard*."

"Li—did you say lizard?" Frank answered, angry now. "Whom do I have the pleasure of addressing? I need a name so I can inform your next of kin."

"I'd say dragon, but I don't recall ever encountering mini-dragons," I answered with a laugh. "Tell me, did you get a choice when you monumentally screwed up the casting? Did you actually choose extra small, or was the size you ended up proportionate to your level of power as a mage? I'm asking for a friend you might know."

"A friend I...might know?" he seethed. "Who the *hell* is this?"

"I'm going to be there in ten minutes...*lizard*," I said. "Then you and I can *discuss* what you've been telling my friend. I'm sure you remember him. His name is Peaches."

A low rumble from the backseat filled the Dark Goat.

"Peaches? I don't know anyone named...Oh, shit."

"Tell Grey I'm on my way...*lizard*. You better be there when I arrive."

The call ended.

<Please don't scare my friend, bondmate.>

<I'm not scaring him. He and I are going to have a conversation. Besides, if he's really a dragon, he has nothing to fear. Dragons—real dragons—are powerful, and don't scare easy.>

<He is powerful...he is just small.>

"Who is Frank and why did he sound scared?" Jessikah asked, looking at me. "Do you make it a habit of threatening people?"

"Only those trying to corrupt my hellhound."

"I see," she said, glancing into the backseat where Sir Peaches Sprawlington, the sprawl master, occupied the entire backseat. "Do you really think your hellhound is capable of being corrupted?"

"It's a long story. I'll deal with it," I said. "I have a question for you."

"Ask," she said. "If I have the answer, I will provide it."

"The orb you used on clueless Richard back there," I started. "Was that the extent of your power?"

She remained silent for a few moments, and I knew the answer before she replied.

"Yes," she said, hesitantly. "With the exception of my farsight ability, which does...unpleasant things to my reality, that was my power."

"I see," I said in my best Monty voice. "We are truly and rightfully bolloxed."

"Excuse me?" Jessikah said. "I don't think that word means what you think it means."

"This farsight ability you have," I said, "does it make you go Super Saiyan or something?"

"I'm not familiar with this term 'Saiyan.' Is it like a mage?"

"When you use your farsight, does it increase your power?" I clarified. "Does it make you like an Arch Mage?"

"Arch Mage?" she asked, shaking her head slowly. "Impossible. I would need at least half a millennia of extensive training to even approximate that level of power. Farsight gives me the ability to sidestep time for three seconds. It can still be thwarted."

"So we really *are* bolloxed."

"That word means..."

"That we are screwed," I said. "In over our heads."

"Fair enough," she conceded. "Why do you make this assessment?"

"Did you know that Monty has faced an Arch Mage?" I asked, quietly. "Along with a few gods, and beings too scary to even describe?"

"The only official Arch Mage we have on record in this city is..."

"Julien, I know," I said, "and his creepy assassin-assistant Claude."

"Arch Mage Julien," Jessikah corrected, "is quite accomplished and powerful. I have to doubt you and Tristan faced him in combat...and survived."

"It wasn't really combat, more like fleeing," I admitted, "but Monty has faced some serious heavy-hitters and walked away from them. Don't take this the wrong way, but you are outclassed...way outclassed. That was before the schism. Now, you're not even in the same galaxy."

She remained silent for a few more seconds.

"How will *you* stop him?" she asked. "You have less ability than I do."

"I don't know," I said as we approached The Dive. "I

have to hope that Monty is still Monty. If anyone is going to get close, I have the best chance of doing it."

"Why? You have no special ability," she said. "In fact, outside of your hellhound and your peculiar gun with runic-suppressing ammunition, you seem quite...ordinary."

"I still have a few surprises."

"I highly doubt these 'surprises' of yours will allow you to confront Mage Montague," she said. "If he's as powerful as you say he is, you're as outclassed as I am."

"Normally, I would agree with you," I said. "If it were just me and you, this would be a suicide mission. It's a good thing we have help."

"Help?" she asked incredulously. "Who? His uncle? The proprietors of Fordey? Your idea of help is misplaced. They are rogue mages who only care for themselves. They are not 'help'. They are dangerous and to be avoided at all costs."

I glared at her before slowing in front of The Dive.

"You're entitled to your opinion, as narrow as it may be," I said, checking my anger. "Just make sure you keep that opinion to yourself. Those people you just named are the closest thing to a family I have...and no one, no one messes with my family."

"Understood," she said, eyeing the matte black 1970 Chevy Camaro parked in front of The Dive as we coasted past. We turned at the intersection and parked across the street. "Is this Grey part of your family as well?"

"Grey?" I said, surprised by the question. "I've never dealt directly with him. I try to keep my mage interactions down to a maximum of one, whenever possible. Monty worked a case with him a while back. If Ezra says I need to see Grey, then I'll see Grey."

"That was a roundabout way of saying no."

"It's not a no and it's not a yes," I said. "If he helps me with Monty, then I'll be indebted to him, and I don't take that lightly."

We came to a stop in front of The Dive.

"That vehicle back there...it's..."

"Cursed," I said. "That's the Beast. Stay away from it. The person who runed the Dark Goat runed that thing, and must have been angry on the day he did it. The runes on that thing are lethal. Don't go near it."

"Right, then," she said, looking out of the passenger window at the entrance to The Dive. "We're here to get help from a dark mage who drives a cursed vehicle, and carries around a sword capable of death and destruction. What could go wrong?"

"I'm going to assume that, like most mages," I said, "he won't be in a pleasant mood."

"That's just a myth," she assured me. "Not *every* mage is continually angry."

"A myth that hasn't been debunked...yet."

"Is this where this Frank person lives as well?" she asked, looking up and down the street. "The one you threatened earlier?"

"If he knows what's good for him, he'll be inside."

"This place looks..."

"Run-down?"

"I was going to say quaint, but run-down fits," Jessikah answered. "It's quite protected. The wards on and around the property are considerable."

"The place is a fortress, if Grey wants it to be," I said, turning off the engine. "Grey moves in some questionable circles."

"The runework is impressive. Outside of the Black Orchid, I've not seen such a level of detail," she said. "There are layers upon layers of defenses, most of them lethal."

"They should be," I said, getting out of the Dark Goat. "It's an unofficial neutral location, and Grey, as a dark mage, has more than a handful of enemies."

"Are you certain this is the person we need to go see?"

I nodded.

"Ezra says see the angry dark mage. I see the angry dark mage."

"You don't sound overly enthused."

"Because I'm not," I said. "I'll ask him questions, but it doesn't mean I have to like it."

"I can just tell this is going to go so well," she answered, giving me a worried look. "Should I wait here? It seems like the safest alternative."

"I would hate to deprive you of the singular experience that is The Dive," I said, shaking my head. "Just remember, this is also neutral ground. Keep your badge and attitude in your pocket. We need help and he can provide it."

"I don't have a badge," she huffed. "I am aware of the protocols of neutral sites."

"Good," I said, getting out and opening the door for Peaches, who bounded out as the Dark Goat groaned in relief. "Make sure you observe them."

We headed to The Dive's entrance.

TEN

The Dive sat in the center of a neighborhood that had radically changed over the years.

Aside from being an unofficial neutral location, The Dive attracted a distinct clientele, which differed from the Randy Rump. The supernatural community that frequented the Rump was mostly part of the Dark Council, or affiliated with it. They didn't mind being seen there, and actually enjoyed frequenting the location.

With the Randy Rump, Jimmy had created a space that felt like the neighborhood bar. It was the kind of place that had regulars, and over time—and in between explosive renovations—had become a place where everyone knew your name. The Randy Rump was a restaurant-bar and butcher shop where you could sit down to a meal without worrying about being attacked for being supernatural. On most days.

The Dive was...different.

There were regulars at The Dive, too. These were the kind of regulars who didn't want to know your name or care. If they did know your name, you were attracting the wrong kind of attention—the kind that paid you a visit in the middle of the night and ended you. The regulars at The Dive lived on the fringes of the supernatural community. They worked in the dark and enjoyed it.

As large as the Dark Council was, there were plenty of supernaturals and magic-users who preferred not to be associated with them. That's where The Dive came in. On occasion, Grey would lend out the space to the Dark Council for non-official meets: allowing for a neutral place to hash out differences without blowing everything up. These meets took place between some of the powerhouses of the community—beings who would rather destroy one another, and the city, than have a civil conversation.

Grey facilitated these get-togethers with a minimal loss of life, or at least, he tried to. There were a few incidents where the talks went sideways. Fortunately, Grey was able to handle them, along with the Dark Council's help.

Making The Dive an unofficial neutral zone also gave Grey some latitude regarding his Night Warden activities. It was true he was officially known as the last Night Warden—at least that's what Monty told me—but I heard he was training an apprentice. I don't know how the Dark Council felt about a new generation of Night Wardens, but I don't think they, or anyone, could stop Grey.

In the end, it was good business. Loaning out The Dive kept the Dark Council out of his hair, while giving them the impression of keeping an eye on Grey and his dealings. I had done some research on The Dive over the years. Grey Stryder, or some proxy of his, had owned the converted carriage house for over a century.

He had converted the top two floors into a residence

with sanctuary rooms, while turning the ground floor into a bar with a small kitchen. As far as I knew, The Dive didn't turn a profit, but from my information, Grey was independently wealthy, owning the building and the property it stood on.

This was a typical story with many mages, at least those who were smarter, and older. They invested their money, or owned property that was worth a fortune compared to the initial sale price decades or centuries ago. I knew Monty had several holdings in the city and abroad, in London.

We never discussed details. It wasn't the polite thing to do. But, the fact that he immediately replaced most of the expensive medical equipment in Haven, without so much as batting an eye, spoke to some small measure of his wealth.

I stood across the street from The Dive and sensed the energy around the place. It was covered in runes and wards; not just the building, but the entire block around it. The street felt charged with power. I wondered how Grey had managed to ward an entire block with the focus being the converted carriage house.

The building itself was located in what had once been called Alphabet City, on 4th Street between Avenue C and D. The neighborhood had changed recently into a cross between upscale and pretentious, with transplants coming in from other parts of the city and buying property to add a new flavor to Lower Manhattan.

The Dive was exactly that...a dive. It stood out like a sore thumb, defiantly reminding the residents of the origins of the neighborhood when it had been a hub for immigrants. I'm sure there were several community meetings held to get rid of the "eyesore" and replace it with something more upscale and aesthetic.

I'm certain every single one of those meetings failed. No one was going to get Grey or The Dive out of this neighborhood.

As I approached the door and looked down the street, a reflexive shudder raced through my body when I saw Grey's vehicle—the Beast—parked several feet away. Even from this distance, I could feel the menace coming off of it in subtle waves. It radiated a subtle feeling of, *Step a little closer and let me devour you.*

If there ever was an evil vehicle, The Beast was it. The car itself was a work of automotive beauty. The 1970 Chevy Camaro was a monster muscle car...this particular one just happened to be more monster than car.

I was about to knock when the door silently opened.

"Get in here, Strong," a voice called out. "Before I change my mind."

It was Grey.

I looked around to see if he had cameras on the door, or some sophisticated hi-tech surveillance, but saw nothing. The runes along the street must have been some kind of early-warning sensor system.

"How did he know?" I muttered under my breath. "I don't see any cameras."

"It's possible he has a different set of sensors," Jessikah answered. "He *is* a dark mage, after all."

"Just like a Sith lord," I said with a nod. "Maybe he sensed a disturbance?"

"It's very likely he sensed a disturbance," Jessikah said, giving me a look. "Or a disturbed individual."

"Maybe it's these runes?"

I noticed the pulsing violet runes on the threshold. I reached out to touch them when Grey called out again.

"Wouldn't do that if I were you," Grey called out again. "Come in and leave the runes alone."

I pulled my hand back and glared at the door.

"He's good," Jessikah said with a small smile. "Better leave those runes alone...they look painful."

I stepped just inside the threshold and let my eyes adjust to the dim lighting. The wards and runes inside were on overdrive. Jessikah stepped in next to me and silently swept her gaze across the interior.

The furniture was a mixture of mahogany tables and cherry-wood chairs, evenly spaced out around the floor in what would have appeared to be a random setup, except for the flow of energy in and around the interior.

"This is feng shui on steroids," I muttered under my breath. "Even more than the Randy Rump."

"It would appear that even the furniture is positioned just so, to facilitate the flow of power in this place. Ingenious."

"It is," I said, following her gaze around the interior. She was right—even the furniture enhanced the power of the runes inside. "Right up to the moment the chairs and tables try to kill you."

"Don't be foolish," Jessikah said. "These are inanimate objects infused with power. They are not capable of attacking you."

The floor appeared to be a deep-red marble, which gave the illusion of standing in a frozen Saharan desert. I let my senses expand slightly, noticing that every surface had been recently runed, creating a magic null space similar to what existed at the Randy Rump...only stronger, much stronger. He really had turned The Dive into a fortress.

"Where's Tea-and-Crumpets?" Grey asked from behind the bar to my right. The aroma of coffee—not just any coffee—but Death Wish coffee, wafted over to where I stood, beckoning. "Is he on his way?"

The tone behind the question set off my radar. Grey knew something was wrong. He wore a pair of faded work jeans and a black T-shirt. His leather duster hung from a coat rack at arm's length from where he stood.

"Monty won't be joining us today," I said, keeping emotion out of my voice. "He's away...on mage business."

"Mage business, right," Grey answered with a nod, as he poured dark liquid into a large black mug covered with a skull-and-crossbones design. "Did you threaten Frank?"

"I told the lizard we needed to speak," I said. "Why?"

"He doesn't like being called a lizard," Grey said, before lifting the mug to his lips for a deep pull. He paused a moment to appreciate the coffee with a small grunt of approval. "He prefers Frank or dragon."

"There's no way I'm calling him a dragon," I said. "I could squish him with one foot."

"Unlikely," Grey said. "He may be small, but that doesn't mean he's powerless. More importantly, he's my friend, and I'd appreciate you showing him some respect."

"As soon as he stops trying to corrupt my hellhound, I will."

"Corrupt your hellhound?" Grey asked, glancing at Peaches. "What are you talking about? How does anyone corrupt a hellhound? Feed it lettuce? Give it healthy meat? Not that anyone would be crazy enough to feed a hellhound meat laced with broccoli, or anything ridiculous like that...right?"

Grey looked at me pointedly. Apparently someone had mentioned the "deathane incident" to him.

"Right...that liz—Frank's been trying to fill Peaches' head with...ideas."

I regretted it the moment the words escaped my lips.

"Oh...no," Grey answered, heavy on the sarcasm. "Not...*ideas*? Is your hellhound okay? Will he recover? Should I call a vet? Where in hell would I even find one for a hellhound?"

Jessikah coughed to hide a laugh.

"Not funny," I said seriously. "You know he tried to get Peaches to form a hellhound union? A union to demand larger meat portions."

"Is that Local 666?" Grey asked, barely able to keep a straight face. "I hear they have chapters in all the lowest places."

A second later, he burst into laughter.

"I'm glad this amuses you," I said, keeping my voice serious. "Frank is a bad influence on Peaches. Ideas travel faster than bullets...and in many cases can be deadlier."

"Understood. Frank is Frank," Grey said with a tight smile. "He's not going to change for you, me, or anyone. I don't control him, no one does. Deal with it. Besides, you should cut him some slack. You *owe* him."

"Excuse me? I owe him what?"

"From what I heard," Grey said, after regaining some of his composure and taking another sip of coffee, "Frank, your hellhound, and a little girl ice mage with her guardian mutt had to rescue a certain detective from captivity."

"You were rescued by a little girl and a menagerie?" Jessikah asked. "Really?"

"I wasn't rescued," I snapped, louder than I wanted to. "They facilitated my exit from some nastiness. That's all."

"Rescued," Grey replied. "Even made up a cute name for their group. The Coo Coo Cachoos, or something like that."

"The Brew & Chew Crew," I corrected, knowing Peaches would comment if I didn't. "That's their name."

"There you go," Grey said, raising his mug with a wicked smile. "The Brew & Chew Crew saved you. That's just adorable."

I remained silent. Grey smiled and nodded before taking another sip of coffee.

"Where is he?" I asked. "I'd like to repay some of my debt...with interest."

"Busy," Grey answered. "Said he had some business to tend to across town. Left here a little while ago in a shower of sparks. Dragon business."

"Bet he did."

"Let it go, Strong," Grey said, suddenly serious as he glanced outside. "Frank is a pain, but he's my friend. I'll speak to him about trying to emancipate your hellhound."

"You do that," I said, partially satisfied as I looked around the interior. It was mostly empty. Judging from the sounds, the kitchen crew was busy in the back. "Slow day?"

"Not even noon yet, Strong," Grey answered, taking another sip from his large mug and looking at Jessikah. "Did you trade in Tea-and-Crumpets for Ms...?"

"Onuris," Jessikah answered with a slight nod. "Jessikah Onuris of the Black Orchid."

"Is there a Black Orchid convention in town?"

"Why do you ask?" Jessikah asked, keeping her voice even.

"A few of your sect were here last night looking for..."

"Monty," I said. "What did you tell them?"

"Coffee?"

"You offered them coffee?"

He narrowed his eyes at me and chuckled.

"You, Strong. Are you really that dense?" Grey asked, pouring me a generous amount of black liquid goodness into a mug matching his. "You look like you could use some. Rough morning?"

"You could say that, thanks," I said, sitting at the large redwood that doubled as a bar. "What kind of wood is this?"

I knocked on the surface of the bar. A subtle, musical chime filled the space around me. It vaguely resembled the doors at the Randy Rump, but this one thrummed with a deep power—something the doors at the Rump had never done, even with all of the runes etched into them.

"That, my friend, is living Buloke Ironwood."

"Impossible," Jessikah said under her breath, as she approached and sat on the stool next to me. "Only the oldest sects have the capability or expertise to fashion living Buloke. The skill to work Buloke Ironwood is beyond all but the most accomplished mage artisans."

"I have some highly skilled friends in very low places," Grey answered. "To answer your question, Strong, I told them I didn't know where Tristan was, but that they were welcome to look around."

"Did they believe you?" I asked. "You let them look around?"

"I know of the Black Orchid, as every mage does. Of course I let them look around."

"How long did that last?" I said, feeling the familiar sensation of ants across my skin. "This place feels like Cecil cut loose in here."

"Something like that," Grey said. "Told him I needed some runes to persuade those who would prefer to do more damage than drink to vacate the premises."

I nodded.

"How long before they were looking for the exit?"

"About three minutes before they felt the sudden urge to leave the premises," Grey said. "Those intentions don't do well in this place."

"Three minutes?" Jessikah asked, surprised. "This place is enormous; there's no way they could have conducted a thorough investigation of the premises in that time."

I had heard the rumors. Grey had Cecil add some special runes to The Dive, runes that would make individuals with negative intentions feel the need to leave the place. The worse the intentions, the sooner the runes would kick in.

"Deterrence runes," I said, removing the glowing flask from my jacket as Grey slid the large mug of the darkest coffee I'd ever seen in front of me. "Like my persuader rounds."

"Only without the mess," he said, looking at my silver flask and raising an eyebrow. The skulls across its surface glowed with a dull blue light. "You need an extra kick?"

"Trust me, there's nothing in here that would compare to this," I said, pausing for a moment to take in the aroma from the mug before pouring in a teaspoon of javambrosia. "This smells..."

"Fresh," Grey said, looking away from my flask. "I get my shipments direct. Helps with my condition. Tea? Ms. Onuris? You seem partial to a good cuppa."

"Jessikah, please, and yes, a cup would be excellent," Jessikah said with a short nod. "Did you say condition? Are you ill?"

Grey narrowed his eyes for a second, and then turned to prepare a cup of tea for Jessikah.

"You could say something like that," Grey answered after a few seconds of silence. "It's complicated."

"Is that why you accepted the sword?" Jessikah asked, as I glared at her. "I apologize if I'm being too forward."

"Rude is probably a little closer," I grumbled. "That's his personal business."

"Not an issue," Grey said, still working on the tea with his back to us. "I'm sure the Orchid has some kind of file on me, just like the Dark Council. Mage goes dark, then gets a kickass blade of power...makes plenty of people nervous."

"The Black Orchid noticed the increase in your power and took the appropriate surveillance measures for a mage of your caliber. The shift was, and is, considerable."

"I'm almost flattered," Grey said with a soft chuckle, before becoming serious again. "My condition is...terminal. The sword makes sure it isn't. I get to hang around long enough for me to deal with the nastiness in the streets and help the people of my city."

"What does the sword get?" Jessikah asked, her voice gentle, but firm. "What is the cost?"

Grey gave her a hard look, which softened a second later.

"Blood," Grey said. "She feeds on the evil I fight. That's about all I'm willing to share on the subject."

"Understood," Jessikah said. "I didn't mean to pry. My apologies."

"None required," Grey said, holding a small cup in front of Jessikah. "I trust it will meet your standards."

"It smells exquisite."

"I get this flown in for some of my patrons. It's Taylors of Harrogate, Yorkshire Gold. Direct from 1 Parliament Street, North Yorkshire," Grey said, with a nod. "I hear it's some of the best. Can't drink it myself, but some of my patrons enjoy it."

Grey placed the delicate cup of tea in front of Jessikah, who let it sit for a few moments before taking a small sip. She closed her eyes with a small hum of approval.

"That...is a proper cup of tea," she said, inhaling more of the aroma. "Thank you."

"My pleasure," Grey said with a nod, before looking down at Peaches. "What do you feed your hound? Small cows? Large moose?"

"Sausage is good, if you have some," I said. "Do you know how Frank manages to communicate with my hellhound?"

Grey gave me a look and then ducked under the bar to a refrigerator unit. He stood up a few seconds later with an armload of sausages.

"Give me a sec and I'll have the kitchen warm these up for you," he said, heading to the rear of The Dive. "Be right back. Then we can discuss how they 'communicate.'"

ELEVEN

"Deterrence runes?" Jessikah asked under her breath when Grey had stepped into the kitchen, out of earshot. "I've never heard of such runes. It sounds made up."

I let my senses expand again and felt the presence of the failsafes around me.

"Not made up," I said. "Grey is scary strong, and Cecil is, well—Cecil."

"I just find it hard to believe that trained Orchid agents would allow themselves to be affected by runic interference," Jessikah said, apparently immune to the effects of the runes in The Dive. "It boggles the imagination."

"Welcome to my world. I'm sure there's plenty you're going to encounter in this city that will boggle your brain and sound made up," I said, empathizing. "Better to roll with it before those 'made up' things squash you dead. Trust me on this one."

"Black Orchid mages are highly trained," Jessikah said.

"How could some runes make them cut an investigation short?"

"Do you recall Grey's car?" I said, before taking another sip of the ink that was my coffee. "The Beast that's parked outside?"

"How could I forget?" Jessikah said with a small shudder. "It's malevolent."

"Exactly," I said. "Grey is the only person who can drive that thing. From what I hear, it's killed previous drivers."

"The car...has killed previous drivers?"

"Not the car, exactly, but the runework *inside* the car," I said, without going into detail about how Cecil had placed some of the same runes in the Dark Goat. "Cecil, who runed the Beast *and* the Dark Goat, is beyond skilled when it comes to runework, wards, and things of that sort."

"Is this 'Cecil' a mage?"

"Good question," I said, scratching my chin. "I don't really know."

"You don't know, but you let him rune your vehicle?" Jessikah asked, incredulous. "That's living dangerously."

"Cecil is something more than just a mage, I think," I said. "He's something old and primal."

"Just not something you can elaborate on?"

"I'm not a mage...like you said. Besides, if Grey says Cecil added runes to this place—runes that pick up on the energetic fluctuation of thought processes and their bodily manifestations in a mage, thereby causing a runic chain reaction expressed in a flight response based on their intentions—I believe him."

Jessikah stared at me for a few seconds before speaking.

"Really?" she asked. "You managed all that from his answer?"

"What?"

"That was actually a particularly magelike explanation," she said, "for someone who is not a mage. Are you feeling ill?"

"I'm fine," I said with a growl. "Did it make sense?"

"Actually, yes," she said with a nod. "I just didn't expect it to make sense coming from *you*."

"I've had a few challenging days as of late," I said, trying to dismiss her words. "Also, Monty is my partner. I'm bound to pick up on the jargon at some point."

"That was more than 'jargon,'" she said, looking at me. "That was an explanation with actual understanding."

She was right. I didn't expect to give her that answer. Whatever was happening to me with my signature was influencing my thought process. I needed to get this treated yesterday—but first, dealing with Darth Monty.

Grey came back with a large bowl of steaming sausages.

"Hope he likes these," Grey said, carrying the enormous bowl. "The kitchen sends its regards."

<The shadow-man brought me meat. Can I eat it now? It smells so good, and I'm starving.>

<You're not starving and never have. Wait until he places the bowl down, at least, and why did you call him the 'shadow-man'?>

<He has shadows around him, but he is good. He brought me meat. He must know...meat is life.>

The term 'shadow-man' was new. Either Peaches' vocabulary was improving or my understanding of him was. I was sure it was related to the answer I had just given Jessikah, and whatever was going on with my energy signature. I looked at the bowl that Grey had used for the sausages, and slowly shook my head.

"Is that a regular aluminum bowl?"

"Yes," Grey answered, placing the bowl down near Peaches. "Only one I had in the house. Why? Does he need a special hellhound bowl? Do those even exist?"

"I'll buy you a new one."

"What are you talking about?"

<*Go ahead, and don't forget to thank Grey.*>

Peaches let out a gentle bark that rattled some of the bottles behind the bar, shattering a few. My eardrums squealed in pain, as I stepped to the side, giving him space for his approach on the bowl of sausages.

"That's some bark," Grey said, raising his voice and shaking his head. "My ears are still ringing."

"That was a low bark," I said, rubbing my ears. "You don't want to hear loud."

Jessikah looked at the bottles, and then at Peaches.

"That...was low?" she asked, rubbing an ear. "That sound was deafening."

"He's still a puppy, so he doesn't have a handle on volume control yet," I said, looking at Peaches go to town with the sausage. "Among other things, like *slowing down* while he eats."

"If that's puppy size, how large does he get?" Jessikah asked, staring transfixed at Peaches in action. "He's quite large now."

"Large," I said, thinking about Cerberus or Peaches XL. "He says, 'Thank you,' by the way." I glanced at Grey.

"You may want to stand back a bit. Just to be safe, and to keep your toes."

Grey took a step back.

One of Peaches' bites removed the outer rim of the bowl. By the time he was done, thirty seconds later, the bowl was a mangled mess, resembling something the Tate Museum would display. In actuality, it looked like someone had taken a soda can, crushed it, ripped it to shreds, and finished it off with a generous drowning of hellhound drool.

"Wow," Grey said, looking at the remains of the bowl. "Is he okay?"

"He'll be hungry again in five minutes," I said, rubbing Peaches behind the ears. "His bowls need to be titanium, or they don't last more than one feeding. Even the titanium ones get a mangling. They just last a little longer."

Jessikah just stared from Peaches to me. Watching him eat took some getting used to, so I understood her shock.

"So, why are you here, Strong?" Grey asked, after sliding back behind the bar and grabbing his mug of coffee. "Don't tell me it's to harass Frank about his conversations with your hellhound."

"I wouldn't make a trip here just for that."

"Good, that would be a waste of time. Besides, I don't know how they communicate. Frank underwent some major changes when he became a dragon."

"Is he stuck in that form?"

"Yes," Grey said. "That's not my story to tell, and he doesn't like to talk about it."

"It's possible the effects of the transfiguration endowed him with the ability to communicate with your hellhound," Jessikah offered. "He is a mage, after all."

"You are well informed," Grey said. "Yes, he's still a mage...a powerful one. Even I wouldn't want to face him in a confrontation. He fights dirty."

"I just wondered if it was something like my bond with Peaches."

"I doubt it, but who knows? I certainly don't," Grey said. "I'm not an animal whisperer. I just know he *can* talk to your hellhound. So, if that's not the reason...what is?"

"Ezra sent me."

Grey narrowed his eyes and looked at me, his expression dark—well, darker than usual.

"Say that again...slow." He put his mug down and stared. "*Who* sent you?"

"Ezra," I said again, my expression just as dark. "You know—*the* Ezra?"

I tried to give Grey a two on the glare-o-meter with a dash of the Clint Glint, but failed. Grey just had a natural mage scowl that couldn't be beat. Dealing with Frank for so long must've transformed his expression into a perpetual look of anger and disgust.

"I *know* who Ezra is," Grey snapped, slipping into full magegrouch mode as he rubbed a temple. "Why would he send you to me? What did you do? Does this have to do with your skewed signature?"

"Skewed signature?" Jessikah said, surprised. "What skewed signature?"

"Monty is in a schism," I said, ignoring her for the moment. "A nasty trap by an old enemy who was supposed to be dead."

"Those are the worst," Grey answered, picking up his mug again. "Did Tea-and-Crumpets—Tristan—step across? Is he dark?"

"No. He's not full Darth Monty...yet," I said, glancing at Jessikah, "but he's close."

"That explains the Black Orchid agents," Grey said, looking at Jessikah. "Why weren't you here last night, with the rest of them?"

"They sent her alone. Against Monty."

"What, like a forward observer?" Grey asked. "You were supposed to scout out his location and then report back to the team?"

"Not exactly," Jessikah answered. "My mission was a bit more direct."

"She was supposed to apprehend and erase Monty if necessary, alone."

Grey looked at Jessikah for a few moments and then shook his head.

"That's a death sentence, no offense," Grey said, raising a hand. "You can't face off against Tristan. He's older, more powerful, more experienced...oh, and a war mage."

"A war mage?" Jessikah asked. "He fought in the...?"

Grey nodded.

"He led a group in the Supernatural War," Grey said. "Something covert. He and his uncle, from what I could tell. I never got more than that from him. He's not exactly the chatty type."

"Sounds like Monty," I said. "How hard is it to be a war mage?"

"War mages are trained to stand and die," Grey said, his voice low and grim. "It's what battlemages are called after they've been blooded. Remind me again what the Black Orchids are trained in?"

"We're trained to...well, not *that*," Jessikah stammered. "Bloody hell. A war mage? Are you certain?"

Grey nodded before raising the mug to his lips again.

"She didn't know, and I doubt any of them are truly prepared…not for Monty."

"They sent her in blind?" Grey stared at Jessikah for a few seconds. A look of pity flitted across his face, replaced by something softer, like granite. "You've become a liability to someone and they want to dust you."

"The rest of the team isn't here to apprehend anyone," I said. "At least not alive."

"Didn't think so," Grey answered after a pause. "Wasn't the impression I got from the team last night. They seemed…capable. Just not battle tested."

"They want to eliminate Monty."

"I'd say that was dangerous without the schism. Approaching him while he's in it. Suicidal," Grey said, slowly. "After helping your vampire…I'm tapped out on my quota of suicide missions for the foreseeable future."

"You saw Chi?" I asked, surprised. "Where?"

"Last place I saw her was downtown. City Hall Park."

My earlier conversation with Ramirez flashed in my memory.

"You guys are responsible for the crater downtown?" I asked, incredulous and somewhat relieved that, for once, someone else would get the blame for the destruction.

"What crater?"

"NYTF called me and informed me the park is now the City Hall crater. Was that you?"

"Not me," Grey said. "That must have been her. She was carrying a dangerous amount of C4. Why would they call you?"

"We're the default when things get exploded in this city."

"Makes sense, especially with your track record," Grey replied. "I'm surprised they haven't locked you up yet."

"Is she okay?"

"That's sweet," Grey said. "You actually think there's something out there"—he waved his arm in front of him—"that can actually *hurt* her. She's fine. Crazy as all get out, but fine."

"I hope you didn't say that to her face."

"I'm insane, not stupid," Grey said. "I only refer to her as *Director*. I hope I don't have to see her or her rookie sidekick for a few years, at least."

"Rookie sidekick?" I asked. "When did she get a rookie sidekick?"

"Don't know...don't care," Grey said. "You'll like her, she reminds me of you."

"No two people can be that amazing on the same plane," I said. "The cosmic energies couldn't handle that much awesomosity."

Grey stared at me for a few seconds before nodding.

"Yep," Grey said with a nod. "She was full of it too, but good in a fight."

"I can't believe Chi is back in the city," I said. "I'm going to need to speak to her."

"You may want to give her a few days...or weeks."

"Why?"

"Last I checked, she was doing some massive house-cleaning in the Dark Council," Grey said. "When we parted ways, she was about to renovate that place they had downtown. The Lotus."

"Never heard of it."

"Doesn't matter now. It's probably rubble. The Director leaves little to chance."

"That sounds like her."

"So, the Black Orchid wants Tristan and this greenhorn dead. We know that much; what we don't know is why."

"The real threat is Evers," I said. "You hear about her?"

"I'm old, but I stay out of politics," Grey said. "The Night Wardens focused on keeping this city in one piece. I didn't have time or the energy to get involved in world affairs, like Tristan. Even during the war, we fought our battles on different fronts."

"So, that's a no?"

"That's a no," Grey said with a growl. "I have enough enemies to deal with. I don't go out of my way to make new ones. My life has been overly exciting the past few days. I was looking forward to a little boring...then Ezra sends you to me."

"So much for boring," I said. "Evers is bad news. Sorry."

"I don't understand why they would go after him with such zeal," Jessikah said. "I mean, I do understand *some* of the motivation; he is nearly a dark mage and dark mages are a clear and present danger."

"I'm sure they are," Grey said. "Please, go on."

"Well," Jessikah continued, oblivious to the fact that she had just insulted Grey. "This almost seems...personal. Tristan has been under surveillance for an extended period of time. Ever since the void vortices. That was a disaster."

"Hey," I said, offended."That was defensive."

"No situation warrants unleashing not one, but two vortices in a populated area," Jessikah said. "It was reckless and incredibly dangerous. I won't even get into London. They're still recovering from your little 'visit' to that city."

"I heard about that," Grey said with a chuckle. "You,

Tristan, and your hound are officially banned from the UK, according to the word on the street."

"The Penumbra Consortium placed a continent-wide D-and-D alert on you three," Jessikah said. "I would strongly advise against visiting Europe for at least a few decades. They have long memories."

"D and D?" I asked, confused. "They want us to play Dungeons and Dragons?"

"Detain and Destroy," Jessikah answered. "They are serious about eliminating you. I can't believe you damaged the Tower of London?"

"I did no such thing," I said. "In case you haven't noticed, I'm not in the magic department. They're just being a bunch of self-entitled rectal nuggets."

"That...is an accurate description," Grey said with a crooked smile. "The PC is full of entrenched stuffed shirts."

"I'm afraid this is a case of guilt by association," Jessikah said. "The Consortium wants you all erased or dead."

"They're going to need to get in line," I said. "It's not going to be that easy."

"Don't give it too much thought," Grey said. "Just don't make any trips across the pond and you should be fine."

"He should be *fine?*" Jessikah asked, raising her voice. "It's a termination order."

"Which is only in effect if he's in their jurisdiction," Grey answered with a look that said, *You need to get out more, kid*, before continuing. "I have a few of them myself. The Consortium needs to get the stick out of their—anyway, I'm more concerned about why Ezra sent you here, Strong...you and your screwed up signature. It reads like you're shifting, which is impossible, because..."

"I'm not a mage, I know."

"Exactly," Grey said. "What happened?"

"I don't know, but I need to focus on Monty right now."

"Ezra thought Monty was here?" Grey asked. "That makes no sense."

"Hello, have you met Ezra?"

"Good point."

"He said you would know where I needed to go," I said. "It doesn't explain why the BO is after Monty like he's a fugitive on the most wanted list."

"The BO?" Jessikah asked. "Really?"

"Yes, really," I said. "They stink."

"Puerile names aside," Jessikah said, giving me a glance, "their motivations are suspect."

"Wish I could help you with the BO, but I can't," Grey said. "This sounds like something that goes back to your elders and the Montagues. I may know something about where Tristan would go."

"Dex did say something about the Black Orchid holding a grudge," I said. "You know anything about that?"

"If Dex is involved, you better believe it's personal. Again, not that I would know," Grey replied after taking a sip of coffee. "My schedule is packed with my being a 'clear and present danger' these days."

Jessikah turned a nice shade of red when she realized Grey had used her words.

"I'm terribly sorry," she said, quickly. "I meant no insult."

"Don't sweat it," Grey said, waving her words away.

"I've been called worse. You may want to watch your words, though. Not every mage is as casual and easygoing as I am. Most of them are touchy about their reputations and pedigrees."

"Most?" I said. "You mean all, right?"

"Dexter being his uncle still doesn't explain the deviation in protocol for this particular mage," Jessikah mused, regaining some of her natural color. "The Black Orchid is going above and beyond to apprehend Tristan."

"By apprehend, you mean erase and kill?" Grey asked. "Didn't seem like they were looking to have a chat over tea last night."

"I don't know what their orders are," Jessikah replied. "We left the sect at different times."

"I might have an idea why they have such an interest in Monty," I said. "It was something Evers said."

"What did she say?" Jessikah asked.

"She said Monty was one of the *original* Black Orchid."

TWELVE

"Bloody hell," Jessikah said. "I think I'm going to need something a little stronger than tea."

"That's going to have to wait. You were followed," Grey said, putting his mug down and grabbing his duster in one smooth, practiced motion. "Too damned early for this, Strong. You realize I haven't finished my coffee?"

"Followed?" Jessikah asked. "By whom?"

"Not you," Grey snarled. "Him." He pointed at me. "This doesn't feel like your Orchid agents. This is someone a little higher on the food chain."

Behind us, a figure emerged. The young man was dressed in a black suit with silver accents. His eyes threw me off. The distinct pupils, elongated and vertical, shone with a subtle yellow energy.

Grey and I both drew our guns. He was faster by a full second. Shit.

"Who are you? You have two seconds," Grey said, then paused. "Strong? Is cat-eyes with you?"

"He's with me," Jessikah said. "Please put your weapons away."

"Strong?" Grey asked, still looking at the young man. "Friend of yours?"

"I'm thinking I should shoot first, and ask questions later."

"Simon," Jessikah said, exasperated, "this...is Ink."

The young man gave me a slight nod. His energy signature was substantial.

"This is your...cat?"

"Her what?" Grey asked. "Come again?"

I noticed neither of us had holstered our weapons.

"I am her companion and her weapon," Ink said in proper English, sounding very much like Jessikah and Monty, "much like your hound and your blades. I'm always there when she needs me."

How did he know about my blade? I never mentioned having another weapon. How could Ink sense Ebonsoul?

"Strong?"

"He's friendly...I think," I said. "How do you know about my blade?"

"Both of your blades are tethered to your energy signatures," Ink replied. "You both hold blades of power. Although,"—he glanced at Grey—"his appears to be the more dangerous of the two."

"She's a bit on the bloodthirsty, psychotic side," Grey answered, "but she serves a purpose."

Grey holstered his gun and I followed his example, bringing the tension down to a nine from fifteen. Grey moved from behind the bar and stepped to the front door.

I turned to face Ink.

"Where were you when Richard wanted to blast her to ashes?"

"She was not in danger from such a low-level mage."

"And now?"

"Now...you are all in danger," Ink answered. "The mage approaching this."—he raised an eyebrow as he looked around—"establishment...is formidable. Retreat would be the wisest course of action."

"I think I liked him more as a cat, and I'm not a fan."

"He's still as cheerful in cat form," Jessikah said. "You just can't hear him."

"I have enough voices in my head," I said. "I don't need another, especially not Mr. Cheerful over here."

"We should leave now," Ink said. "Is there another exit?"

"You want me to *run* from my home?" Grey asked. "You think I'm going to let some mage come into my house?"

"Are those rhetorical questions?" Ink asked, moving closer to Jessikah. "If not, the answer is yes, to both."

"He's not going to," I said. "Grey, do you still have the sanctuary room?"

"Upstairs, first door to the right of the stairs," Grey said, while focusing on the door. "Do not make the mistake of trying the other doors. I don't want to have to wipe up what's left of you."

"Your job is to keep her safe, right?" I asked Ink. "You're her guardian?"

"Well, that's an oversimplification of the myriad facets regarding my duties," Ink said. "My tasks are clear. Her safety is paramount, and she is a Daughter—"

"Take her upstairs to the sanctuary room and keep her

safe, now," I said, cutting him off. "You can explain your duties later."

"Absolutely not," Jessikah protested. "I'm a mage and you aren't." She pointed to me. "If anyone should be taking shelter in some sanctuary room, it should be you."

"Not everything is as it seems, Miss," Ink said, pulling Jessikah away by the arm. "I'm certain these gentlemen"—he glanced down—"and their hellhound are more than capable of dealing with the impending threat."

"Are you saying I'm not?" Jessikah answered, wrenching her arm away from Ink's grasp. "Is that what you're insinuating?"

"I just think that it would be best..."

"Shut it," Grey said from the door. "She wants to stay and fight, let her. If she falls, we'll honor her death. What we will not do, is waste time yapping when someone is on their way to dust us."

Jessikah gave us a self-satisfied nod. Ink sighed and shook his head. I turned to face Grey and drew Grim Whisper.

"How bad is it?" I asked. "Can you tell what we're up against?"

"I've ascertained..." Ink started and promptly stopped as both Grey and I gave him a look. "Please, do carry on."

"Bad," Grey said, glancing at Ink. "The cat boy is right. Whatever is headed this way is nasty and powerful."

"How do you figure we were followed?" I asked. "I mean...?"

"Simple," Grey said, "None of the Orchid that were here last night read this strong. You just told me Ezra sent you to me. Ezra's isn't exactly what *I* would call a secure location. The conversation could have been overheard. Did he mention me by name?"

I thought back to Ezra's and nodded.

"Yes, he mentioned you by name."

"There's that, plus the fact that your signature is one screaming 'come find me' beacon, if someone knows how to look," Grey said. "Are you sure you don't know the cause?"

"Don't know," I said. "But if it's going to attract this kind of attention, I better deal with it before I look for Monty."

"Sounds like a good idea," Grey said, drawing his gun. "We may not get to speak later. When I went dark, or close to it, I needed to find a place that was familiar, a place that felt like home. Does Tristan have a place like that?"

"The closest place besides the Moscow would be the Golden Circle," I said. "Why would he need a place that felt like home?"

"It's the change," Grey answered. "It will take him back to the deepest memory of the familiar before forcing him in one direction or the other. If he's anywhere, it's the Golden Circle. Now, move back."

We stepped away from the door and headed to the other side of the floor, near the staircase.

"I still think discretion is the better part of valor in this instance," Ink said, drawing two guns about the size of Grim Whisper. "But if we must fight, we fight to the last breath."

I gave him a short nod and looked down at my hellhound.

<*Someone bad is coming.*>

<I know. I can smell him.>

<When he gets here, you take the cat-lady and her cat some place safe. Far from here.>

<They will want to fight.>

<They're scared, and the cat-lady might get hurt. I can't worry about her and simultaneously stop the bad guy.>

<You might get hurt, bondmate, and I can't take you some place safe. You still smell.>

<I'll be fine. Take them away, and then come back and help me face whatever is coming.>

<Will I get extra meat after? Can you have the shadow-man bring me two bowls?>

<If we manage to survive this, I'll make sure you get two bowls of the best meat.>

"How about we fight until their last breath?" Grey asked. "I'm attached to breathing."

"Fair enough," Ink answered. "We fight until their last..."

An explosion rocked the front of The Dive. I turned as the door was ripped off its hinges. It hung, suspended in mid-air for a split second, before being launched inward. The runes were bright on its surface, as the large wooden slab of pain and destruction was cast forth.

Heading directly for me.

THIRTEEN

Before I could press the main bead on my mala bracelet, and materialize my shield, Peaches blinked out.

He intercepted the door, but it was a matter of physics. The heavy door outweighed him by several hundred pounds. He crashed into it head-first. His maneuver managed to deflect it, knocking it off its trajectory, but the impact with the door bounced him across the room.

It tossed him into the area behind the bar, slamming him against the wall, before he fell behind the bar with a crash. The door caromed off my hellhound and punched into the wall, shattering into small, lethal pieces of runic shrapnel.

Grey waved a hand, creating a shield in front of us and stopping the pieces from converting us into pin-cushions. I made to run to the bar, but Grey grabbed me by the shoulder with a vise-like grip, pulling me back.

"I need to go get him," I said, straining against his hand. "He's hurt."

"He's a hellhound," Grey said, his voice grim as he held

me in place. “The wood of the door just knocked him for a loop. He’ll be good, but right now he’s safer behind the bar.”

“What the hell kind of wood was that?”

I had never seen anything knock the wind out of Peaches like that. The pieces of the door, scattered all over the floor of The Dive, vibrated with a low hum of power.

“Same as the bar,” Grey answered, holstering his gun, drawing a black sword, and heading to the now empty doorway. “That thing would have done serious damage if it had hit you. You must have someone very pissed off looking for you.”

<*Are you okay, boy?*>

<*I am hurt, but I will get better. The wood hurt. I will need extra meat to get better faster.*>

<*Nice try. Once you feel better, remember the plan.*>

<*Take the cat and the cat-lady away.*>

<*Right—now stay back there until you’re better.*>

“That list is going to be hard to narrow down,” I said. “Can we block the doorway somehow?”

“On it,” Grey answered. “Stay back.”

Grey gestured again with a grunt of pain. Black tendrils shot out from the sword, filling the doorway and closing the gap, creating a door of dark, living energy.

“What the hell is that?” I said, pointing at the doorway. “That looks dangerous and deadly.”

“Dark magic,” Jessikah hissed. “Is that a dark gateway?”

“You don’t want to know,” Grey said. “More importantly, someone just blew through my door like it was tissue paper. I have serious runes, Strong. Powerful, heart-stopping runes.”

“Not powerful enough,” I said, looking at the new

undulating doorway of darkness. "What could blast your door like that?"

"Can't think of much, short of a negomancer...or a god," Grey said.

I glanced over at Jessikah, who had visibly paled as she looked from the door to Grey with an expression of fear and respect. On-the-job training sucked when you were a mage.

"Negomancer...like Beck?"

"Beck couldn't even scratch my door," Grey scoffed. "Whoever is out there makes Beck look like a novice."

"So, it's not Beck?"

"Not even close," Grey said. "You piss off any gods lately?"

"That a serious question?" I asked, staring at Grey. "Are we talking about today, or in general?"

"Do I sound like I'm joking?" Grey answered. "Today, as in the last twenty-four hours."

"Perhaps now would be a good time for that sanctuary area?" Ink asked. "The integrity of this level seems to have been compromised."

"Anything that can get through that door that fast will make short work of the runes upstairs," Grey snapped. "This is the safest place in the building."

Ink glanced at the doorway.

"It doesn't feel very safe at the moment."

Grey shot him a glare and then looked at me.

"Strong, is this a god?" Grey asked, calmly. "Is Kali coming to pay you a house call? Did you do something to piss her off?"

"It's not like we hang out," I snapped. "Why is it me, all of a sudden?"

"Destruction follows you like odor on a skunk," Grey answered. "Black Orchid don't usually possess this kind of firepower. So I'm leaning to those who would want you eliminated."

"What about you?" I asked. "You said it yourself, you have plenty of enemies."

"My enemies are more the intimate type," Grey said. "They would prefer to carve out my heart, not blow up my door."

"Wow," I said, "I think I'll keep my enemies."

"I'm fairly certain this wasn't Black Orchid," Grey answered, pensively. "At least not the three who were here last night."

"I don't think it was a god," I said. "The deities I know, and have the pleasure of pissing off, aren't the dramatic type. They wouldn't blow off your door, either." I recalled my last interaction with Kali. "They just hit you with massive power and death. We'd be in the middle of a very large, very deep crater right now, especially if it was Kali."

"Hmm, then maybe it's not just you," Grey said, turning to Jessikah. "I bought us some time; not much, but some. What exactly did *you* do to the Black Orchid?"

Jessikah turned her head away.

"I'm Farsight," she said after a moment.

"Good for you," Grey said. "Get some glasses? How does that help us?"

"She can see three seconds into the future," I clarified. "Farsight, not farsighted."

"You're a precog?" Grey asked. "Rare, sure, especially among mages, but why would that get you killed?"

Jessikah glanced over at Ink. The realization slowly dawned on Grey's face.

"You're a Daughter of Bast?"

She nodded.

"Well...that explains some of this. No wonder they want you dead." He cursed under his breath. "Someone is out there with your friends. They weren't here last night just looking for Tristan."

"They probably were," she answered quickly, "but it would seem they were testing your defenses, looking for weaknesses."

"It would seem?" Grey asked, getting angry. "I'd say it would *seem*...damn. Black Orchid *and* a Daughter of Bast? I should've stayed in bed today."

He took a deep breath and let it out slow, calming himself down.

"They knew I would come here," she said, "eventually."

"Right, and you're supposed to die in the line of duty."

Jessikah nodded.

"I believe that's the plan," Jessikah said, looking around. "What better place than in the lair of a dark mage while searching for another?"

"This is not a lair. This is my home, and that door was expensive, not to mention the rune work. Still, I didn't think the Orchid had that kind of..."

Something flew through the dark tendrils covering the doorway with a scream, and impacted forcefully against the far wall with a wet, sick sound. The mangled mess that made it through the tendrils vaguely resembled a human. I walked over to the remains to get a better look, but there wasn't much to see.

"Whoever that was, they went quick," I said, stepping around the blood and bits of bone, looking at Jessikah. "You recognize him?"

"That...that was one of..."Jessikah started but couldn't finish. "That was Henry. He was a Black Orchid agent."

"Not anymore," I said, crouching down to get a better look. "Was Henry powerful enough to disintegrate the door?"

"No," Jessikah said. "I don't know. He was strong."

I stood and turned to Grey.

"What the hell kind of dark magic is that?" I asked, pointing at the tendrils.

"The kind that's keeping me alive," Grey said, narrowing his eyes at me. "That door is now a dark siphon. I'm sure you're familiar with the concept."

"Not like that, I'm not."

"Nothing is coming through that door and staying alive...for long."

"Tell me you have another exit, some sort of emergency exit or back door to this place."

"Can't use the back door. It's sealed," Grey said. "There's another way."

"They killed him...Henry," Jessikah said. "He was one of the—"

"Henry is among the dead now," Grey said, turning to the door. "I think you need to listen to your cat."

"Grey, I'm going to guess that the Black Orchid didn't disintegrate your door," I said. "That means—"

"Whoever or whatever is out there, is looking for you," Grey finished, his voice low.

"Strong," called a voice from outside. "I know you're in there, Simon Strong."

Everyone turned to look at me.

"Friend of yours?" Grey asked. "Something you need to share, before the dying starts?"

I looked over at the dead Orchid agent.

"I'd say we passed that part," I said. "I don't know who's out there."

"You don't know me, but I know of you," the voice said. "My name is Talin. I'm here to deliver a message from Evers."

"I got your message loud and clear," I said, glancing over at the dead body. "Did you have to kill him?"

"Oh, that? That's not the message for you," Talin answered after a short laugh. "That was a message to the Black Orchid agent inside there with you. Her insult of a sect is going to be destroyed, right after we deal with the Montagues."

"Henry must have been tasked with surveillance after last night," Grey said. "This Talin must have found him scoping out The Dive."

"Why do you say that?" Jessikah asked.

"If it had been the whole team,"—Grey glanced at Henry's body—"three bodies would be stacked over there right now."

I nodded.

"You need to come out now, Strong," Talin said. "We can make this quick and easy, or just hard and painful. Your death will bring us Tristan."

"Doubt it," I said. "Haven't you heard? He's all Darthy now."

"Cute, but incorrect. He is in a schism, not dark, which means he still has attachments...vulnerabilities...weaknesses. Like you and the Director at Haven."

"You must have the wrong Montague. Monty doesn't have vulnerabilities."

"After we kill you and his love, we will destroy his uncle and obliterate the Golden Circle, before ending his life."

"Seems like you have a full schedule," I said. "Where is Evers?"

"I'm afraid she's busy at the moment," Talin replied. "You should make this easy on yourself. I don't want to kill you. I'm inviting you to death."

"Well, when you put it that way, how could I refuse?"

"Precisely. Resistance is futile."

"He killed...he killed Henry," Jessikah muttered, still in shock. "Who is that?"

"Someone who is going to kill us all, if we let him," I said, turning to Grey. "What is the other way out?"

"Behind the bar. Pull up the trapdoor and follow the tunnel all the way out."

"What about you?" Jessikah said. "Are you going to the sanctuary room?"

"Don't need to," Grey said. "I can lock down the entire place. The door is a crumple zone. I designed it as a point of failure."

"Why on earth would you do that?" Jessikah asked. "They'll walk right in."

"I know," Grey said, pressing a palm on the floor, igniting all of the runes around us with red energy. "You better head out before he gets impatient. I doubt he's going to wait all day."

"I owe you," I said, moving to the bar with Jessikah and Ink in tow. I found the trap door and opened it, letting a groggy Peaches down first, before the rest followed. "Kick his ass, but if it gets dicey, get the hell out of here."

"He may be strong, but he's in *my* house," Grey said

with a growl. "No one attacks me in my home...and survives."

I paused at the top of the stairs.

"It gets bad, you bug out. I'll make sure the damage is repaired."

"Damn straight you will. I'm going to expect a new, runed door, Strong," Grey said, holding up his sword. "Go find Tea-and-Crumpets and make sure he doesn't step over. Go—now."

I ran down the stairs.

A few seconds later, the sounds of destruction followed.

FOURTEEN

"Where does this lead?" Jessikah asked as we ran down the tunnel. "Will he make it?"

"Don't know," I said, and I didn't. I knew Grey was tough and powerful, but whoever redecorated the entrance to The Dive was at least on his level if not stronger. "We need to put distance between us and The Dive."

"You're not going to help him?"

I stopped running and stared at her.

"What did you say?" I asked. "You want me to go back and help him?"

"Yes, it's the right thing to do," she said with a nod. "Whatever destroyed that door is clearly powerful, possibly more powerful than the Night Warden. He needs help."

I shook my head. Apparently, she had just missed the horror show of watching one of her Black Orchid sect mates going through a lethal doorway. Serious trauma had a way of doing that. The brain can only take so much before it starts deleting the bad parts.

We needed to get this straight now, or I was going to have to cut her loose, which would be a death sentence for her. She was strong, but not nearly strong enough to deal with Talin or Evers.

Neither was I.

"The right thing to do?" I asked, hearing the destruction behind us. "What are you talking about?"

"You're just going to leave him alone?" she asked, glancing back down the tunnel. "He sounds like he needs help."

"I strongly advise against returning to that establishment," Ink said. "The threat level is considerably higher than expected. We should—"

"Yes, I'm just going to leave him alone," I said, measuring my words. "Grey can probably stand against Talin. You and me? Not a chance."

"If we stayed, all of us could stop this Talin," she said. "Together, we are strong enough."

"Did you hit your head on the way down the stairs?"

"What are you talking about?" she asked. "I'm perfectly fine. I just don't think running is the best strategy here...it's cowardice."

"Cowardice?" I said, taking a deep breath and counting backward from a hundred by sevens. I let out the breath and managed to keep myself under control. "So what you're saying is that you're a battle-tested mage...right?"

"Well, no...what I meant—"

"What you *meant* is that you"—I pointed at her chest—"a veteran of dozens of these attacks, thinks it's cowardice to run away and stay alive?"

"I wouldn't say dozens."

"Hundreds?" I asked, feigning surprise. "Now I'm

impressed. No wonder they unleashed you on Monty. You must be one fierce mage destroyer. With that much firepower, I'm surprised the entire sect isn't out here looking for you."

"It's not hundreds either."

"How many mage battles *have* you been in?" I asked, letting the anger loose just enough to get the point across. "I mean real fights, where your life was on the line?"

"I daresay more than you," Jessikah answered, pushing her chin forward. "I was born and raised as a mage. I mean no offense, but you were not."

"Funny how the words that usually follow that statement of not being offensive usually are," I said, keeping my anger in check. "You didn't answer my question."

"Two battles," she said, staring me down hard. "The first was a fight for my life, and the second was the one when..."

"When you screwed up and almost got everyone killed?"

"Yes, and that wasn't my fault. There were circumstances beyond my control."

"Of course there were," I said. "There usually are when mages are involved."

"It may not be much, but I have actual mage training," she said. "I am equipped to deal with these circumstances. It's not something I expect you to understand."

"You remind me of someone I know," I said, keeping my voice even. "He didn't know how deep this world was until he was into it up to his neck."

"My lack of experience doesn't change the fact that you aren't a mage," she said. "I know you have some tenuous connection to Tristan, but you should really leave this to the mages."

"Monty is my friend, and more importantly, he's my family," I said, extending a hand, palm up, gathering energy. "I may not be a mage like you are, but I've learned in my short experience not to judge people by outward appearances."

"Miss, please step back," Ink said. "I'm registering a large accumulation of power."

"Of course you are," Jessikah said, exasperated. "There's a dark mage risking his life fighting some creature behind us and we're here jabbering."

"Not behind us," Ink said, pointing at me. "Him."

I had formed a smallish, violet sphere of power in my palm.

It was the orb that formed when I used my *ignisvitae* command, except this time I had only thought the command. The sphere whirled in my hand, radiating intense energy and nearly blinding me with its intensity. A few more seconds, and I wouldn't be able to hold it. I ran back to the stairs and poked my head just above the bar.

Grey was surrounded by dark tendrils.

Never a good sign. The light around him seemed dimmer, as if it were struggling to get away from being absorbed by the sword in his hands. Talin—I assumed it was Talin—was in trouble, and his expression showed it.

He was looking for a way out.

He was dressed in the usual black on black mageiform, but was looking a little worse for wear. There were ragged holes in his suit, one of the sleeves was torn, and he was wearing a few painful bruises across his face.

The sphere in my hand jumped, and I knew I had

seconds before it released the energy it contained. I focused on Talin and let it go. I felt the aftereffects of the energy in my palm, as it left my hand and slammed into the unsuspecting Talin.

He turned in my direction at the last second, a look of surprise on his face as the orb punched into his chest, blasting him through the nearby wall, destroying it. Rubble from the damage fell into the Talin-shaped hole, covering his body.

Grey laughed at the scene, except I knew it wasn't Grey. His laugh sounded like a blending of several laughs. Some were high pitched, others were low, but all of them creeped me the hell out.

It looked like Grey, but it was someone...something else.

Something incredibly powerful and lethal.

"Cursed one," Grey said in his blended voice, turning his head from the newly redecorated wall and looking at me. His eyes fluctuated from deep red to solid black. Waves of power washed off him. "Have you come to play?"

I shook my head slowly.

"Not even a little bit," I said slowly, backing up. "Is that you, Grey?"

"My vessel is present." Grey narrowed his eyes at me. "You hold a part of me within? Fascinating."

Then Scary Grey smiled.

Oh, shit.

The rubble started to shift, and I saw dark energy form around the debris.

"I'm just going to....you know"—I thumbed over my shoulder and headed back to the stairs—"leave this way."

"Leave me, cursed one," Creepy Grey answered, as

more tendrils shot out from the sword and into the debris. I heard Talin scream. "We will meet again...soon."

"Not too soon, I hope," I said under my breath, as I rushed down the stairs, pulling the trap door closed behind me and nearly crashing into Jessikah. "That's going to give me nightmares for a few years."

I saw the fear in her eyes.

"How did you...?" she asked. "What...what are you?"

"Right now? I'm in a rush to get away from this place. You can stay and 'help' all you want, but I can guarantee you that Grey, or whatever that is up there, doesn't need our help."

"Did he release her?" Jessikah asked as she ran behind me. "Did he release the sword?"

"I don't know what you're talking about," I said, picking up the pace. "I didn't see her. All I saw was Scary Grey with black tendrils all around him, and enough power pouring out of him to melt my brain."

"That was Izanami," Jessikah said. "I've only read the reports, but I didn't think it was true. She's a goddess contained within the sword. The sword is sentient and dangerous."

"I agree on both parts," I said, still moving fast. "I'm sure Talin agrees, too. He was getting his ass kicked. He probably still is, or he's dead by now. It didn't look like Scary Grey was in a hurry to finish him off."

"If Talin doesn't escape, she will feed on him."

"That sounds like a horrible way to go," I said. "Better Talin than us."

Jessikah glanced back when we reached another set of stairs at the end of the tunnel.

“They will blame the Night Warden for Henry’s death.”

“I wish them luck trying to make that stick,” I said moving to the stairs. “Grey isn’t in the mood right now to take anything but lives.”

I climbed the stairs two at time. Another door sealed the top of the stairs, and I really hoped it didn’t require some special rune sequence to open. That would defeat the purpose of this being an emergency exit.

I pushed on the door and it barely budged. I pushed again, shoving my shoulder into the door, and it flew open.

A pair of hands grabbed me, the world flashed white, and everything disappeared.

FIFTEEN

"What the hell?" I said as I looked around. "Where am I?"

I was standing in the middle of a mid-sized, green lawn. Surrounding the perimeter of the lawn were large stone globes covered with symbols. Each one pulsed with a subtle white energy. The symbols on the surface moved and rotated slowly around each of the spheres.

"What did you do?" a vaguely familiar voice asked. "Really?"

"You said you needed to speak to him," another voice replied. "Here he is."

"I didn't say right this moment," the first voice answered with a sigh. "You plucked him out of his stream?"

I didn't see anyone, but I was hearing voices, which meant I could be going through a few scenarios.

I might still be in the tunnel, and had begun spontaneously hallucinating—a strong possibility after meeting Scary Grey.

Another option was that I somehow made it out of the tunnel, but had been immediately blindsided by a taxicab

—not entirely beyond the realm of possibility in my city. If that was the case, I was currently in a bed at Haven and this was all a fever dream. A really vivid fever dream.

Option three was that my brain had finally had enough, had packed its bags and left the building, leaving me to ponder my madness in the middle of a green lawn with glowing globes around me. However, I was really lucid for someone who had just disconnected his brain from reality.

It's true, I had no context—it's not like I lost my mind on a regular basis—so I had nothing to compare it against, but this didn't feel like madness. Not any more than my usual days, that is.

"What did you expect me to do?" the second voice said. "Did you see what he did?"

"Of course I saw," the first voice said with a chuckle. "The Night Warden is going to be so pissed at him."

"I'm glad you find this entertaining, sir," the second voice answered. "His progression is in flux."

"It's his signature. He hasn't used the totem. This is troublesome."

"Hello?" I said, taking a chance I hadn't completely lost my mind. "Who are you? Where am I?"

Two figures materialized in front of me.

I recognized one of them immediately.

It was Sid Rat. The Lead Designer, Sid Rat.

"Hello, Simon," Sid said with a smile. "Been some time since we spoke. How are you?"

"Confused?"

"That's to be expected," Sid said with a nod. "This can be disconcerting. I apologize."

"What is going on?"

"It's a little hard to explain." Sid looked at the

young man next to him. "This place is sort of a parenthesis, an interstice of sorts, in your timestream's current events."

"Are you going to Zillerfry me?"

Sid laughed, and then looked at his watch and frowned. He wore a Limited Edition Steffon Carlson Patek Philippe time piece that glimmered with white light when he moved his wrist.

"Rey, we don't have much time."

"Understood," the other man said. "The time juncture?"

Sid nodded and then looked back at me as if remembering I was standing there.

"The explanation of this place is beyond even Professor Ziller," Sid said, picking up where he left off. "In simple terms, this place is similar to what happens to you when you press your mark, sort of like a pocket dimension of time. Without the personification of causality paying you a visit."

He gave me a short nod with a subtle smile.

"So, where am I right now? Or is it when?"

"Astute," Sid answered with a nod of approval. "When is more appropriate."

"So when am I?"

"Hmm," Sid said, tapping his chin. "That's a hard question."

"You *are* going to Zillerfry me, aren't you?"

"Do you mean when are you now in terms of your timestream, or the parallel streams that have been designed to intersect with yours?"

"What?"

"There is also the factoring of which 'you' we are

discussing," Sid continued his brain-melting assault. "Are you positing the theory of—"

"Sir?" the young man next to him said. "I think you lost him."

I nodded silently.

"Sorry," Sid said, holding up a hand. "Sometimes I get carried away. I forget—the adherence to the concept of linear time is ingrained in most. Thank you, Rey."

Rey was a tall, young man with a deep intelligence in his eyes. He looked at me with a small degree of pity. He was dressed similar to Sid, wearing a blue blazer over a white shirt and blue jeans. There was a small, silver emblem on the blazer: three interlocked circles—a triquetra.

"Did you want to accelerate the process?" Rey asked. "The box?"

"Oh, yes!" Sid said, turning to face me. "Why didn't you use the box?"

"What box?" I asked. "What are you talking about?"

"That box," Sid said, pointing at my jacket pocket. "The one I gave you. I did give it to you, didn't I?"

I reached into my pocket and pulled out the keepsaker Sid had given me.

"This?" I asked. "You were kind of vague when you gave it to me. I don't even know how to open it."

"I apologize," Sid said. "Sometimes I don't have the luxury of exhaustive explanations. If you'll excuse me, I'm dealing with a delicate situation...Rey?"

Sid moved off to a corner of the lawn, mumbling something to himself. I caught something about bifurcating timestreams at positional junctions, and then he lost me.

"Got it," Rey said, glancing at Sid as he approached

me. "You'll have to excuse him; he can come across as distracted at times."

"You think?" I asked. "Is he okay? He seemed much more put together the last time I saw him. Granted, it was only for a few minutes—I think—but he wasn't talking to himself."

"He does that sometimes," Rey answered with a nod, glancing in Sid's direction. "How did you know he was talking to himself?"

"Excuse me, what?"

"Oh, you meant 'talking to himself' as if he were alone, right?"

"Is there another method of talking to yourself?"

"He's a Lead Designer," Rey said with admiration. "He's talking to 'himself' across different timestreams. Different versions of himself."

"Oh," I said, because sometimes my mastery of language astounds even me. "That's almost impossible to wrap my head around. I think I'd prefer an afternoon chat with Professor Ziller at this point. Probably safer for my remaining brain cell."

I touched my ears repeatedly.

"What are you doing?" Rey asked. "Is something wrong with your ears?"

"I'm checking to see if my brain is leaking out," I said, glancing at Sid. "Does he do that often?"

"I know he seems a little off at times," Rey said with a knowing smile. "I can assure you, he's sharper than he appears."

"Not exactly filling me with confidence here," I said. "He gave me a box and neglected to tell me how to open it. Do you know how to open it?"

"We're going to address that now," Rey replied. "Try to understand, as a Lead Designer, he monitors countless timestreams at one time. Anyone else would be driven mad; it takes centuries of training."

"Centuries?" I said, with a new appreciation for Sid's abilities. "How old is he?"

"That's not a rabbit hole you want to jump into. Easy answer? Lead Designers count their birthdays in millennia."

"He doesn't look a day over a thousand," I said, glancing at Sid again. "How does he do it without losing his mind?"

"Practice and focus," Rey said. "Anyway, that's why he can come across as distracted. His focus is everywhen, literally at times."

"Are you a designer, too?"

"Not really, I'm a Temporal Realignment and Interdiction Operative—TRIO. You'd understand it more as Time Police," Rey said. "Before you ask, I don't know any Doctors, never went to med school, and make all my phone calls on a cell phone, pretty much like yours—not in a blue police box that happens to be bigger on the inside than on the outside."

"I wasn't going to ask any of that."

"Sure you weren't," Rey answered. "My job is simple: I make sure the streams aren't violated. Basically, I watch the streams to prevent splintering or blatant abuse."

"Blatant abuse of time?" I asked. "Seriously?"

"Yes. In any case, let's get you working on the TEST."

"I have to take a test?" I asked. "I'm not ready for a test...wait, what kind of test?"

"Temporal Energy Signature Totem. A TEST is an artifact that will help regulate the fluctuation you are going through," Rey said. "It's what Sid gave you in the box."

"A totem? What kind of totem?"

"That's up to you," Rey said. "It will take shape according to how you view objects of power." Rey looked at the keepsaker. "In this case, small objects of power."

"So it could be anything?"

"It's usually something from your memory, and wearable," Rey answered. "Something that made an impression on you and remains with you, even to this day."

"That could be anything," I said. "Especially after meeting Monty."

"It could be, but it won't be."

"Good thing that's not cryptic at all," I said with a glare."That's all well and good, but why am I going through this?"

"Wow, that's a whole other subject we really can't get into right now."

"Are you going to tell me we don't have time?"

"Yes and no," Rey said, with a crooked smile. "I can't tell you, but I can help you open this"—he pointed to the keepsaker—"and that will set you on the path to answers. Fair enough?"

I nodded.

"Fair enough," I said. "How do I open it?"

"First things first. TESTs have a limited amount of uses," Rey said. "It depends on your current level of power, and how far off alignment your signature is currently operating."

"That, I kind of understand."

"Okay, good," Rey said. "The next part is not so fun... the initial adjustment period kind of hurts. The greater the amount of uses, the greater the pain. There's always a cost."

"Hurts how?"

"Try opening the box."

"I tried this a few times before. I got nothing, except nearly spraining my wrists."

"Try opening it the same way you created the sphere of power a little while ago," Rey coaxed. "Focus the energy with your mind and into the box."

I tried to focus energy into the keepsaker, picturing energy flowing from me into the palm of my hand...nothing.

"It's not working."

"I think I see the problem," Rey said with a nod. "You're not a mage."

"Oh, is that all?" I said, frustrated. "I could've saved you all this trouble."

"No, no, no," Rey said, raising a hand. "Hear me out. Mages are foci for the energy they manipulate, which is why they don't use wands or staves or other methods of focus. The mage is the focus. With me so far?"

"Yes," I said, remembering when Monty had to use a focus during his shift. "I follow you."

"Good," Rey continued. "Since you aren't a mage, you can't think of yourself as the focus—you have to go beyond. This is both easier and harder. You can be both weaker and stronger over time."

"Beyond, how?"

"Instead of viewing yourself as the source of energy—which mages do with their will, by spooling energy into their bodies and then tapping into it—you have to invert that thought process. The source of energy is all around you; all you're doing is aligning to the flow and channeling it, not storing it in your body."

"Easier and harder...? More on the harder side, I think," I said. "Are you sure you didn't study with Professor Ziller?"

"I'll tell you a secret," Rey said, looking back at where Sid stood. "Ziller was one of the few mages to ever make it through the Lead Designer novice program."

"Novice...program? Professor Ziller?"

"Yes, Sid even invited him to take the intermediate level in a few centuries, when he matured more."

"That is staggeringly mind-blowing on levels I can't even voice."

"I know," Rey said. "Ready to try again?"

"The whole energy concept is throwing me off."

"Think of it like the ocean," Rey said. "A mage is a container and can carry the water with him wherever he goes. You, not being a mage, have to stay in the water and splash it where you want it to go. Is that easier to grasp?"

"Somewhat," I said. "I need to tap into the energy all around me and then direct it?"

"You've done it a few times already," Rey said. "Much to our surprise. Now you have to be intentional, not reactive. Precise, not scattershot."

I let my senses expand and felt the energy around me. I nudged the energy to the keepsaker in my hand, and felt it wrap itself around the box. I felt it shift in my hand and open slightly.

"There you go," Rey said with a nod of approval. "Remember what I said about the cost? When you put on the TEST, you won't be able to remove it until it's exhausted, or..."

He paused.

"Or?"

"Or you're killed. Which for you would be quite difficult, considering your curse."

"How bad is it?"

"Try to recall the worst pain you've ever felt," he said. "Got it?"

"Yes," I said, recalling some of my most agonizing moments. "That bad?"

"That's where you begin," Rey said with a nod. "Make sure you're safe before you put it on. It can take you out of play for a bit."

"I opened it," I said, looking down at the keepsaker. "Does this mean the box is open out there?"

"Out where?" Rey asked. "This isn't a dream. This is the same effect as you pressing your mark and briefly stepping out of time. This is still you...the corporeal you. Only this time, *I* pulled you out of the timestream."

"Why are you doing this?"

"It's what *Sid* does," Rey said. "I'm just on loan at his request. TRIO usually takes a more...surgical approach to temporal entanglements."

"A surgical approach? Like?"

"If we find an abrupt deviation in a timestream, we cap it, and move to a parallel stream with relocations."

"Why does that sound devastatingly painful and lethal?"

"Because it is," Rey said, his expression grim. "We don't waste time."

"You think he's wasting time?"

"With you? No," Rey said. "But we don't really understand Lead Designers, anyway. We basically stay out of their way and do as they request."

"How strong is he?" I asked as we headed back to where Sid stood. "Is he stronger than an Arch Mage?"

"Lead Designers like him, because of their exposure to the timestreams, eventually become embodiments of Time...capital T," Rey said. "What do you think?"

"Much, much stronger than any Arch Mage."

"Sid has probably forgotten more runes, castings, and wards than any Arch Mage will ever learn in their lifetime."

"Right, making a mental note to never piss off Sid."

"Always a good policy," Rey said with a smile. "You ready?"

"Ready? Ready for what?"

Rey nodded to Sid, who nodded back.

"I apologize for the abruptness, Simon," Sid said. "But we'll speak again soon. I look forward to it. Brace yourself...this might sting a bit."

"What? What are you..."

A white flash blinded me, and I found myself pushing up on the door at the top of the stairs leading away from The Dive. I shoved the door open, and rolled out into the afternoon heat, coming just short of the busy street.

"We should get off the street," Jessikah said from behind me as she looked around. "This city *is* peculiar. Did no one see you exit and tumble out of an underground tunnel?"

"If it doesn't directly impact us, we don't care," I said. "Especially if it's going to make us late somewhere. Then, we don't even acknowledge its presence, no matter how bizarre it can be."

I turned back to look at the exit we had just stepped out of, but it had disappeared. I couldn't even sense where the tunnel was. Whatever runes Grey had used, they were excellent at camouflage.

"You're right though," I said, looking around. "We do need to get off the street. We need to go somewhere your friends, or my enemies, would think twice about attacking."

"You know another run-down, seedy clubhouse we can go to?"

I pulled out my phone and pressed a button.

"You destroyed it?" Cecil answered, with a certain amount of restrained joy. "Did you kill the Dark Goat? How did you survive? Tell me everything."

"Always great to hear your voice too, Cecil," I said. "Good morning, how has your day gone? Oh, mine? Thanks for asking. Well, aside from the fact that some maniac is out there trying to blow me to bits..."

"You're going to need to be a bit more specific, Simon," Cecil said. "That sounds like a normal day for you and Tristan."

"Tristan is in trouble," I said. "I'm headed to Erik's and need the Dark Goat delivered there."

"You mean it's still intact?" he asked, sounding somewhat defeated. "I thought you called to tell me it was in pieces. You know, your usual."

"Still in one glorious piece of automotive art," I said. "I don't think the Dark Goat *can* be destroyed."

"What happened to Tristan?"

"Schism, but I'm not going to let him go dark if I can help it."

"Damnation," Cecil answered. "A schism is tricky business. Do you know what you're doing?"

"Not really, but I figure I'm the best chance he has."

Silence.

"Call Dex," he said after a good twenty seconds of empty air. "There are things happening here that you need to know. He can help you with Tristan, as well."

"I will," I said, intrigued. "In the meantime, I need a ride. Can you send Robert?"

"Robert is away on a delivery," he answered, and I heard him punching some keys. "I have your location. I'll send one of the other drivers in one of our new experimental models—the LUMPS edition. We've had good results with it so far."

"LUMPS?" I asked, confused. "Do I even want to know?"

"No, you don't."

"Is this driver any good?" I said, looking down the street. "We may have some nastiness after us."

"I would feel more confident about the vehicle returning intact, if *he* drove," Cecil answered. "I think you'll like him. He drives like you. Wear your seatbelt."

"Thanks, I think?"

"Five minutes. Sit tight."

"Thanks, Cecil...really."

"You can thank me by helping Tristan," Cecil answered. "Call Dex."

He hung up.

SIXTEEN

Five minutes later, a dark purple Lamborghini Urus screeched up to where we stood and stopped exactly where we were standing.

A young man unlocked the doors and beckoned us to enter the vehicle. It was an exact replica of the one we destroyed in London. I say "destroyed," but it was really a victim of circumstance. The circumstance was we were driving it—the demons attacking us preferred we were dead, so they blew it up.

I want to say it was a misunderstanding, but we understood the intent pretty clearly. Cecil was livid with Monty for weeks after that. The fact that he sent me another Lamborghini only demonstrated how worried he was.

The young man gave us a grin as we got in.

"Nice ride," I said, as the young man opened the doors. "I'll ride shotgun. Jessikah, will you and...?"

Ink was gone.

"He's close," she said. "Don't worry."

"Not worried," I said, worried. "Just hope Peaches doesn't start poofing off on his own."

"I don't think hellhounds 'poof' anywhere," Jessikah said, looking down at Peaches, who approached the back seat like he owned it. "They more or less *whomp* wherever they want, especially this one."

Peaches jumped into the back seat, but left some room for Jessikah. He was a Sprawlmeister with style, and yes, he did sort of *whomp* when he finally settled in. Jessikah sat next to him. He placed his enormous head on her lap, giving her the puppy-dog look and a nudge of her hand to get some head rubs. She looked down with a smile and obliged the ham. He gave off a low rumble of pleasure.

<You made some room for her. That was nice of you.>

<She still smells scared. Being next to me will calm her down.>

<You are many things, boy. Calming is not one of them.>

< I think she's scared of you.>

<Me? Why would she be scared of me?>

<You made a ball of energy. It was scary. Plus, you smell.>

<I don't smell.>

<I think your smell scared the cat man away. Is your nose broken? I can smell you from here.>

<I'm working on the smell.>

<I don't smell like you. I smell calm. You smell angry.>

<Right, I'm sure her fear has nothing to do with the immense, aluminum-chewing hellhound next to her. There's no way she would be scared of you.>

<I'm too cute to be feared. You smell, and it's a scary, angry smell. Should I lick you?>

<Just behave until I figure out what's going on.>

The driver was young, almost too young to be driving in the city, kind of young. His blondish brown hair was a mess under his black cap, which read *Formula 1 for Life*. This did not set me at ease.

"You're into racing?" I asked nonchalantly, as I started strapping myself in. "Formula 1?"

"Quite," he said, touching the brim of his cap. "Oh, the cap. It was a gift from my uncle. Love F1. Currently following Hamilton, but love them all, past and present."

"Are you sure you have a license to drive?" I asked, concerned. "How old are you?"

"In *your* years?"

That question alone should've been enough to stop my line of questioning, but no, I kept going forward. I liked to live dangerously.

"Yes, in *my* years," I said, matching his tone. "You're barely sprouting fuzz on your chin. So I'm thinking you're barely old enough to get behind a wheel, especially the wheel of this vehicle. I don't want Cecil blaming me for any scratches on this thing."

"Scratches? On a LUMPS? Impossible. Do you know what LUMPS stands for?"

"Not really, no."

"Uncle Cecil didn't tell you?"

"Uncle...Cecil?" I asked. "He's your uncle?"

"He's everyone's uncle," the driver said with a wink. "Anyway, I thought he would've told you, of all people."

"I asked him not to, but now I'm not so sure about that," I said warily. "Cecil has a knack for giving me heart attacks when he describes the runework he installs on vehicles."

"Do you want to know?" he asked. "It's pretty boss."

"Sure. Does it define the state of my body when I leave this thing?"

He laughed.

"No," he said, caressing the dash. "It stands for: Lamborghini Urus Montague Peaches Strong edition. This baby is a tank disguised as a jet, and he named it after you."

"I don't know if I should be flattered or insulted," I said, shaking my head. "And you're old enough and qualified to drive this tank-jet?"

"True, I look young, but I do all the SuNaTran automotive stress testing," he said with a wicked grin. "I'm Ayrton, by the way, and I'm about"—he scrunched his face up making the calculations—"about ninety-five of your years old ."

He didn't look a day over twenty.

"Right," I said, clearly taken by surprise. "Ayrton is it... like the F1 driver?"

He nodded, and beamed with an infectious smile.

"Where to, sir?"

"Don't 'sir' me," I said with a smile. "You're old enough to be my dad. The name is Simon, or call me Strong. We're going to the Hellfire Club. Do you know where that is?"

"Of course, Strong, sir," Ayrton said with a smile in return. "Please finish strapping in."

I pulled the five-point harness over my body and locked it in place. He started the engine with a roar, and basked in the purr and rumble of runically enhanced Italian engineering. I took a moment to sit in the rumble with him. I was liking him more by the second.

"Now *that* is an engine," I said. "Never get tired of that sound."

"Agreed, sir," Ayrton said with a nod, pulling his cap down a little lower over his head. "Are you ready?"

"Ready? For what?"

"There seem to be several vehicles strategically placed at our rear," Ayrton answered, without looking back. "I'm going to assume you want me to lose them?"

I glanced in the rearview mirror and saw three large, black sedans parked about a block way. They were driving what appeared to be ultra-enhanced 1990 Chevy Impala SS Interceptors. The black tint on the windows only added to the air of menace.

"Black Orchid?" I asked Jessikah. "Is that what they drive?"

Jessikah nodded.

"Those are Interceptors—special Black Orchid vehicles," she said. "I'm afraid we won't be able to lose them. They are fast and dangerous. This is a pretty vehicle, but no one escapes the Black Orchid Interceptors."

I glanced over at Ayrton, who was wearing a smile. It was a smile I recognized, because I wore it every time I drove the Dark Goat.

"I think you'd better strap in," I said to Jessikah. "Ayrton here may be one of the first drivers to escape the Black Orchid."

"I highly doubt..."

"With all due respect, ma'am," Ayrton answered with a slight smile. "This is a SuNaTran vehicle, and I'm the best driver SuNaTran has. We'll lose them. Please strap in."

Jessikah strapped in and Ayrton crushed the gas.

SEVENTEEN

Italian engineering, unlike American muscle, believes an automobile should get from point A to point B in the shortest time mechanically possible, all while looking good doing it. American muscle is fast and powerful. The Dark Goat was a monster on the road, but this LUMPS was about as close to sitting in a rocket car as I wanted to get.

The Black Orchid Interceptors never stood a chance.

Ayrton shot down 1st Avenue and flipped a series of switches, which caused the LUMPS to drop down low on its chassis, lowering its center of gravity.

"Hydraulics?" I barely managed over the roar of the engine. "This thing has hydraulics?"

"Yes, sir," Ayrton said. "If we don't lower the COG, I can't do things like this."

He pulled the steering wheel hard to one side while simultaneously using the emergency brake. The LUMPS pulled a tight one-eighty turn and Ayrton nosed into the entrance to the FDR Drive. He released the brake and stepped on the gas in one practiced motion as we put even more distance between us and the Black Orchid.

Jessikah looked behind us in shock.

The Interceptors appeared to be standing still as we accelerated. I gripped the door handle tight enough to turn my knuckles white. Ayrton glanced at me and laughed.

"Eyes on the road," I said, a little louder than I intended. "I don't want to end up a mangled, flaming wreck because you're distracted."

"Yes, sir," Ayrton answered, weaving through afternoon traffic. "Don't worry, I never get distracted."

I looked behind us, expecting to see the team of Interceptors, but the Black Orchid was gone.

"How fast is this thing?"

"Fast enough," Ayrton said. "Uncle Cecil made some 'modifications' to the engine for the LUMPS edition."

"Modifications? What? Like swapping it out for an F-35 engine?"

"I wish," Ayrton said, accelerating even more. "A Pratt & Whitney would really give her some kick."

I couldn't tell if he was serious or kidding. All I knew is that he could drive.

"Don't go giving Cecil any ideas, please," I said, barely holding on to my breakfast. "She can really fly."

Ayrton nodded, taking the 23rd Street exit at the last possible second, nearly smashing us into the concrete berm. He sped down 23rd and made a hard left on Park Avenue South, following it until it led to Broadway.

"I'm going to take a bit of a roundabout route, if you don't mind, sir," Ayrton answered with a tight smile. "I want to make sure we aren't followed."

"I don't think there's anything on four wheels that can follow us in this thing."

"That's the plan, sir. Please brace yourself."

I didn't think it was possible, but he managed to squeeze more power from the engine, pushing us faster. I kept stepping on the imaginary brake pedal on my side every time I saw him get too close to another car, only to slip to the side, avoiding it altogether.

Even taxis made room for the LUMPS barreling down the city streets.

"How are you doing that?" I asked, amazed. "Taxis don't usually move out of the way like that for anyone."

"Avoidance runes," Ayrton answered, as traffic parted for us. "Sends out an omnidirectional pulse saying to get out of the way. It makes life easier, that's for sure."

"No kidding," I said. "I might have to have Cecil put some of those on the Dark Goat."

"You have those on steroids," Ayrton said. "Everything and everyone wants to avoid that car. Only the Beast is worse."

He was right. The Dark Goat sent out some not-so-subtle *stay the hell away from me* vibes. I figured it was part of the rune package, but I didn't realize they were specifically designed to keep people away.

"That would explain some of the reactions I get," I said, thinking about it. "Still, I wouldn't trade her in for anything...not even a LUMPS."

"The Dark Goat is a sweet ride," Ayrton said. "Shame I can't drive her...I like breathing."

"That is one downside," I said. "At least you get to drive this monster."

"That I do," he said with another grin. "Cecil wanted

me to tell you that your vehicle will be waiting for you at the Club within the hour. It needs to be transported."

"Thanks," I said with a nod. "Maybe one day he'll lend me a LUMPS?"

Ayrton laughed.

"He said you'd say that," Ayrton answered. "He said, when you bring him the steering wheel, and *only* the steering wheel of the destroyed Dark Goat, he'll consider it. Otherwise don't even dream about it."

"I don't see that happening anytime soon. The Dark Goat is invincible, I think."

"Cecil says that about the Beast, too," Ayrton said, squeezing between two cars, barely grazing them. "Says he's starting a Lamborghini abstract art museum with your wrecks...an expensive one."

"Sounds like Cecil."

We had to stop a few blocks away from City Hall because the area was cordoned off due to NYTF activity.

"This is as far as I can go," Ayrton said, parking near the cordon. "NYTF has the area around City Hall closed off. All the streets heading south are blocked. Apparently, there was an explosion."

"I heard something about that."

"Did you have anything to do with it?" Ayrton asked. "Cecil says if you were in the neighborhood. You were probably involved."

"I was *not* involved, or even near the area, thank you very much."

"I'll let him know," Ayrton said, smiling and unlocking the doors. "You'd better get in the Club. If anyone is following you, your signature will give you away soon enough."

"Even in here?" I asked, looking around the LUMPS. "You can sense it?"

Ayrton narrowed his eyes and stared at me.

"Whatever you have going on, it's powerful," Ayrton said after a few seconds. "I can't see much in here because of the runes, but out there? You'll be shining like a small star."

"A small star with a target on its back," I said, worried. "I'm working on it. The Hellfire Club should shield me enough to deal with it."

Ayrton nodded.

"I hope so, sir," Ayrton said, serious. "Last time I saw that kind of energy, the client exploded in one of our cars."

"That's encouraging," I said, getting out of the LUMPS. "Thanks again. I'd say drive safely, but that's probably not one of your skills."

Ayrton laughed again, and waited for Jessikah and Peaches to exit the SUV.

"I'm always safe," Ayrton said, giving the engine some gas and increasing the roar. "It's just not safe for those who try to follow."

He locked the doors and pulled away slowly, before gunning the engine and disappearing around the corner in a blaze of speed.

"I can't believe he evaded the Interceptors," Jessikah said, still in awe. "No one has ever outrun the Black Orchid."

"I'd say they've never come across that particular driver in that particular vehicle," I said, moving down the street. "Let's not waste the time he bought us. Hellfire is a few blocks from here."

"Isn't the Hellfire Club part of the Dark Council?"

Jessikah asked as we moved quickly down the street. "The mage division?"

I nodded.

"Something like that," I said. "The person who runs the Hellfire, Erik, heads the mage division of the Dark Council, but the Hellfire Club is a separate entity from the Dark Council."

"And this Erik can help you?"

"I think so," I said. "The real question is...will he?"

"Why wouldn't he? Jessikah asked. "You're a friend in need. It's the most natural thing."

"I wouldn't exactly say we're friends," I said with a grimace. "More like acquaintances, very loose acquaintances. He's closer to Monty than me."

"Tristan is a mage after all," Jessikah added. "Mages don't like to mix with non-mages—it leads to complications. You're not a mage, but you're not entirely powerless either."

"I can hold my own, most of the time."

"What did the driver mean when he said he couldn't drive your car because he likes breathing?" Jessikah asked. "Is your car dangerous too?"

She was sharp. I hadn't expected her to catch that. If I lied, I'd only have to explain it later. Better to come clean now...well mostly clean.

"Cecil runed the Dark Goat so that only I could drive it," I said. "It's keyed to my signature. Anyone else trying to drive it gets a nasty reminder why that's a bad idea."

It was mostly the truth. I didn't want to have to explain how the nasty reminder was potential death, and how I managed to avoid it. I had a feeling she'd have a hard time grasping it all, coming from a non-mage.

"You're the only one who can drive it?"

"Yes, it's safer that way."

"Does Tristan drive?"

"I wouldn't call what he does driving exactly," I said. "I think he prefers those backward cars with the steering wheel on the right."

"You mean proper automobiles?"

"I mean backward automobiles," I said. "You're almost as bad as Monty. Anyway, on this side of the pond, we drive with steering wheels on the left."

"One more thing you've taken and perverted," she grumbled. "It's astounding."

"One more thing? What did we take and pervert?"

"We don't have that kind of time, I think," she said. "Let's just start and end with language. You say you speak English, but what you really speak is some kind of strange dialect that vaguely resembles English."

I didn't have a comeback for that...she was right.

"I'll give you that one. As I've told Monty many times, I don't speak English, I speak American and proud of it."

"Which is why no one in the civilized world understands you...not without a translator. It's simply incredible."

We moved fast down the street, and I saw the kiosk that signaled the entrance to the Hellfire Club. No one really stood in our way as we moved. I didn't have personal avoidance runes, but what I did have, was a Peaches. People parted before us when they saw him coming. I would've, too, if I'd run into a large hellhound on the street.

"Erik should be able to help me deal with my signature issue," I said, giving the NYTF cordon a wide berth. The last thing I wanted was to be seen anywhere near the site of the recent destruction. I made a mental note to ask Chi why she blew up the park. "He'll either help me or blast me...depends on how he's feeling today. We'll find out soon enough."

EIGHTEEN

We were up the block from the entrance to the Hellfire, when I pulled out my phone and dialed.

"Who are you calling now?" Jessikah asked, looking around furtively. "You said we needed to get off the streets."

"I can't just drop in on Erik," I said, waiting for the call to connect. "He doesn't like unannounced visitors."

"Is that the entrance over there?" Jessikah pointed to the Harlequin standing guard at the entrance. "Is she the door person?"

"Yes and no," I said, watching Jessikah approach the Harlequin. "What are you doing?"

Jessikah stood before the kiosk that led to the entrance of the Hellfire Club.

She gestured and formed an intricate rune that hung in the air.

In front of the kiosk stood a woman dressed in a skintight black-and-white checkered costume. Her face was hidden behind a black mask. The mask was a combination of tragedy and comedy.

This was one of the Harlequin—protectors of the Hellfire.

When she saw the runic symbol Jessikah had created, she bowed with a flourish and twirled the pair of rune-covered tonfas she held.

"The Black Orchid is always welcome," the Harlequin said. "Please step inside the circle."

She stood to one side of the large, rune-inscribed circle that rested at the top of the stairs. In order to get into the Hellfire, you needed to step in that circle—no exceptions. We stepped in. I took a deep breath, preparing for digestive torture.

"I need to see him," I said, calming myself and giving her a slight bow. "Is he in?"

The Harlequin nodded.

"He's expecting you."

The Harlequin returned the bow and slammed both tonfas into the ground. The circle we stood in flared to life. A second later, we stood at the foot of a flight of stairs that led to a large wooden door. This time there was no nausea, just a white-hot pain trying to split my skull open.

I fell to my knees, grabbing my head, and vaguely registered arms supporting me.

"Bring him inside," I heard Erik order. "Now, before it's too late."

I felt myself being carried as the world became one large blur. I looked to one side and saw a tall figure...Erik.

"Oh, hey, Erik," I said, through the mind-numbing pain. "Wash...wash...wash going on?"

“Get him to the null room, now. The secure one, downstairs.”

More movement and then a cool darkness. I closed my eyes and for a few seconds my brain didn’t feel like it was trying to escape through my skull.

“This is nice,” I said, mostly to myself. “Can I just lay here for a few decades?”

“Tell me you have a totem, Strong,” Erik said, the strain clear in his voice. “You’re too far along for me to arrest this.”

“Don’t arrest me,” I said, getting my bearings. “Jacket pocket. Keepsaker. There’s a TEST inside. Ow, my head. Did you change the teleportation sequence?”

“Your signature is reacting to the security measures of the Hellfire Club,” Erik answered in his usual clipped manner. “Why didn’t you call me first?”

I glanced at Jessikah with an *I told you so* look.

“What’s wrong with him?” Jessikah said. “He looks bad.”

“Thanks,” I said with a groan. “Kick a man when he’s down.”

“She’s right,” Erik said. “You’re crashing.” I could feel him going through my jacket pockets. “Are you sure you have...Never mind, I found it.”

“What...is the totem not there?” I asked, taking in the dimly lit room. I saw whips, cuffs and various implements of restraint and pain. “I’m not into you that way, Erik. I thought you said the null room...not the pain room?”

“He’s delirious,” Jessikah said. “Help him.”

“Bloody hell, Strong,” Erik said, as the worry in his voice kicked up a few levels into t*his is really bad* territory. “Where did you get this?”

"Get what?" I asked, confused. The pain in my head had returned with friends, and they were all swinging sledgehammers inside my skull. I placed a palm against my temple in an effort to alleviate the pain. "What are you talking about?"

Erik held the open keepsaker in his hand. A soft golden glow escaped from the small box.

"This totem," Erik said. "Who gave it to you?"

"What's wrong? Is it broken?"

"Broken?" Erik said with a shake of his head. "No, but if this is your totem, we may have to strap you down."

He removed a golden, rune-covered ring from the box.

NINETEEN

"Where did you get this?" Erik asked, holding up the totem. "I swear, if you answer Sauron, Gandalf, or anything to that effect, you will regret it. I mean it."

From the tone in his voice, he meant it.

When I saw Erik hold up the *one* ring, my brain raced through so many response opportunities in that one moment. They were all lost...because the moment I saw the ring, an ice pick of pain drove itself deeper into my skull, robbing me of speech.

Erik gestured and I suddenly felt cooler. I felt my arms and legs being strapped down. I realized I was lying on a padded St. Andrews cross. This one was nearly horizontal, as opposed to the usual vertical models I was used to seeing in the Hellfire. On the fringes of my awareness, I heard Peaches whine nearby.

No, I was not the kinky sort, unless you counted the fact that I was involved with an angry, ancient vampire as some sort of kink...then yes, I was extremely kinky. The reason I headed to the Hellfire, aside from it being close to Ezra's, was Rey's warning: "*Make sure you're safe before you put it on. It can take you out of play for a bit.*"

Being "out of play" while Evers and Talin were out there looking for us sounded like a bad idea. There was no way I could help Monty if Evers turned me into a smear on the sidewalk. I needed someplace I could be out of commission without having to worry about an impending attack.

This far downtown, that meant the Hellfire Club.

The Hellfire was many things, but the most important of them was that it was safe—at the very least, safe enough for this. Erik had a destruction tolerance that had probably exceeded its limit with Monty and me, but he would still help us when he could.

"Is this some kind of joke?" Jessikah asked. "That looks like the..."

"It's no joke," Erik answered, turning to the several Harlequin who stood nearby. "Make sure he's secure. This is going to be pain...not the good kind."

The pain in my head subsided for a few seconds, and I reached the shore of clarity, if only for a moment. Just enough time for me to capitalize on the presence of this particular totem.

"One ring to rule them all?"

"Didn't realize you were such a Tolkien fanboy," Erik said. "Should I expect a tall old man wielding a staff?"

"Hope not," I said, "but you never know."

Erik held up the ring again, admiring it.

"Of all the things your brain could have picked, you chose this symbol?" he said, turning it in his fingers. "I don't know if I should be impressed or concerned."

"With my brain? Probably both, but I didn't choose it."

"You didn't?"

"At least, I don't think I did."

"I do not envy you the pain you will experience today."

"Can we just pass on the pain...good or otherwise?"

"You shall not pass...on any of this pain," Erik said with a tight smile. "It's part of the signature-aligning process."

"Really? Now?"

"Apologies, couldn't resist my inner Gandalf. If it's anything like a mage shift, you'll wish you were dead many times over."

"I'm not a mage."

"I'm aware, and for someone who doesn't wield energy the way mages do, you do experience many of the situations otherwise exclusive to mages. Is it possible you're in the closet, or is it more like a wardrobe?"

"I swear if you slide into Narnia, I'll smack you myself."

"Just trying to raise your spirits a bit. This is going to be a major suckfest for you."

"Have I ever mentioned how mage morale building sucks?" I asked as I felt another tsunami of pain cresting. "This is hurting, and I haven't even put that thing on."

"This is a particularly powerful totem, Strong," Erik answered after a moment. "We won't be able to be in here for long after I put it on you. Do you have any last words?"

"I do?"

"You must not be feeling that much pain if you can still be a smartass," Erik said, his face grim. "I won't try and move your hellhound—I do enjoy my fingers attached to my hands—but if it gets bad, you have to send him away, Strong."

"That bad?"

Erik gave me one slow nod.

"Beyond."

"Shit."

"The power in this ring is staggering," Erik answered. "Any spillover or backlash will hurt even your hellhound. The design of this particular room"—he glanced around—"should mitigate most of the energy released, but I'm not certain. If you manage to survive this, I want to know how you came to possess it."

"If?"

"Yes, if. I've never seen a totem with this much power... ever," Erik answered, after looking down at the ring again. "I don't know what it's going to do to you, or if this room will be enough to contain the adjustment to your scattered signature."

"That...that sounds promising."

"I don't know what you're mixed up in this time," Erik answered. "But this—"

"Monty...schism," I managed. "This should help me help him."

"Was that you at Haven earlier?"

"Friends of his," I said, holding off the pain. "Turns out they have some unfinished business with Monty."

"That explains the Black Orchid," he said, glancing at Jessikah. "Unfinished business is usually lethal business. Is she here to erase him?"

"She's one of the good guys," I said. "There are others...not so good. Those want to take out Monty."

Erik stared at me for a few seconds.

"I swear," he said, letting out a long breath. "Do you two *actively* look for danger?"

"Not Monty's fault this time...I think."

"Bullshit," Erik said, making sure the straps were extra

tight. "When the shit hits the fan, you two are either flinging the shit or you're the fan. There's no middle ground with you two—three, if you count your hellhound."

"This time I want to unplug the fan, and dodge the shit altogether," I said with a weak smile. "Thanks for your help."

"Don't thank me," he said, continuing to tighten the straps. "Thank Director Nakatomi. The Dark Council has moved to a Blood Rule; she is in full control of the vampire division and locking things down. She put out the official word that you were off-limits to all Dark Council personnel."

"Off-limits? Meaning what, exactly?"

"Anyone who moved against you in retaliation would be exterminated with extreme and merciless precision," Erik said. "By her hand...personally."

"That sounds scary and dangerous," I said. "What about unofficially?"

"You have several packs of weres that would like to eviscerate you repeatedly," he answered. "Along with a group of mages that still remember downtown and Tartarus. They would like to have a conversation with you. Unofficially, of course."

"Tartarsauce wasn't my fault." I smiled and then grew serious. "I didn't summon him, and more importantly, he needed to be stopped. The Dark Council was sleeping on him."

"As I understand it, you took it upon yourself to make a phone call and raise an army?" Erik asked.

"Tartarus was—is dangerous," I said. "He needed to be stopped."

"By who?" Erik asked. "You lured the Dark Council Enforcers into a trap."

"I did no such thing."

"They were racing downtown to stop a rogue mage, not an old god," Erik answered with an edge. "An old god, who soundly beat them to a pulp...many died that day. Who do you think they blame—unofficially, of course?"

"Me, of course," I noticed how he forgot to mention how many were racing downtown to take out one rogue mage. "Unofficially, they had it coming. They wanted to erase Monty and kill Peaches."

He stared at me, then slowly shook his head.

"We can discuss that later. Right now"—he held up the ring and moved to my extended arm—"this."

"I need you to make a call," I said. "This is important."

"Who do you want me to call, now of all moments?"

"Dex. He can help me."

"That may not be possible right now."

"What are you talking about? This is Monty, his nephew, his family."

"Dex has gone rogue...really rogue this time."

"What does that even mean?"

"The Golden Circle is gone," Erik said, lowering his voice. "The entire place."

"Call LD and TK. If anyone can find him, it's them."

"I wouldn't get my hopes up, but I'll see what I can do," Erik said. "Anything in particular you want me to say to him?"

"I need help."

"Short and to the point," Erik answered. "That should work."

"How does an entire sect disappear? That place was enormous."

"I don't know."

"Dexter is a master teleporter," Jessikah broke in. "He could do it. It's almost impossible, but he can do it."

"Shit, this complicates everything," I said. "I think Monty is at the Golden Circle."

Peaches let out another small whine. I could tell he was worried.

"I meant what I said earlier," Erik said, looking at Peaches. "It's going to be too dangerous in here, even for him. I know hellhounds are nearly indestructible, but this..."He shook his head. "This is an unknown quantity."

"I don't want him to get hurt. Give me a moment."

<Hey boy. You're going to have to go with Erik and Jessikah.>

<I'm your bondmate. I go where you go.>

<I know. I know, but right now Erik is going to put that ring on me, and it's going to hurt real bad.>

<Should I bite him? I can stop him.>

<No, but thank you. Maybe later. He needs to put it on so I won't smell bad anymore. It will help make me better. Understand?
>

<Should I lick you? It won't hurt. My saliva is better than a ring.>

<I know it is, but for now, you have to go with Erik. I'll make sure he gives you some meat.>

<Right now you're hurt. I can eat later.>

That's when I knew it was bad. My hellhound had just turned down an offer of meat.

<He'll make extra meat, and I'll feel better knowing that you're safe.>

<I won't feel better knowing you are hurt. I go where you go.>

Hellhound logic was hard to counter. I was going to need a different strategy.

<Do you see the cat-man?>

<No. He is not here. I don't smell him.>

<That means Jessikah is in danger. I promised to keep her safe. Right now, I can't keep her safe. It's up to you. As my bondmate, you have to keep her safe. I promised.>

I could almost hear the hellhound wheels turning in his head. I had no illusion as to his intelligence—Peaches XL came across as a genius-level intellect, reminding me many times that he communicated in a rudimentary way so that *I* could understand *him*. Not the other way around. Still, my logic was sound, and I had boxed him in...for now.

<I will keep her safe, but I will stay close to you. When you get better, you can give me two bowls of meat.>

<Solid plan. Erik and Jessikah will leave soon. Please go with them when they do.>

He chuffed and slobbered my face before padding away to stand next to Jessikah...because healthy saliva.

"Hellhound situation squared away," I said, peering at Erik through the haze of impending agony squeezing my brain. Speaking to Peaches had accelerated the pain train. "Whenever you're ready."

"This is really going to hurt," Erik said, holding the ring gingerly. "Ready?"

"No. Do it anyway."

TWENTY

Life is pain.

Anyone who tries to tell you different is lying.

Yes, life is full of good things—family, friends, hungry hellhounds, and deep, rich mugs of javambrosia—special moments, and the like. But beneath it all, at the foundation...lies pain.

Never far and only a heartbeat away.

Pain and loss are the only way we learn to appreciate the things we have and those we don't. Right now, what I had was an impending blitz of misery. What I didn't have was another way to deal with this situation and help Monty.

I decided Winston had the best plan for this one: *If you're going through hell, keep going.*

I intended to keep going.

I nodded to Erik and he placed the ring on my finger. For a few seconds, all I felt was warmth expanding through my hand. I looked over and noticed the area brightening as the ring gave off a dull glow, pulsing every few seconds with subtle, golden light.

Then it started.

I had felt pain before. All kinds of pain. Nothing prepared me for this. I saw Erik gesture and back up with Jessikah and Peaches beside him.

"Good luck," he said. "We'll speak on the other side...hopefully."

Regular mage of optimism, that Erik. Moments later, they were gone.

Those were the last words I heard before everything became white noise and pain.

I was alone.

I don't know how I knew, but I knew I was in the room alone. My senses were on overdrive. Smells surrounded me. I felt the leather straps chafe against my wrists, biceps, thighs, and ankles.

I looked down and realized I was only wearing a pair of shorts.

When did that happen?

The pain quickly focused my attention on the white-hot sun blossoming on my hand. I glanced over at the ring and nearly blinded myself, the energy was so intense. I closed my eyes, turning my head away from the light, and tracking the afterimage against my closed eyelids.

That's when the festivities kicked up a notch.

My body spasmed. Each of my muscles seized as I strained hard against the straps, arching my back. It felt like an army of dwarves, armed with hammers, had decided I was a nail, and needed to be beaten into the ground...repeatedly. Every part of my body screamed with tension.

The pain subsided a few agonizing seconds later, only to be replaced with a searing heat that made me actually look around to see if I was ablaze. I figured it was my curse trying to heal me, and failing. My eyes were next; it felt like the heat wasn't content with just incinerating my body. It raced up to my face and focused on melting my eyes.

I took a few deep breaths and tried to ride the waves of pain. It was working to a certain extent; I could feel the crest approaching and tried to breathe through the worst of the agony.

That didn't last long.

The army of dwarves was replaced with fire ants riding wasps, and they all stung my eyes at once. I started screaming then. I screamed until I lost the ability to make a sound, and then I screamed some more.

"That looks painful," a familiar voice said next to me, in between my screams. "Is he really worth it?"

I tried focusing my eyes and failed. Everything was a blur. It didn't matter: I knew who it was by the voice and air of menace.

Kali.

"He would do the same...the same for me," I said hoarsely. "Why are you here?"

"You are *my* cursed," Kali said. "Your current increase in power caught my attention. I came to see if you were actively trying to end your existence. Do you seek death?"

For a split second, I almost said yes...the pain was that bad.

"No," I said, and gritted my teeth. "It'd be great if you...if you could do something about the pain, though."

"Would you like more?" she asked. I could tell she was

serious by her tone. "I'm certain I could increase the level of discomfort exponentially."

"This...this is way past discomfort," I answered with a groan. "This is really up there with intolerable agony."

"Perfect," she said, and I could almost hear the smile. "Pain at that level is cleansing, pure. It peels away all pretenses and reveals your true nature. It is in the white-hot crucible of suffering that the dross is burned away. This is good for you."

"Good? How is this good?"

"Well, in the long term, if it doesn't kill you, you will be tempered, made stronger," she said. "Short term, nothing focuses a mind more than pain. Singular focus at that level is good."

"No...not good," I said, shaking my head. "Can we dial down the dross-burning?"

"Why?" she asked. "You knew this was going to be pain. Several people advised you, yet you chose to continue upon this exquisite path. Why would I deprive you of this singular experience of purity?"

"Because it's killing me?"

"Killing you?" she asked, glancing down at the glowing supernova on my finger. "Are you certain? You have proven quite resilient in the past."

"Are you serious?" I asked, getting angry and momentarily forgetting who I was speaking to. "This thing is melting me from the inside out. Take it off."

"Impossible," she said, stepping close enough that I could feel her breath on my face. "If I remove it, I *will* have to kill you...permanently. Is that your wish?"

"Is it yours?" I asked. "If you don't get this off me, I'm

pretty sure I'm dying here...on a cross...in a dungeon... Wonderful. Is that what you want?"

"I will get what *I* want, my Cursed," she said in a soft voice. "*You* will help me."

"I can't do that if I'm dead."

"Stop being so precious," she said dismissively. "You've withstood and survived worse. Power always comes at a cost. This is a law that cannot be broken—bent, perhaps, but not broken. Out of the seven laws, that one is the most irrefutable. That one encompasses them all."

"I don't *want* this power."

Even shaping the thoughts to form the words hurt.

"Really?" she asked, as I heard her pulling over some piece of furniture. "Do you think you possess enough? Enough to save Tristan? To defeat Evers and her minion?"

"I don't know."

"You don't *know*?" she said with a small laugh. "Then this entire exercise is for what? Practice? Try again. This time, be honest."

"No," I said. "I don't possess enough power to save Monty, or to stop Evers. In case you haven't noticed...I'm not a mage."

"Yet you have accomplished much without being a mage."

"Monty is in trouble," I said. "He needs help."

"Is that why?" she asked. "Why you put yourself through this?"

"I don't *want* power, but I *need* it...to do what I must."

"You *must*?" she scoffed. "You are going to risk it all, to save the one who abandoned you? He even threatened you with death. This is who you want to save?"

"No... he didn't...He wasn't thinking straight."

"If you seek me out," Kali said in Monty's voice, "I will end your immortal existence."

"That's...that's just creepy."

"Those were his words. I was there," she said. "He sounded serious."

"Monty always sounds serious. It's a mage thing," I said. "The schism is messing with his mind."

She laughed, and the sound drove cold needles of fear into me.

"A schism reveals the darker nature, the things that are hidden, the things that are true," she said. "Perhaps he envies your immortality. Can you imagine? An immortal mage? Living long enough to discover all of the secrets of power?"

"That's not him."

"He would never age, never grow ill," she continued. "He would become the most powerful mage in existence. Nothing and no one could stop him."

"That's...not...who he is," I said, gritting my teeth against the pain. "Monty isn't some power-hungry mage."

"You think you *know* him?" Kali asked. "You only know what he has chosen to show you."

"He's shown me plenty, when it counted the most."

"You know nothing. Have you seen Montague the War Mage? Have you experienced the Scourge of the Banshee?"

"That's not Monty...not anymore."

"Are you trying to convince me...or yourself?"

She waved a hand in my direction.

The pain subsided from my body and I let out a long breath.

"I know him. He is good," I said as the vision slowly returned to my eyes. "He will not become a dark mage."

"Perhaps what he needs is a shield against the impending darkness," Kali said, gently taking hold of the enso pendant hanging from my neck. It shone a deep violet in her palm. "This is what you are...his shieldbearer, yes?"

"What are you doing?"

"Redefining and refining your purpose. You *will* become a shieldbearer, but of a different sort."

"I'm not crazy about the shieldbearer I am now."

"You voice your opinion like you have a choice in the matter," she said. "You made the choice long ago. These are the consequences."

"I don't recall making the choice to be tortured," I said. "Or to be a shieldbearer."

"The day you stood beside the mage to fight off impending destruction, you made your choice. That day and every day since."

She closed her hand around the enso pendant. The chain attached to it came apart and disintegrated, leaving the pendant in her hand. The enso was an open circle, symbolizing perfection in imperfection.

"That's not mine," I said. "That belongs to Monty."

"It was given to you, shieldbearer," Kali answered, hefting the pendant in her palm. "Do you know why I cursed you?"

"You were pissed?" I said and paused, giving it thought, hopefully before she blasted me for my default answer. "Not really I figured it was because I messed up your plan against Shiva?"

"Partially, yes," she said. "Your interference deserved an adequate response."

"I did notice how you conveniently forgot to curse Monty, though."

"Convenient? It was anything but," she said. "Cursing you meant abrogating laws of time and space. There were several who felt I...overreacted."

"They dared to say that to your face?"

"They did," she said, unleashing another chilling smile.

I knew in that moment that whoever or whatever had dared to inform her of their opinion was a memory.

"Cursing me immortal was adequate?" I asked taking my immortal life into my hands. "Seems like it *was* a bit of overkill. Why not just blast me to dust?"

"I *was* pissed," she said, waving my words away. "How would you react if some idiot, well meaning as you were, interrupted a plan that took five thousand years to implement?"

"Good point," I admitted with a brief nod that sent small ripples of pain everywhere. "I'd be pissed too. Maybe not 'cursing people alive' angry, but I'd be upset."

"Blasting you to dust for your interference would have been...adequate," she answered, "but there is more at play here than you can imagine."

"Can't you just tell me?" I asked. "Why do mages and gods speak in riddles?"

"Mages speak in convolution out of habit. Gods obfuscate because we are cunning."

"Would it kill you, just once, to state things plainly?"

"No, it wouldn't, but it may kill you," she answered. "Human brains are such frail things. You barely comprehend the four dimensions you inhabit; to speak plainly would only confuse you further."

"So, you speak in riddles because the truth would melt my brain?"

"You *know* the truth," she said. "Understanding it is another matter entirely."

"How can I know what I don't know?" I said, frustrated. "That makes no sense."

She smiled, and it was worse than the laugh. For a moment, I wished my vision would blur again. Her beauty as a goddess was impossible to look away from. It wasn't the beauty, though. Behind it, mixed in with it, I was gripped by a profound feeling of death and foreboding.

This was fear...real, mind-numbing, blood-curdling, run-away-screaming fear.

I was getting a glimpse at the goddess of creation and destruction, and my mind could barely keep it together. A few more minutes of this, and I'd be a drooling vegetable.

"You know the answer," she said, opening the hand holding the pendant. "What you must learn...is the question."

"The question?"

"Do you know the question?"

"At this point, I barely know my own name, much less some hidden question."

"Some things are hidden plainly," she said, forming a fist around the pendant. "Like this 'key.'"

"Could you not destroy that?" I said, concerned that getting a replacement would be nearly impossible. "Nana would be really pissed if I broke Monty's key."

"You still don't understand," Kali said, raising her fist. "But you will. For now, I will take matters into my hands."

She drove her hand and the pendant into my chest.

My torso erupted in violet light. The Pain—which up to this moment, had been taking a break—came back... with friends, Agony and Torture. The violet light in my torso exploded and outshone the light from the ring.

I couldn't even scream in agony, it was that intense and sudden, ripping the breath from my lungs.

"Your totem has three uses," Kali said when she removed her hand a few agonizing seconds later. "Only three."

"Why only three?" I managed between gasps. "How do I even use them?"

"Three, because four would have meant collecting your remains," she said. "Even immortals have limits. How did you open the box containing the ring?"

"With...with difficulty."

"I would imagine it required viewing energy differently?"

"I don't know how to do that regularly," I said. "I had help."

"Then practice," she said. "Utilize the ring wisely. The power of this pendant"—she placed a hand on my chest—"is now yours to master and refine. You will no longer need this."

She touched my mala bracelet, and it became dust.

"I kind of needed that," I said, feeling surprisingly naked without my shield. "It was an effective defense."

"A shield does not require a shield," she answered. "You are not a mage and never will be, my Cursed, but you *will* bear my mark and be feared."

"I thought I already bore your mark? Endless knot on my hand?"

"That is the mark of your curse, not *my* mark. My mark is all encompassing and will be visible to those who can see."

"Another one of those hidden in plain sight things, I'm guessing?"

"You're learning," she said with a nod. "The power you possess will rival that of any mage, once you understand how to use it."

"That sounds like more pain."

"There are some who would see magic and its use removed from this plane."

"Evers and Talin," I managed. "They want to erase magic. Is that even possible?"

"Do you want to find out?"

"No."

"You will become the shieldbearer against those who would try to transform and twist this energy," she said. "You will be the one in the gap, no longer a shieldbearer. You will be *my aspis*—a shield-warrior.

She placed a finger on each of my eyes—her index and ring finger—and a third, her middle finger, on my forehead in some strange variation of a Vulcan mind-meld. The icepick that was burrowing into my head earlier decided now was a good time to explode.

Violet and gold light blinded me, robbing me of my sight again, as the straps holding me in place melted away. I fell to the ground in a heap of mangled pain and agony.

The sobs came then, uncontrolled and unrestrained.

"Just...just kill me," I said in-between wracking sobs. "I can't...I can't do this."

"That day will come," Kali said gently. "But it is not

today. You will have to endure a little longer. It is not only Tristan that depends on you now."

Another wave of pain crested and crashed into me as I spasmed on the floor, blinded by power and pain.

I was alone again.

TWENTY-ONE

The first thing I felt and heard was Peaches' wet muzzle push my face with a worried whine. Then he growled. I felt the tremor race across the floor, originating in his chest, and radiating outward from him in sonic ripples. He spread his forelegs and blocked my view.

"Strong," Erik said slowly. "Inform your hellhound we're trying to help you."

"It's okay, boy," I said, patting my hellhound's flanks weakly. "Let them pass."

<He hurt you. Can I bite him now?>

"Later," I said softly. "Not now."

"Strong, we can't do this later," Erik said. "You need attention now."

"Sorry, not you," I said weakly. "Was talking to my hellhound."

I didn't chance communicating with Peaches in our normal way...my brain still felt tender, and I ached all over.

<You're hurt. I will lick you and that will help.>

I winced as his voice slammed into my head.

<Let's talk later, boy. My everything hurts right now, especially my head.>

<If I lick you, you will get better.>

<Not so loud. Save the licking for later. I'll get better, I just need time.>

<You don't smell bad anymore. You smell like you.>

<Thanks, I think. Let Erik pass. He wants to help me.>

Peaches moved over to the side with a low rumble, allowing Erik and several of the Harlequin access to my mangled body. They gently scooped me up from the floor and suspended me in mid-air, before placing me on the table. I hadn't realized how strong the Harlequin were, but it made sense. They weren't window dressing; they were the security for the Hellfire Club.

Erik wouldn't pick a group of weak women to protect his mage club—he'd get the best, which also meant the strongest. I was pretty certain they were all like Master Yat, wielding their tonfa the way he wielded his staff, skillfully and painfully when the situation required it.

"Secure him," Erik said, his voice distant. "Make sure the table is horizontal. I don't want him falling off. How did you break free?"

"I didn't," I said, looking at the ruined straps. "They just fell apart. Maybe get better quality next time?"

"Strong, that was the highest quality leather," Erik answered. "I runed and reinforced those straps myself. There was no way you should have been able to destroy them."

"Probably wasn't me then," I said, my voice raspy. "Could they have just been worn out from too much use?"

"What happened to him?" Jessikah asked. "He looks awful, like he's been beaten...severely and repeatedly."

“Thanks,” I said, barely able to form the word. “I feel that way, too. Some water would be good.”

Erik glanced at one of the Harlequin, and motioned with a hand. She left the room only to return a few seconds later, with a silver pitcher and a large glass, setting it to one side.

“What happened, Strong?” Erik asked as he poured me half a glass of water, holding it out to me. “Here, drink this, slowly. Do *not* guzzle it.”

“I don’t think you’d believe me if I told you,” I said, after taking a few sips of the water. It was delicious. “What is this?” I held up the glass. “This isn’t water.”

“It’s Rejuven,” Erik said. “Looks like water, tastes like heaven. On occasion, some of the patrons ‘tax’ themselves past the point of wisdom. We give them that to help them recover.”

“Whatever it is,” I said, taking another sip, “it’s excellent. Can I have more?”

“No,” Erik said, motioning to one of the Harlequin with a nod. The Harlequin gently removed the glass from my hand and the pitcher, silently stepping out of the room. “It’s highly effective and incredibly addictive. A little goes a long way. You should be feeling its effects.”

“Feeling much better already,” I said, as the low-grade warmth rushed through my body. I still ached, but now I only felt gently mangled, instead of chewed up, spit out and stomped on.

“Tell me what happened,” Erik said. “Leave nothing out, even the things you feel are incredible.”

“What happened to your eyes?” Jessikah asked, pointing at my face with a look of surprise. “They didn’t look like that before.”

Erik gave Jessikah a glance and shook his head.

"What's wrong with my eyes?" I said, concerned. "What do you see?"

"They're glowing...purple," Jessikah answered. "I'm certain I would have remembered if you had glowing purple eyes."

"Glowing eyes? Nice."

"Nice?" Jessikah said, evidently upset. "Normal eyes do not glow purple, or any other color for that matter."

"I left normal long ago," I said, keeping my voice calm. I didn't want her launching from upset into hysterical. "I've never claimed to be normal. In fact, I've never even *met* normal. Can you describe what normal looks like?"

"I don't understand," she said, shaking her head. "You're not a mage. How is this happening to you?"

"I'm abnormal?"

"Truest thing you've said all day," Erik said. "Starting with your brain."

Jessikah opened her mouth to answer and closed it again.

"Surely, you can appreciate how out of the ordinary this is," Jessikah said, when she found her voice. "These events, his signature, the hellhound, and the fact that he can manipulate energy without being a mage...it's not proper."

She was beginning to get on my nerves.

"I'm sure we'll get to that in a moment," Erik said, focusing on me again. "Strong, start from the moment we left the room."

I explained what had happened with the totem, the pendant, the agony, and Kali.

Erik looked at me and narrowed his eyes.

"It tracks," he said. "Your signature is slowly aligning. Whatever she did to you seems to have set you right in the scariest way possible. I still can't entirely tell what's going on. If you were a mage I'd say you shifted, but..."

"I'm not a mage," I finished, glancing at the disturbed Jessikah. "I know."

"No, you're not," he said. "Whatever she did, untangled the mess with your bonds." He narrowed his eyes again. "There are three clear lines of resonance, overlapped and intertwined with some new thread of energy—a separate bond...Incredible. How do you feel?"

"Like one of Peaches' chew toys," I said, assessing the damage to my body. I was sore everywhere, but functional. "I feel like I went a few rounds with an angry troll and lost."

"Is there another kind of troll?"

"That...is a valid point," I said, remembering my date. "Trolls are not known for their cheerful dispositions."

"Are we supposed to believe that the *actual* goddess, Kali, paid him a visit?" Jessikah asked, incredulously. "Why would a goddess visit *you* and leave you alive? Especially a goddess like Kali?"

Erik and I turned to look at her.

I could understand her reluctance and surprise. It's not that she disbelieved in the existence of gods; she was a mage, after all. It was, however, becoming clear that her worldview was shaped by those she perceived as superior—those who wielded energy—and everyone else.

Also, Kali did have a reputation for being cranky on a homicidal level unsurpassed by most. Jessikah's skepticism made sense, even though her tone irked me.

In her mind, I fell into the unworthy *everyone else* category.

"What do *you* think happened here?" Erik asked. "As an Orchid agent, how do you explain his energy signature? You're trained to observe and assess. Execute your powers of observation and extrapolate why Kali would visit Strong."

"I...I really don't know," Jessikah answered. "His situation refutes all my training. Technically, he should be dead even before encountering a goddess, if that even happened."

"Trust me, it did," I said with a slight groan. "Her visit was no dream."

"His energy signature displayed high levels of activity and complete inactivity simultaneously. In addition, he's bound to a spawn of hell, and works cases with a dark mage. All improbable occurrences, yet factual."

"Monty is not dark...yet," I corrected. "He's on the verge."

"Semantics," Jessikah said, waving my words away. "He used blood magic. It's only a matter of time. The power is a slippery slope few can resist."

"He will resist it."

"Correct on the facts regarding Strong," Erik said. "Let's leave opinion out of Tristan's situation. The fact is that he is in the midst of a schism. He hasn't gone dark yet. Strong is correct in his response. What is *your* assessment?"

"Honestly? It seems safer to place Tristan under restraint."

"Safer?" I asked. "For who?"

"For whom," she corrected. "For him *and* for the

general populace. Do you know the power of a dark mage? It's staggering. The entire city is in danger once he goes dark."

"Monty is not going dark."

"You can't guarantee that," she said, her voice low. "Not unless..."

"If he does, I'll make sure he can't hurt anyone, starting with himself."

"He'll kill you," Jessikah said. "You don't know the potential power you're facing. Are you insane?" She looked at Erik. "Tell him how dangerous this is."

"She doesn't know," I said under my breath to Erik. "She assumes I'm just weird, some kind of mutant...probably like Wolverine."

"Strong...don't," Erik warned. "This is serious. She doesn't know about your curse?"

"We never got around to discussing it?"

"Curse? What curse?" Jessikah asked, glancing in my direction. "Should I be taking precautionary measures? How are you cursed?"

"You are incredible," Erik reprimanded me. "How could you not tell her?"

"We didn't meet under the best of circumstances," I shot back. "She's Black Orchid, and they are *currently* trying to kill Monty. You know, the Monty that's my friend?"

"They know about the schism," Erik said. "And you didn't tell her?"

"What did you want me to say?" I asked, getting angry. "She literally appeared *in* the Moscow, past our defenses. How did you want the intros to go? 'Hey, nice to meet you, I'm Simon, I hear you and your buddies want to kill my friend and partner, by the way...not happening. Also, I've been cursed alive by Kali?' Seems a bit awkward, don't you think?"

"You do have a point," Erik said, shaking his head. "Apologies."

"Given the circumstances, I wasn't feeling especially warm and open. I didn't know who she was, and then things kind of...took off. Dex, LD, and TK appeared, and I never got around to explaining things like my curse."

"Why are you cursed?" Jessikah asked. "More importantly: who cursed you?"

"Same person you doubt ever paid me a visit: Kali."

"She cursed you, and then you claim she helped you? Are you ill?"

"See?" I said, looking at Erik. "Easy to explain, right?"

Erik nodded and held up a hand.

"Are you trying to kill Tristan?" Erik asked, looking at Jessikah. "Yes or no?"

"No," Jessikah said. "My priorities shifted once I realized I was being sent to my death."

"Your priority shift notwithstanding, I want you to understand what you will be facing if this is a deception on your part," Erik said. "Please look at Strong. Use your true-sight."

"My what?" Jessikah asked. "Are you referring to my farsight?"

"She's a little new," I said. "He means that squinty thing you mages do, when you shift your focus and see past the veil of things to the 'real world.'"

"I don't do a 'squinty' thing. My eyes are in perfect working condition," she answered. "I haven't been adequately trained in true-sight. The Farsight training came first, and then was interrupted when I was tasked with apprehending Tristan."

Erik just stared at Jessikah for a few seconds.

"Apprehending Tristan seems to be code for 'extermination' in the Black Orchid," I said. "I think she pissed off the wrong people. I should know, I'm an expert at it."

"Indeed you are," Erik said. "That explains much. Can you see a basic unveiling?"

"Yes," Jessikah answered with a nod. "I can see up to an intermediate unveiling."

"That will work," Erik said, pointing at me. "Please focus on Strong."

Jessikah turned, focusing on me for a few seconds and then let her gaze go soft. She was looking in my direction, but it appeared as though she was looking past me, to some fixed point in the distance.

"I have him in my sight," she said. "Please begin."

"We'll stick to a basic unveiling," Erik said. "I don't know how extensive your training is, and this should suffice to reveal what you need to know."

"I'm ready," she answered, "though I don't understand the point to this. What do you expect me to see? It's not like he's a mage. Outside of some aberrant energy signature, he doesn't possess much of a threat. Honestly, this is all a waste of..."

Erik gestured next to me, and for a few seconds she held that thousand-mile stare. It slowly shifted as Jessikah's eyes opened wide before she looked away in shock.

"Are you okay?" Erik asked, holding onto Jessikah's arm to steady her. "Did you see?"

"That was a *basic* unveiling?" she asked, her voice trembling slightly. "How is he still alive? Pardon me"—she looked in my direction—"how *are* you alive?"

"*That* is his curse," Erik said, letting his voice become hard. "It makes Strong very difficult to exterminate. That curse, along with his hellhound, and the fact that he has worked some of the most dangerous cases alongside a mage, make him resilient enough to deal with most threats —mages included. I will ask you one more time. Do you intend Tristan harm?"

Jessikah was unsettled.

It could've been my imagination, or the fact that she took several small steps away from me and refused to look in my direction. Maybe it was the micro-tremors in her hands as she smoothed out her hair that made me feel like I had just contracted a major case of cooties.

Whatever she had seen had unnerved her, which I think was Erik's intention all along. Not being a mage, I had no way to determine what exactly she saw, or what Erik allowed her to see regarding my signature and curse.

Kali words came to mind: *you will bear my mark and be feared.*

"My priority is survival outside of the Black Orchid now," she said once she managed to get herself under control. "Tristan Montague outclasses my ability, and evidently"—she glanced my way—"has powerful friends who would make me regret any decision to bring harm upon him."

"That sounds accurate," I said. "If we get past this, we'll help you get resettled here. It's less murdery for Black Orchid rookie agents."

"Do you understand now why Kali would visit Strong?" Erik asked.

"I have some understanding, yes," Jessikah said. "It would seem this is a case of not judging the book by the cover. I have to confess, I still find it odd she would visit him. Why not one of the Arch Mages?"

"If you ever get the chance, perhaps you can ask her," Erik said. "I'm sure she'd love to explain her reasoning to you."

"Are you saying it's not my charming personality?" I asked, looking down at my body. "I'm practically irresistible. By the way, Erik, clothes?"

"Oh yes, right," he said, waving a hand. "Apologies, I was thinking about the ramifications of this."

My clothes reappeared instantly.

"My irresistible allure? I get all sorts of unsolicited attention—most of it unwanted, all of it dangerous."

"Stop spouting nonsense," Erik said. "You know Director Nakatomi would skewer any female who got too close to you."

"Excuse me?" Jessikah asked, suddenly even more concerned. "Am I in danger?"

"Only if your intentions toward Strong are anything other than professional."

"My intentions are *strictly* professional," she said, raising a hand with a mild look of disgust. It was the expression you wore when you discovered your milk was now a chunky semi-liquid, as the rancid odor punched you in the nose. "No offense meant."

"Some taken," I said, turning to Erik. "What do you mean? What ramifications?"

"I wasn't able to reach Dex," Erik answered. "It seems he is avoiding any organized group at the moment."

"That would make sense," I said, looking at Jessikah.

"The Black Orchid threatened him and the Golden Circle if he interfered with their mission."

"Talin alluded to the destruction of the Golden Circle as well," Jessikah said. "It would makes sense that Dexter has gone into hiding."

"You don't know Dex too well," I said. "He's not big on hiding. He leans closer to the 'raze everything to the ground' method of doing things."

"I did manage to contact LD," Erik said. "He'll be here shortly. Also, Cecil left your automotive atrocity outside. Make sure you take it with you when you leave, or it'll scare away everyone."

"The Dark Goat is not an atrocity...she's a work of art. An artrocity, if you will."

"If that art was designed to maim and kill, then yes, it's art. Right up there with the Night Warden's abomination. What *was* Cecil thinking?"

"Cecil is a man with a plan," I said. "How soon before LD gets here?"

"Why?"

"Is this the strongest null room you have in the club?"

"Why?" Erik asked again, with an undertone of urgency. "I just had the lower floors redone, Strong. It cost a fortune and shut us down for weeks."

"Yes or no?" I asked. "I need to test something."

"No," Erik said. "Whatever it is...no. Test it elsewhere."

"It *should* be safe," I said. "You yourself said Kali set me straight; my bonds are untangled."

"I also said she set you right in the *scariest way* possible," Erik replied. "We don't know how your body will react to this change in your signature."

"I'm pretty sure it'll be fine," I said, moving my tenderized body around slowly. "I'm still sore, but I don't intend to unleash any Club-destroying energy."

"Oh, forgive me, *Mage* Strong," Erik answered, heavy on the sarcasm. "I hadn't realized you graduated top of the class in energy manipulation from Imaginary U."

"I'm just going to materialize Ebonsoul," I answered with a glare. "Should cause no destruction and minimal energy expenditure."

"Those sounds like famous last words," Erik answered with a sigh. "If you sense anything is amiss, you stop, understood?"

"Understood," I said with a nod. "You may want to give me some privacy for this...just in case."

"Just in case of what?"

"Nothing, nothing," I said, quickly raising a hand. "I just prefer doing this alone, in case it doesn't work."

"Your hellhound stays here," Erik answered, glancing at Peaches. "You need to get him some training."

"We tried that," I said. "It didn't go so well."

"Try it again. He gently mangled through one of my chairs. A Gehry Power Play. It has been reduced to abstract art. I expect it to be replaced."

"I'll add it to my to-do list, right after facing homicidal mages and walking Monty back from the brink of darkness."

Erik shook his head and pinched the bridge of his nose.

"You do your test in here," Erik said, adding some curses under his breath. "I swear, Strong, if you destroy this room, I'm holding you personally responsible."

"What else is new?"

"LD will be here inside the hour," Erik said. "Conduct your test when he arrives...not before. At least that way he can prevent any major destruction."

"Got it, and thank you...for everything."

"Thank me by leaving the club the same way you found it: intact," he snapped. "Let's go, Miss Orchid. You have some things to learn while Strong is trying his 'test.' Some of it may actually be beneficial."

Erik, Jessikah, and the Harlequins stepped out of the room, leaving me alone with my hellhound.

TWENTY-TWO

"You chewed one of his chairs?" I said, looking down at my sheepish hellhound. "Why?"

<It looked chewy. He had many of them. I didn't think he would mind if I gently bit one of them.>

"How much of it was left when you were done?"

<I stopped when he turned red and started talking loudly about me turning his Power Play to trash. I thought it was for chewing. It was soft and chewy. I was worried about you being hurt.>

"I'm okay now, but that is...was a very expensive chair," I said, holding back a small laugh and keeping a straight face. "I'm sure he was upset."

<If you get him some meat from the place, he will be happy again. I know I would be.>

"It's not that simple," I said. "Don't worry about it. We'll get him another one of his froufrou chairs. Right after we help Monty."

A gray circle of energy formed on the floor next to us. I made sure we moved out of the way. It increased in intensity until I had to look away. When I could see again, LD stood in the null room. It spoke to the level of his power that he could teleport into a room designed to negate all runic energy.

"Hola, hombre," LD said, giving me the once-over as he stepped out of the circle. "You look like you've been playing in traffic and lost...a few times. What happened?"

"Kali."

"Where's Farsight?" LD asked, looking around. "I keyed into your location. Why are we in a dungeon?"

"Jessikah is with Erik," I said. "I needed someplace safe to put this thing on."

I showed him the ring.

"So, when are you planning the trip to Mordor?" he asked with a grin.

"Oh, ha, ha," I said with a grimace. "This thing hurt like hell...worse than hell."

"How many uses does it have?"

"Three," I said. "Which would mean something if I knew how to use it."

"You'd better learn quick," he said, serious. "Things are developing quickly, and you don't have the luxury of the extended training version. This is more like the crash course—emphasis on crash."

"Kali said as much. I need to learn how to use several things, and I have no idea how to do that, except to think differently about energy."

"That makes sense," he said with a nod. "I have bad news and worse news. What do you want first?"

"Bad news," I said. "I'll ease into the worse, considering how my day is going."

"Bad news is: we don't know Evers' location," LD said,

his voice grim. "TK is tailing Talin, hoping he will lead us to her, but Evers is a skilled masker."

"Talin survived Grey?" I asked, surprised. "It didn't look good the last time I saw him. He was buried under a mountain of rubble that used to be a wall."

"When did you see him last?"

I explained what happened at The Dive with Grey and his psycho-sword.

"Talin survived," LD said, "barely. For a few moments, TK considered dusting him, but we need him to locate Evers. She's the real threat."

"How did he survive against Scary Grey and his sword?" I asked, confused. "Grey had a serious energy signature when I saw him last."

LD nodded.

"Izanami is a goddess," LD said. "Unlike, say, Kali, she is not in corporeal form, so her power is limited to the wielder of the weapon. Grey is pretty banged up from his last mission with your vampire."

"So I heard," I said. "They were busy redecorating the park at City Hall."

"In true Montague and Strong fashion, too. Big crater where the park once was. You'd be proud at the amount of destruction and devastation."

"You *do* realize I'm not the destructive part of the Duo of Destruction, right?"

"Sorry, hombre, guilt by association. Besides, from the looks of things"—he narrowed his eyes at me—"it seems like you've untangled that mess you had in there...and upgraded? How did that happen?"

"Kali did something with Monty's enso pendant shield-bearer thing," I said. "She took it from being a pendant and shoved it into my chest. It's like Ebonsoul, floating around in there somewhere, except it feels permanent." I tapped my chest lightly. "Solid inside. At this rate, I'm going to be a rare artifact warehouse."

"Well, if you were a target before, now you're a blazing beacon. No way you can hide now. Whatever she did is... whoa, off the charts intricate."

"So Grey was too wiped out to stop Talin?" I asked. "He had mentioned the whole City Hall thing."

"That's how Talin managed to escape," LD answered. "Grey wasn't at one hundred. That gave Talin the opportunity to retreat once he realized he was outclassed."

"And now he has TK tailing him?" I asked. "I think I'd prefer Ezra to TK after me."

"Agreed," LD said, "she has to be subtle. Talin has skill, but TK is an accomplished tracker. He won't escape her. Sooner or later he will lead her to Evers."

"This is like the ultimate game of hide-and-seek."

"Sure, where the loser dies," LD answered. "We need to find Evers soon, before she unleashes her revenge on Tristan."

"Not knowing where Evers is, is bad. What's worse?"

"There are varying degrees of worse. Ready?"

"Why would I expect it to be any other way?" I said, mostly to myself. "Go for it."

"Monty's schism has put him on a sect-wide blacklist. If we don't stop him, some heavy-hitters will be coming for him, not just the Black Orchid."

"That sounds worse. Can't we just email them, or something, that we have it under control?"

"Normally, the Black Orchid being on the case would calm the other sects down, but Dex managed to *Dex* the situation," LD said with a dark smile. "He removed the Golden Circle from all the sects."

"He did what?" I asked. "Erik said he moved the Golden Circle, but this sounds...deeper. Is he really powerful enough to move the entire Golden Circle?"

"You've experienced the Living Library and Moving Market, right?" LD asked. "Open a door and discover an entire world behind it, kind of thing?"

"Yes," I said with a small shudder. "Each time it was unnerving. Those places are immense and mobile. He has a room at our place...not really a room, but a world."

"Same principle, except Dex is a Master Teleporter," LD replied. "I've never seen a mage weaponize teleportation circles like he does, and I know some skilled mages."

"So, he basically 'poofed' the Golden Circle away?"

"The runic theories driving the Moving Market, the Living Library, and even Fordey, were perfected by Dexter first," LD said, letting the words sink in. "He is an old, powerful mage. In the area of teleportation, Ziller studies Dex."

"Who is now on the defensive."

"That's just it—Dex is never on the defensive. Even when he looks like it. That's what makes him dangerous and deceptive."

"Was it the entire complex?" I asked. "I seem to remember that place being huge, and he just winked it out of the plane?"

"He hid it, and if *he* hid it...we aren't finding it, until he wants us to."

"This sounds bad," I said. "Real bad, like 'mage warfare' type of bad."

"It is," LD said. "All of the mage sects are united in

purpose. They don't always agree, but they form a loose union...unofficially. It keeps things peaceful."

"Dex just ended that, didn't he?"

LD nodded.

"The Golden Circle is no longer part of that unofficial union," LD answered. "The Golden Circle, much like Dexter, who is currently the highest-ranking mage in the sect, has gone rogue."

"Does he have the authority to do something like that? What about the Elders?"

"Two things: One, Dex is in the highest position in the Golden Circle after Connor passed. Two, the Golden Circle was founded by a Montague—some even say it was Dex himself, though I doubt he's that old."

"The Elders can't stop him? Aren't they just as old as he is?"

"Have you met Dex? He's stronger than all of the Elders combined. You'd need a few sects of Elders to even have a chance at taking him down."

"That many?"

"If he was in a good mood. But now, with Tristan in danger? Let's just say that's not a war I'm willing to entertain...ever."

"A war?" I asked. "He's just one mage."

"You should always fear an old man in a profession where people die young."

"Good point. Is Dex an Arch Mage?"

"You're not paying attention, Strong. Focus. What do you know about Dex?"

"He has a dislike for clothing most of the time, is cranky all of the time, and really, really looks out for those who he considers family."

"You're missing one thing...one very *scary* thing that should illuminate it all for you," LD added. "Who is he currently 'seeing'—and I use that term loosely."

"Shit. The Morrigan," I said, as the realization hit me. "What are you saying?"

"She's a goddess, and has chosen to be with him. *A goddess of Death,"* LD emphasized. "Do you really, for a second, think she would be with someone she considered weak?"

"Well, she's not with him for his good looks, that's for sure," I said. "This defection was because of the Black Orchid letter, wasn't it? The threat?"

"In part," LD said. "I think this was a long time coming. Dex doesn't do well with authority, never has. Not even in the Ten, and we're as lax as it gets with rules. Dex rebels against them, which is why he never really joined us, despite numerous invitations."

"Then he gets placed in charge of the Golden Circle," I said. "He must have hated it."

"Hated? Not really," LD said. "He hates the trappings of the Order, the constraints; but he actually loves the Circle, just not the rules there."

"Grey said Monty may have gone there to sort things out during his schism. He said he'd want to be somewhere familiar, somewhere that felt like home."

"Makes sense," LD said. "The only problem is..."

"We can't find it right now."

"Exactly. Which is good and bad," LD said, pensively. "If we can't find it, neither can Evers. It also means *we* can't help Tristan during the schism."

"How do we help Monty, if we can't even find him?"

"When I said *we*, I meant everyone but *you*," LD said,

handing me a small, off-white card covered in runes I couldn't decipher. "This appeared suddenly, about half an hour ago. Seems like your presence is requested."

I took the card. It felt heavy in my hand. Instinctively, I knew it was from Dex. I didn't know how I knew, but I knew. There was only one line on the card I could understand. The rest was in some kind of magealphabet.

It read: *Send me the shieldbearer*.

TWENTY-THREE

"Dex sent this," I said, turning the card over. "It feels like him."

"You can sense the energy?"

"Yes, powerful with a heavy dose of cranky," I answered. "It's hard to explain, but it's Dex."

"Yes, and it seems he wants you, wherever he is."

"Wonderful," I said, exasperated, turning the card over in my hand again. "Should I just jump into the Dark Goat and drive off to the plane where he is? Did he happen to send a map, too? Maybe GPS coordinates? How am I supposed to find him?"

"*You* aren't."

"LD, I swear, if you start magespeaking me, I *will* shoot you."

"Take a breath," LD said, holding up a hand. "If anyone can find Dex, it's you, or rather"—he pointed at Peaches—"him."

"Are you serious?" I asked, looking down at my hellhound. "We don't even know where he is."

"You don't," LD said, looking down at Peaches and scratching his head behind the ears. "I'm sure this awesome hellhound knows how to find the cranky old man. Isn't that right?"

Peaches gave off a low rumble and chuffed. The ham.

<He said I'm awesome. He must really know me.>

<I think he's just being polite.>

<Ask him if he can make some meat. I'm so hungry. Are you trying to fast me again? Did you know I'm a growing hellhound?>

<I'm aware. Can you find Monty's uncle?>

<I can't find anyone on an empty stomach. It doesn't let me concentrate. My stomach is so empty.>

<This is serious, boy.>

<Nothing is more serious than meat.>

<What about your bondmate and your pack?>

<They are serious too, but meat is even more serious. Meat makes me strong. If I'm strong, I can protect my bondmate and my pack. Meat is life.>

<That actually makes sense. He's not going to make meat if you can't find Dex. As awesome as he thinks you are.>

Peaches moved into pounce mode and sniffed the air. For a second, I thought he fell asleep— he was special that way. After a few more seconds, he gave off another low rumble.

<I found him, but I can only take you, my bondmate. The old man is far away.>

"He found him," I said, looking down at my hellhound with awe. "Don't ask me how, and he says he can only take me there, but he did."

"Dex is probably helping with the locating on his end," LD said, rubbing Peaches' massive head. "Are you hungry, boy? Hellhounds are always hungry. Here."

LD gestured and created two large sausages, placing them in front of a barely contained Peaches.

<Can I eat them now? They smell so good.>

<You earned them. Dig in.>

<Why do you want me to dig? I want to eat them?>

<What I meant was, enjoy your sausages. Eat.>

He didn't wait to be told twice. The enormous sausages disappeared inside five seconds.

"Wow," LD said, shaking his head. "I hope you can find a larger space when he gets to full size, and maybe buy a few sausage factories to keep him fed."

"Or I could just learn how to make him his meat."

LD stared at me for a good three seconds.

"I have one word for you...deathane. Let's not try that again for a few decades."

"What do I do if Monty is there?" I asked, concerned. "The last time we spoke, he wasn't exactly himself."

"Did he threaten you?"

"He promised to end my existence."

"Let me ask you a different question," LD said. "Why do you think Dex is asking for you?"

"I don't know. It doesn't make sense," I said. "I mean, if Monty is there, why doesn't he just smack some sense into him and fix him?"

"He didn't ask for Strong or Simon, he asked for the shieldbearer," LD said. "I think this has something to do specifically with you and Monty. It's possible Dex can't help Monty; maybe that's *your* job."

"I'm not a mage or a mage doctor. I don't know the first thing about how to help him," I said, frustrated. "All I know is that he used blood magic to save us, and now he's in a schism."

"Don't forget Evers, who wants to kill him and probably you now, along with getting rid of magic altogether."

"Right, no pressure," I said, looking at the softly glowing ring on my finger. "Why did he use blood magic?"

"He must have felt it was the only choice at the moment," LD said. "Tristan has never been what I'd call impulsive."

"Maybe he wanted the power? Blood magic is off-the-charts power."

"He picked an odd time to go power mad, don't you think?" LD asked. "He must have had a reason. The runes we saw on the skywalk should have shredded Haven to pieces. I don't know how he didn't activate the sequence."

"Kali said Evers wanted to remove magic from this plane," I said. "Is that even possible?"

"Possible?" LD asked. "I don't know. Probable? I guess anything is probable. She's strong, but so are we. If she targeted Tristan, there must be a reason."

"You mean aside from being just this side of a psycho-sandwich of revenge and insanity?"

"We'll find her," LD said, his voice certain. "Right now, you need to find Dex and bring Tristan back from the edge."

"Right," I said, crouching down close to my temporarily satiated hellhound. "What if I can't help him? What if it's too late?"

"What do you think Tristan would want?" LD asked me gently. "Do you think he's dark? I mean deep, where it counts. Do you think he'd want to be a dark mage?"

"No, absolutely not," I said without hesitation. "Monty may be many things, but dark is not one of them."

"Then fight for him," LD said. "Help him see what he can't see right now."

Then, I asked the questions that had been tugging in the back of my mind all along.

"What if I fail? What if I try to help him and make things worse...force him over to the dark side?"

"This is a schism, not mind-control," LD said. "You can't 'force him' to go anywhere he doesn't want to go. If he goes dark, your job at that point is not to convince him."

"What are you saying?"

"If Tristan goes dark, despite your attempts to bring him off the edge into the light, you're going to have a small window of time to stop him."

"Stop him?" I asked. "Stop him how?"

"Do you know why Grey isn't hunted down by the rest of the sects or the Dark Council?" LD asked. "Everyone says he's a dark mage. Why not just put him away?"

"Because Grey, a dark mage, happens to wield a dangerous, goddess-powered sword?" I said. "Have you seen Scary Grey? I wouldn't tangle with him."

"Me neither," LD said. "But that's not it. Grey is a dark mage who has managed not to succumb to the darkness; there's still good there. He fights the darkness everyday. It's why he doesn't cast often, much less give that sword freedom. As long as he manages to win that battle..."

"He remains Grey."

"He remains alive."

"What happens if one day he slips, or loses the battle?"

"The moment that battle is lost, if he gives into the power of the sword and steps fully over to the darkness..."

"He has to die?"

"Before he kills hundreds, if not thousands of innocents," LD said, his expression dark and tinged with sadness. "If Monty can't be brought back from the edge..."

"Fuck you, LD," I said with venom. "I am not going to kill Monty. He's family."

"You say that like he'll give you a choice," LD said. "If he steps over and surrenders to the darkness, the Tristan you know will be gone, buried by the darkness."

"Buried, but not gone," I said. "If Grey can do it, so can Monty."

"Grey's darkness is now focused in the sword," LD said. "Tristan doesn't wield a goddess-powered dark weapon."

I thought hard about what LD was saying, when a solution presented itself.

"But I do," I said, slowly. "If I use Ebonsoul, I can siphon the energy of the schism from Monty and help him."

"Or kill him," LD said. "You don't know how your weapon will react to him in a schism—or to you, for that matter."

"Do you?"

"No, I don't, but I'm not his shieldbearer. You are," LD said. "Ultimately, this is your choice. To use Ebonsoul, you're going to have to get close. Close enough for him to hurt you. Your odds are slim to none."

"Never tell me the odds."

"This isn't a movie, hombre. Tristan is powerful in his right mind. If he's lost it, chances are he's going to blast first without bothering to ask questions. This is beyond risky...it's suicidal."

"What if it was TK?"

"Excuse me?" LD asked. "What do you mean?"

"What if it was TK who had gone dark?" I asked. "What would you do?"

"Bring her back or die in the process," LD said without hesitation. "She's scary and dangerous, but she's not dark. She was close, but she didn't step off the cliff into the abyss."

"Then you understand," I said. "Monty is family. He would do the same for me."

"I know," LD answered with a nod. "I needed to make sure you did."

"When did TK almost go dark?" I asked. "Was that when she was with Badb?"

LD nodded.

"Before the Ten. That's a story for another time," he said. "I suggest you never bring that up to her, if you enjoy breathing without mechanical assistance."

"Understood," I said. "I'll bring him back."

"We'll keep tracking Talin. Once he leads us to Evers, or TK loses her patience and forces it out of him, I'll let you know."

"Tell Erik I had to leave," I said, touching Peaches lightly on the head. "Besides, I think Jessikah would be safer here."

"You mean out of the way."

"She's clueless and a mageist," I said. "Her attitude is going to her killed out there. Or I'm just going to feed her to my hellhound."

"He'd probably get indigestion. Don't be cruel."

"How can she be so blind to the obvious?" I asked.

"And what's with the superiority complex? I get she's a mage, but...wow."

LD nodded.

"Black Orchid aren't trained," he said. "They are indoctrinated from an early age. They are taught to believe that they are the best sect, the most pure, and the most honorable. It's the only way they can justify the actions they take."

"You don't sound like a fan."

"The Black Orchid is universally hated by mages," LD said. "Any group that runs around calling themselves superior is instantly blacklisted by me."

"Agreed, that whole 'I'm better than anyone' attitude lasts right up to the moment an orb smashes into your face."

"No matter how badass you are, hombre," LD said with a nod, "in this world, there is always someone or something more badass."

"I learned that the hard way, several times," I said. "Maybe you and TK can polish some of Jessikah's rough edges?"

LD stared at me for a second, before shaking his head.

"TK doesn't suffer fools lightly, even if they've been conditioned," LD said. "Farsight is going to have to learn the hard way. The world is a hard and cruel place. The sooner she breaks from her current way of thinking, the easier it will be for her."

"Either she breaks from it or the world will break her," I said. "Especially the world of mages and monsters."

"It would be good to have a Daughter of Bast out of their control," LD said. "They're powerful when fully trained, if they make it that far. Most don't, which makes them rare."

"The Black Orchid doesn't feel that way," I said, "They want her eliminated."

"The Black Orchid fears what it can't control," LD said with a wry smile. "Bast mages are an anomaly to them. If they can't understand it, they erase it."

"Sounds like they are the ones who need to be erased."

"One of the reasons they hate Dex," LD answered. "He checked them a while back. Stopped them cold in their plans. Plenty of Black Orchid were retired that day and they won't let it go, ever."

Mage politics were worse than normal politics.

"I may not be a mage, but I know from personal experience when someone is green and dangerous," I said. "She'll end up getting herself or someone else killed. That's not a risk I'm willing to take right now."

"Duly noted," LD said. "I'll let Erik know your hellhound could only take you. That should defuse any protests from Farsight."

LD moved back, giving Peaches and me some room.

"Tell TK to be careful with Evers."

"I think you have that backward," LD answered with a slight shake of his head. "I'd be worried if TK were after me."

"Me, too," I said. "Thanks again."

"For what? I just came to deliver a card," LD said with a tight smile. "Don't get yourself dead, hombre. Bring Tristan back, if you can."

I nodded.

"Failure is not an option."

LD stepped back even farther and nodded. I looked

down at my hellhound. The runes along his flanks were glowing, along with his eyes.

<Let's go, boy. Take us to Uncle Dex.>

A low rumble escaped from him, followed by a bark. I saw LD wince, covering his ears, before the world went black.

TWENTY-FOUR

Traveling in-between with Peaches was a singular experience. Normally, it felt like a runaway rollercoaster ride where I was hanging on for dear life.

This time it was different.

It didn't feel like my insides were trying to escape my body.

I didn't understand how my hellhound managed planewalking. I figured it was a feature with hellhounds, but Hades never took the time to explain those abilities or how they evolved as they matured. I think Hades wanted me to be pleasantly surprised as I discovered them...in the midst of breathtaking heart attacks. God humor seriously sucked.

I was still adjusting to the fact that Peaches was a puppy. Images of Cerberus flashed in my memory, and I realized that LD was right. Peaches was going to outgrow the Moscow at some point. Unlike Hades, we didn't have access to unlimited space, unless we started knocking down some walls or created another *Dex room* in the office.

Olga would love that, right before she froze us solid.

As his bondmate, I needed to take a more proactive role in our relationship, aside from being his meat dealer. I really needed to study hellhounds and their abilities.

I'm sure if I sat down with Prof. Ziller, he could break down the quantum aspects of planewalking for me in simple language I could comprehend.

I reflexively shuddered at the thought. There wasn't enough coffee in the world that could convince me *that* was a good idea. I was going to have to attempt another training session with Mori, if we managed to get out of this situation relatively unscathed.

The idea of facing a Darth Monty had my stomach tied in knots. I didn't think he would actually try and hurt me: or worse, dust me. But a part of me—a small part of me—knew it was possible.

That small voice explained that I was in way over my head, dealing with forces I couldn't comprehend, and confronting someone who may be operating with a radically altered mental state.

A lethal mental state.

I grabbed the voice by the neck, strangled it and kicked it out of my head. This needed to happen or Monty was going dark. If that happened, all bets were off.

The sense of velocity suddenly diminished, and I found myself outside, in a large, hazy, empty, stone courtyard. The sun blazed overhead, its light diffuse as a cloudy sky blocked most of it. I looked around, confused.

There was nothing here...except for a large structure I could barely make out at the far end of the courtyard. The Sanctuary at the Golden Circle was an exact replica of Angkor Wat, the latter being the actual replica.

This didn't look like Angkor Wat, or any other place I knew for that matter.

<Are you sure this is the right place, boy?>

<The old man with the good sausages is close. Can you ask him for meat when you see him?>

<Sure, as soon as I figure out where we are. Do you smell him nearby?>

<Over there.>

Peaches sniffed the air and began walking away, heading to the other end of the large courtyard. At the other end, stood a large Torii gate. This one was made of black, rune-covered stone, and towered high above the granite walls that enclosed the space.

After closer examination, I noticed the wall was solid. There was no opening to exit the courtyard; the space was enclosed on four sides.

Sitting in the center of the gate, on the ground, was a figure.

It was Dex.

He was wearing a black robe with runes that matched the ones on the Torii gate. He opened his eyes as I approached, and stood with a grunt. He gestured and formed a large sausage, placing it on the ground in front of my shameless hellhound, who proceeded to chomp on it.

"Ach, took you long enough," Dex said, bending backward and twisting his torso. "This is a young mage's work. I'm getting too old for this shite."

"Nice to see you, too?"

"Enough with the pleasantries," Dex said, waving my words away. "We have work ahead of us—and by we, I mean you."

He narrowed his eyes at me and nodded.

"Where are we?" I said, taking another look around and ending on the immense gate in front of us. It stood nearly forty feet in height and about half as wide. The black stone thrummed with power I could feel in my lower abdomen, like a bass beat. "Where is this place?"

"Everywhere and nowhere," Dex said. "You understand the concept of a mind palace?"

"Vaguely?" I answered, fearing we were entering brain-melting territory. "Are we in your mind?"

"Don't be daft," Dex said. "This place is a construct, a doorway."

I looked around, not seeing any doors leading anywhere.

"A doorway...right," I said. "Shouldn't a doorway contain—oh, I don't know, a door?"

"This place is like a mind palace, in that it's based on a mental construct," Dex answered. "There is no time here."

"We're running out of time?" I asked, confused. "Where is Monty?"

"Not running out, boy," Dex answered curtly. "Here, in this place, we are in stasis. It was the only way to hide Monty from Evers during his schism."

"If there's no time, that means my curse...?"

"Is inactive in here, yes," Dex said. "For someone with your particular condition"—he glanced around—"a place like this can be fatal."

That didn't sound ominous at all. Dex was looking at me with a heavy dose of stink-eye. I figured he was upset about Monty and was having difficulty processing the schism. I know I was.

"Where's Monty?" I asked, not exactly enjoying Dex's tone of voice. "I don't see him."

"We'll get to that in a second," Dex said, his voice serious. "Tell me how you became untangled."

I shared about my last meeting with Kali, and how she took matters "into her own hands" with my bonds the totem, and the enso pendant. I left out the exciting parts, like the excruciating, mind-numbing pain.

"Doesn't sound like it was a pleasant experience."

"It wasn't," I said. "She redefined the concept of pain and took it to new heights for me."

"Pain is good for you," he said. "Helps you focus."

"Sounds like you two would get along just fine," I said, before handing him the card. "I got your message. You wanted to see me?"

He glanced down at the ring on my finger.

"How many uses does the totem have?"

"Three."

"That'll do," Dex said with a nod. "Do you know how to use it?"

"No," I said, looking down at the ring. "I'm supposed to channel energy into it, but I missed that lesson, apparently."

"What *do* you understand about it?" Dex asked. "This is important."

Rey's words came back to me: *You have to invert that thought process. The source of energy is all around you. All you're doing is aligning to the flow and channeling it, not storing it in your body*.

"I'm not a mage," I said after a few seconds of thought. "I have to view the energy around me differently."

"So far so good. Differently, how?"

"The energy is all around me; all I'm doing is aligning to the flow and channeling it," I said. "Like jumping in the ocean and splashing around. That last part is a little sketchy, though."

"I don't know about any ocean," Dex said, "but the first part is close enough. You've done this. Remember Rene's plane? The Strix?"

"You mean the one that ended up in little parts after the orb I made punched a hole in it?" I asked. "The orb *you* suggested I practice?"

"Yes, that one," he said with a grimace. "You recall how you formed the orb?"

"Yes, you gave me a new word of power: *ignis*..."

"What are you doing?" he asked, cutting me off. "I didn't say to form the damn thing."

"You asked me how I formed the orb. I was showing you how."

"I didn't say show me this exact second," Dex snapped. "You do remember the right word, right?"

"Yes, it's...*ignisvi*..."

"Stop," he said, suddenly, cutting me off again, this time with more force. "Not yet, and that's not what I meant."

"What did you mean?" I asked. "That is the word."

"I asked you how you formed the orb, not the word you used," Dex said. ""Do you recall *how* you formed it? The orb...not the word."

"No, I just said the word and it happened," I said. "You were there. You said it tapped into my life force. Since I have an abundance, it appeared. Doesn't make sense, but little does in my life."

"Tapping into your life force isn't the same as you having control over the energy," Dex replied. "Don't you understand that yet?"

"I'm starting to get it, yes," I said, concerned. "What's wrong?"

"My nephew is fighting for his life, and the only person who has a chance of helping him has no grasp of the basics of energy manipulation."

"What are you talking about? You're here," I said, still confused. "You're much better at this than I am."

"You haven't been paying attention," Dex said. "I'm keeping hidden, not just my nephew, but the entire damned Golden Circle."

"I'm hearing the words, but they aren't making sense," I said. "How are you hiding the entire Golden Circle?"

"The details would fry what little brain you have left," he said. "Judging what you went through with Kali, that would leave you in a coma. Let's just say, I can't leave this place, at least not yet. You're the best shot Tristan has."

"*I'm* the best shot?" I asked. "What about the other sects? You're running the Golden Circle now. Can't you make some calls? Call in some favors?"

He stared at me like I had spit in his coffee.

"What part of 'hidden' is escaping that brain of yours, boy?" he asked, the frustration clear in his voice. "My nephew is blacklisted."

"I thought that only happened if he went dark?"

"How would you deal with an impending threat?" he asked. "Wait until it becomes powerful enough to destroy you, or nip it in the bud?"

"They're not waiting until Monty goes dark...Shit. It's not just the Black Orchid. They've been waiting for this opportunity to take him out. Why?"

"Mostly my fault," Dex admitted. "They can't move

against me directly, the bastards, so they go for the next best thing."

"This is why you removed the Golden Circle."

Dex tapped the side of his nose and pointed at me.

"Sharp as a brick you are," he said with an undertone of anger. "Only one sect stood beside us, but even they can't act. Best thing was to break the agreement."

"Which sect?"

"White Phoenix. They can't do anything without taking on the rest of the sects. It would start—"

"A mage war," I finished. "Isn't taking the Golden Circle out of the agreement a little rash?"

"A little rash?" Dex asked. "They want their vengeance by killing my nephew. I'd say I'm taking the high road here."

"What's the low road?"

"I go to each sect and reduce it to ashes," Dex answered, his voice low. "Aye, maybe even bring Mo along. She always enjoys a good killing."

I shuddered at the thought of a Dex-and-Morrigan team-up. Alone, each one was a force to be reckoned with. Together, the other sects wouldn't stand a chance.

"Can we leave the 'obliterate everything' plan as the last option?" I asked. "It sounds extra homicidal."

"Let me try to explain this to you in small words, so you can understand," Dex answered after a short pause. "If you can't help my nephew, it may be the *only* option."

"How am I supposed to do that?" I asked, getting as frustrated as Dex sounded. "Do you have some rune you can give me? Some 'step away from darkness and re-enter the light' cast designed to help Monty before it's too late?"

"No," Dex said. "Even if I did, you couldn't use it. I

don't have a few hundred years to teach you. If I leave this place, Tristan will be found inside the hour. I have to stay here, which means his shieldbearer must take on his primary function."

"Which is?"

"What? Are you daft?" he yelled. "What do you mean 'Which is'? You're his shieldbearer."

"I'm learning this as I go," I said, offended by the tone of his voice. "This isn't intuitive, and I didn't study with Ziller for several thousand years like some people I know."

"How are you going to help Tristan?" Dex asked, as I felt the shift in the air around us. He was gathering energy around him. "You can't even help yourself."

"What are you talking about?" I asked, taking a step back. "Dex, where *is* Monty?"

"You're useless, do you know that? This was a mistake. You...are a mistake."

"Excuse me?" I said, feeling my own anger rise. He wasn't joking. "In case you haven't noticed, I'm not a—"

"I'm not a mage. *I'm not a mage*," he mocked. "How long are you going to cling to that poor crutch of an excuse? Why are you even *here*, boy?"

Now I was confused.

"What are you talking about? *You* sent for me."

"No, I sent for the *shieldbearer*, not the diaper-wearer," he snapped. "If you're going to bemoan how unfair things are, just go back. I have no use for you."

"I *am* the shieldbearer."

"No," Dex said, stepping close and putting a finger in my face. "You're *a* shieldbearer, and a bloody bad one at that. I'd feel safer holding up toilet paper for protection, than depending on your ability."

"What?" I asked, barely controlling the anger now. "I didn't *ask* to be anyone's shieldbearer. No one asked me."

"I didn't ask...no one asked me," Dex scoffed, raising his voice. "I'm sorry, *Your Highness.* Were you not consulted? No one asked your permission? Oh, woe is me. No wonder my nephew is in a schism! *You* were supposed to watch out for him, and what did you do when it mattered? You ran."

"You...need...to...stop. Now."

"Coward," Dex spat and he stepped closer. "When he needed you, where were you? How long did it take before you ran with your tail tucked between your legs? Worthless"—he threw up a hand—"you're a worthless waste of space. Do you know what I have to do now?"

"Besides back the hell up away from me?" I said, letting my hand drift to Grim Whisper. "You need to stop. You don't want to do this."

"I'm quaking in fear, boy," Dex said with a short laugh. "I now have to go kill my nephew, because you are clueless, and worse, spineless."

"No, I won't let—"

"You won't let me?" Dex cut me off. "The time for you to act has long passed. You think you can stop me? You think I *want* to do this?"

"No, I don't think—"

"Exactly," he said, cutting me off again. "You...don't... think, and when you do, it's all about you. The universe revolves around you, doesn't it, you myopic, egocentric, little shite."

"I know you're upset," I said, raising a hand in surrender, while keeping the other close to my weapon. "I don't want this either. Let's stay calm. Monty needs us."

All around us, the energy level kept increasing at a steady pace. Dex always had a scary edge; right now that edge was exposed, and it was sharp.

Sharp enough to cut...sharp enough to kill.

"Monty *needed* us—needed you. It's too late now."

"What are you talking about?"

"How dense are you?" he asked, his voice laced with venom. "I have to destroy my own flesh and blood, because you, his *supposed* shieldbearer, were too weak. I now have to do the unthinkable, because you...you...are a poor excuse of a friend and brother. Go back to whatever hole you crawled out of. I'll do you the favor of killing you, once I'm done with Tristan."

I heard Peaches whine, and then saw him crumple over on his side.

"Peaches! What did you do to him?" I asked as the anger surged. "What did you do?"

"I put a little something in his sausage," Dex said, stepping back as I ran to Peaches' side. "Even something as simple as feeding your bondmate, even in that, you're incompetent. Removing you will be doing the world a favor."

"I take care of him just fine," I said, checking Peaches. "C'mon, boy."

"Ignorance in the world is a bad thing. Willful ignorance with power...well, that's a dangerous and lethal thing, and should be destroyed whenever encountered."

"Destroyed?"

"Even now, boy," he said, looking down at me and shaking his head. "You don't understand. Some people are truly too stupid to live."

"What did you do?" I asked again, focusing on my hellhound. Peaches was still breathing, but he was knocked out cold. "You drugged him?"

"I removed him from the equation," Dex answered, his voice grim. "I don't need him trying to rescue you when you're undone. After your bond is broken, sadly, I'll have to put him down, too. He's too dangerous to leave alive. A shame, really. At least he was honorable; he knew what it meant to protect his own, unlike the bloody Chosen Victim of Kali."

"You know what, old man?" I said, standing slowly and shaking out my hands as the anger took over. "Let's not wait. I'm here now. You want to 'remove' me? Do it."

I never saw the blast.

That's how fast he was. One moment I was standing up and daring him to remove me, and the next, I was sailing across the courtyard. I hit the far wall hard and fell to the ground, with the wind knocked out of me.

"You think you can challenge me, boy?" Dex called out as he walked toward me. "I'm not old because I'm lucky; I'm old because I fight dirty. No rules and no quarter given. You may not be a mage, but at least you can die like one."

"No quarter asked," I said, getting into a crouch, drawing Grim Whisper and firing in one smooth motion. Ever since the attack at Haven, I was using entropy rounds. I wasn't going to waste time trying to persuade someone out to kill me.

He waved his hand, creating a wall of green light and deflecting the rounds.

"That's the best you have?" he jeered. "No wonder you failed Tristan. Just quit, accept your fate and end it, boy.

You're outclassed, outmatched, and outwitted. You have no hope...it's over."

"I'm not dead yet."

"Yes, you are," he said, his voice low. "The message just hasn't reached that thick skull of yours."

He muttered something under his breath and formed a group of six green orbs around his body. The grapefruit-sized orbs were crackling with power and energy, and slowly hovered around him. Every single one of them looked deadly, and somehow I knew, if one of them hit me, it was over...literally.

"Don't do this, Dex. I don't want to hurt you."

"Child, not even in your wildest imaginations does there exist a place where you can hurt me," Dex said, looking around. "Much less in this place. It pains me to do this, but it must be done. I'll make it quick."

I saw him take a deep breath and let it out slow. As he exhaled, a thin shield of green energy covered his body completely.

"What the hell is wrong with you?" I asked, suddenly very aware of Dex's deadly intent. "We both care about Monty."

"Don't you dare," he hissed. "If you cared, my nephew would be whole right now. He's in this situation because of you."

"You're wrong," I said, trying to find some reason in the madness. "He made a choice. I'm here to help him."

"This is for the best, really," he said, with a hint of sadness. "You've been a failure, a screw-up, your whole life. It's why you're on your own—no family, no friends, no one and nothing."

"That's not true and you know it, you old bastard."

The words stung because they hit close to home.

"I checked, boy," he said. "They bounced you out of the NYTF—the Shadow Company, for dereliction of duty, wasn't it? They counted on you, but their trust was misplaced. You failed when it mattered the most...just like with Tristan."

He had done his homework. Shadow Company and my involvement in it had been scrubbed clean from every database, or so I had been told. Apparently, it hadn't been scrubbed hard enough.

"You don't know what you're talking about."

I could feel my jaw clench involuntarily. We weren't going to find a resolution today—not while we were both still breathing.

"Oh, I *know*," he said, getting closer. "I can smell the fear coming off you, boy. You're a lying coward if I've ever seen one. I've seen plenty in my years and you, boy, are the worst of the lot."

"I may be scared, but I'm no coward."

"Empty words," he said with a sneer. "I'll make sure they're your last."

With a nod, the orbs raced at me.

TWENTY-FIVE

The rage broiling inside of me broke, replaced by something else—a calm, calculated coldness. I had no illusion of who and what I was facing. Dex was a skilled, experienced mage. My odds at facing him were abysmal. Worse, he blamed me for Monty's schism.

The small voice that always ran away, shrieking in fear, stood its ground, faced me, and nodded. This place could very well be where I bought it, but I wasn't going to show Dex fear, no matter how I felt. If he blamed me, fine. I knew who I was, and I knew what was at stake, even if he was blinded by emotion.

I was mortal in this place, but I had no intention of dying here, not today.

I backpedaled away from the orbs, shooting two and destroying them as the other four broke off in pairs to flank me. They arced around the courtyard, hugging the walls on an indirect trajectory to crush me. I waited until the last possible second before diving forward into a roll.

They missed, but not by much, searing parts of my jacket, and picking up speed as they blazed past.

The orbs swept across the floor and homed in again. I needed to know if they were on auto-pilot, or if Dex was actively controlling them. I was hoping for the latter, but I needed to make sure.

I opened fire again on Dex, emptying the magazine and reloading as I slid forward, dodging to the side to avoid another swipe from the orbs. At this rate, I wouldn't last long. The only cover in the entire courtyard was the huge Torii gate at the other end.

Dex didn't even bother to dodge the rounds I fired. They hit his shield and evaporated with little to no damage. That wasn't the point; I needed to see if the orb's trajectories were affected by diverting his attention. If I could distract him, I could make a run for the gate.

I noticed two of the orbs had slowed down.

It wasn't much, but it was enough. I stood still and aimed for Dex's head. In my peripheral vision, I could see the orbs closing. They were moving too fast for me to hit now, but if I could slow them down, I had a chance to run for cover.

I fired and missed.

I never miss, not when I'm focused, and there's nothing more focusing than orbs of death closing in on your location to blast you to bits. I took a deep breath and slowed everything down.

Slow is smooth, and smooth is fast.

Everything, except Dex, became background noise: the crackling of the orbs, the ambient energy pulsing around me, the cold stone beneath me. It all blended into the background, unimportant. All that mattered was hitting this shot.

I fired again, twice, and ran for the gate.

This time Dex moved and gestured. The orbs veered away and lost me before regrouping some distance away. He was controlling them, which was both good and bad news. The crackling was increasing in volume as they flew around. Beneath the sound of the orbs, I heard something else, something that kicked me into overdrive.

A high-pitched tone sliced through the air behind me. I slid on my stomach as it got closer, just in time to see an angry, green teleportation circle hiss by. I saw it head for the gate and then veer off to the side, into the courtyard wall, punching a hole in it. After a few seconds, the hole slowly repaired itself. I doubted I would have the same reaction if Dex managed to slam me with one of those circles.

The crackling orbs had reacquired my location and were blazing in my direction. I got to my feet, continuing my dash as I processed what just happened. I had heard a teleportation circle, not something I remember ever doing.

More importantly, Dex didn't want the gate damaged. He had deliberately altered the trajectory of the teleportation circle to avoid the gate, and smash into the courtyard wall.

The gate was important to Dex, which meant it was important to me. A few seconds later, I slid into cover behind the gate.

"You've gotten better at running," Dex called out. "I would expect no less from a coward."

Goading tactics. He was trying to get in my head, but I

knew this game and had played it all my life. I crouched behind one of the enormous gate legs, the *hashira,* and tried to catch my breath. The crackling of the orbs diminished and then disappeared entirely, throwing the courtyard into an eerie silence.

If my theory was correct, he wouldn't fling orbs or teleportation circles this close to the gate. His next attack would be the up-close-and-personal kind. He wasn't going to risk destroying the gate. At least, I hoped he wouldn't.

"When Monty needed someone to look out for him," I called out, facing the nearest wall so my voice would bounce off, hopefully disguising my exact location. "Where were you? Did you even care about him? You abandoned him."

Silence.

Usually a good thing, but with a master teleporter... silence was a bad thing.

I felt the energy before I saw the green circle form next to me. I dove out of the way as a large mace cratered the ground where I had crouched moments earlier.

Another circle formed under my feet, and I found myself launched to the other end of the courtyard at speed. I bounced off the stone floor and crashed into the wall, managing to twist my body so my shoulder took the brunt of the impact.

There was no flush of warmth to indicate my curse was acting to repair the damage. He wasn't lying. I was mortal in this place.

"I'm going to do this the old-fashioned way," Dex said as he appeared several feet away, holding a softly glowing weapon in his hand. "This is going to hurt you, much more than it's going to hurt me."

The weapon he held was a nasty-looking hybrid mace-axe.

The two-foot handle of the weapon was covered in glowing, green runes, which matched the symbols along the oversized blade. The mace side, forming the back of the deadly bladed end, was a large semi-circle of steel, covered in spikes.

Getting hit by either side would be detrimental to living. As fearsome as the weapon was, it didn't compare to the shrieks coming from it. For a moment, I thought I was hallucinating.

"What the hell?" I said, scrambling back and rolling to my feet, putting some distance between us. "What is that?"

Dex hefted the axe in his hand.

"This here is Nemain," he said, with a small measure of pride. "Had it cursed by Badb herself. Use it too long and it drives you mad. It's designed to make you piss your pants, before I cleave you in half."

"I'm going to guess that you've been using it too long," I said, backing up even more. "Considering your present behavior."

"Ach, boy," he said with a grin. "I rarely find the need for it. I brought this out special...for you."

"Really?" I said. "There's no need to go through all that trouble."

"Trouble? That's all you've been since you met Tristan."

"All I've been?" I snapped back, raising my voice. "Now I know that thing is baking your brain."

"Every time I used this weapon," Dex said. "You know what they called me?"

"You mean besides crazy?"

"Harbinger. The Harbinger of Destruction."

"You're a Montague," I said, trying to step off at an angle, putting even more distance between us. "Destruction is a feature with your family. Why not choose a peaceful resolution? You could transform that into the Harbinger of Goodwill or Strong Coffee."

He smiled.

"I can smell your fear, boy," Dex said with a short nod. "I know you're scared. No one wants to die, but this has to happen. You have to pay for your failure."

"I didn't fail," I said. "Monty made a choice, and I'm here to help him, even if you're not."

"No matter," Dex said, looking down at his weapon. "It all ends today."

The runes along its haft pulsed green as he gave it a practice swing. The shrieks sounded like someone was strangling a group of angry cats, while clawing nails down a chalkboard. It was blood-curdling.

Nemain made Monty's Sorrows sound like an angelic choir in comparison. I tried to block the noise out, but it cut through me on a visceral level. If I hadn't been exposed to the Sorrows, I'd probably be running away in fear and panic. As it stood, the sound of Nemain was assaulting my limbic brain and pushing for a strong case of flight while screaming in fright.

I slid back to the nearest wall as Dex began to close the distance. I reached for my mala bracelet, only to remember, Kali had disintegrated it.

I pressed my mark.

Nothing happened.

No reaction. No flash of power or light, Karma didn't appear, and time didn't stop.

"Well, shit."

"Out of tricks, boy?" Dex asked over the shrieks of Nemain. "Your hellhound is napping, and my nephew is otherwise occupied. No one is coming to save you. You're going to die...alone."

The small voice that had been so brave at the outset, was slowly backing up with me, when it whispered one last, defiant word...Ebonsoul.

In a few seconds, Dex was going to cut me down to size...literally. I was mortal, with no shield, and no way to freeze time. I only had one option left. I reached inside and felt for the power of my weapon. The energy of Ebonsoul exploded in my mind, as the blade began forming. The silver mist wrapped itself around my hand as a transparent, violet dome, five feet in diameter formed around me.

"A dawnward isn't going to save you, boy," Dex said, slamming Nemain down on the dome of violet energy. "Nemain can cut through anything."

He sliced through the dome with some effort, as I raised the newly formed Ebonsoul to parry his strike. Violet and green energy flashed between us as I held up Ebonsoul, stopping his downward swing, even as the force of his momentum brought me to one knee. The look of surprise on his face was only matched by the surprise I felt.

"Not anything," I said, recovering quickly and driving a kick into his midsection. "Maybe you should check the warranty."

Dex backpedaled several feet out of the violet dome of energy and chuckled, unfazed by my strike, which had been designed to break all of his ribs. I should've known it wouldn't be that easy.

"I'm going to enjoy ending you, boy," he said, swinging Nemain. "Come, show me you have the courage to die."

I stayed crouched inside the dawnward and remembered Rey's words again: *The source of energy is all around you. All you're doing is aligning to the flow and channeling it.*

I thought about Monty going dark and being hunted. About Peaches, and Dex putting him down, Roxanne in danger for being close to Monty, Chi for caring about me. All the people who depended on us, and were knowingly or not, protected by what we did or who we stood against. If I failed here, they were all in danger.

I got to my feet and let myself step into the power around me. It felt like jumping into a freezing lake. I saw Dex's expression harden as I tapped into the power. He began gesturing with his free hand as the ambient energy in the courtyard crashed into me.

I returned his glare and whispered one word.

Ignisvitae.

TWENTY-SIX

Fear will make you do some amazingly stupid things.

After I whispered the word of power, the dome compressed into Ebonsoul, wrapping the blade in violet energy as the red runes along its blade exploded with power.

The energy raced through my body, looking for an outlet. I extended an arm in Dex's direction. I felt the power travel down my arm and blast out of my hand in a violet beam.

Heading straight for Dex.

I let all the anger and fear I felt race into that beam, and it took on a darker undertone. The power smelled like burning flesh, which I found strange.

Why would it smell like burning flesh?

I looked at my arm, enveloped in a violet-black cocoon of energy and answered my own question.

My arm was ablaze with violet flames.

I didn't have much time to ponder burning my arm off as the beam slammed into Dex. He held up Nemain as a shield, and it worked...for about two seconds, before knocking it out of his hands and punching into his chest.

Dex rolled with the blow, and twisted his body, raising a hand to deflect the beam. The violet energy impacted his hand and shot off at an angle.

Right into the Torii gate.

The beam cut into one of the legs, blowing a large chunk of the supporting stone away. The gate creaked slightly, swaying from the impact of the blast.

"No!" he yelled, looking away from me and focusing on the compromised gate. "Shut it down, boy!"

"No," I said, my voice full of both fear and determination. "You're trying to kill me, which means you get to die first."

"Don't be daft," Dex said, looking at me and angling the beam away from the gate into a nearby wall. "If I wanted you dead, I could have ended you several times over by now. Now, shut it down, or both you *and* Tristan are lost."

"What are you talking about?" I asked. "You're trying to kill me."

"Listen carefully," Dex said, keeping his voice calm while still deflecting the beam. "If that gate falls, Tristan will be exposed, and you will be trapped here, with me until I can reopen the passage. By the time I can create another gate, it will be too late; Evers or the other sects will have found him, and then I *will* kill you."

"That's not very motivational."

"I'm glad you're understanding the severity of your situation, boy," Dex said with a grimace. "Now shut it down."

"A few moments ago, you wanted to blast me."

"What makes you think that's changed?"

"Lowering my defenses doesn't sound like a smart plan."

"But burning your arm off is?" Dex asked, pointing at my arm. "You keep this up, you're going to lose that limb, boy."

I looked down. The violet energy had burned away my jacket sleeve. Wisps of violet colored smoke wafted off the surface of my now darkened arm. I had jumped past sunburn, into sunbaked with a light charbroiling.

"Shit, that can't be good," I muttered. "Fine, I'll stop, but if you start getting murdery, I'm blasting you."

"Aye, I'm properly warned," Dex said. "I need to repair the gate, before it collapses. Do you have enough control to stop it?"

"I think so."

"Now would be a good time," he said, looking at the gate. "I need to repair that damage before it's too late."

I nodded.

I took a deep breath and slowly forced myself to step away from the energy around me. It was difficult, and felt like running in thigh-deep mud. The power wanted to hold on, wanted to continue coursing through my body.

Part of me wanted it to.

I forced myself away finally, with a grunt, falling to one knee. Dex raced to the gate and began gesturing. He had his back to me as he focused intently on repairing the stone.

If I attacked now, he'd never see it coming.

That little voice in my head cracked its knuckles and nodded. It pointed out how vulnerable Dex was, with his back turned, and his focus diverted.

Take him now. He won't expect an attack—he's too focused on the gate. This is your chance...kill him. That old fart tried to blast you to little bits. He threatened Peaches. For that alone, you should put the old bastard out of his misery.

No one threatens your hellhound...and lives.

I looked down from my charred arm to the still-furiously working Dex. The energy around me was still there. A sense of anticipation filled me. It was only a word away, and I could be using the power again. It beckoned me to channel it again, enticing me to wield it. With a shudder, I closed my eyes and got my breathing under control.

"No," I said under my breath. "No, he may be psycho-batshit crazy right now, but that would be wrong. Even if he did threaten Peaches and try to blast me to bits."

"Good choice," Dex said, clapping me on the shoulder as he stood next to me, nearly startling me into a heart attack. "That's all I needed to know."

"I just nearly shot you," I said, keeping my voice calm despite the fact that my heart was stomping out a sprint in my chest. "How is that possible?"

I looked over and saw the Dex at the gate disappear. The damaged gate shimmered for a few seconds and settled into solidity. The damage from my blast was nowhere to be seen on the gate.

Next to me, stood Dex.

I reached out slowly and poked him in the chest.

"Aye," Dex said, slowly pushing my poking finger away. "It's me."

"You...are a dangerous, old man," I said. "This was all an illusion?"

"Not everything," Dex said, looking at my arm. "You did real damage to yourself."

"The beam?" I said, looking at my burned arm. "Are you saying it wasn't...?"

"It was real," Dex said, shaking his head. "In a few more centuries, you may actually be dangerous."

"How did you get over here so fast without a teleportation circle?" I asked, looking over from the gate to where Dex now stood beside me. "You were over there. I saw you over there."

"By now, you should know enough to see with your proper eye," he said, tapping my forehead. "You saw what I needed you to see."

"It was an illusion?"

"A third-order simulacrum," Dex said. "Let's just say, I refracted light to create a likeness of myself. A quite handsome likeness, if I have to be honest."

"But it looked, no...it *felt* real."

"Because you're using the wrong sense to see," Dex answered. "The illusion precedes and informs reality. I'd explain it to you, but then, frankly, most of it would be beyond you, at your current level of understanding."

"Are you saying I wouldn't understand you?" I asked, not understanding what he was saying. "I may not be a mage, but I can grasp some of the concepts."

"I'm saying that delicate structure you call a brain would snap," he answered. "I need you firing on all cylinders." He gave me a look. "Well, as many as possible, considering the circumstances."

"You deflected my beam from here?"

"Actually from over there," he said, pointing several yards away, across the courtyard. "Like I said, with a few centuries of training, you will be a minor threat. Except, we don't—"

"Have a few centuries to train me?"

"Not even a few hours," Dex said, shaking his head. "Time still flows for my nephew. Every second he is in the Sanctuary, he's one second closer to discovering my ruse. Once he does, he will begin to unravel and grow stronger."

"When did you create the simulacrum?" I asked, still shocked by how real it felt. "I didn't see you..."

"When you saw me gesture," Dex said. "Right before your blast."

It took a few seconds for my brain to catch up.

"What the hell, Dex?" I asked, raising my voice. "What was the mind-game for?"

"Tell me why you didn't take the opportunity," Dex asked, his voice stern. "I was open and I had tried to kill you. I even threatened your hellhound."

"I know. Trust me, it was tempting," I said. "I thought you were lying, until I saw the gate."

"It could have been a ruse to get your guard down," he answered. "Get you to stop attacking, then end you."

"Yes, true," I said, "I may have pushed it, if you hadn't been deflecting my magic missile of might with one hand."

"That, and your 'magic missile' was mightily melting your arm off," Dex added with a glance at my destroyed jacket. "Is that why you stopped? Fear I was too powerful?"

"It was wrong," I said after a moment of thought. "I wanted to, but it was wrong."

"You wanted to?" he asked, narrowing his gaze. "Was it you, or the power?"

"More like the power made it easier to consider obliterating you," I said. "Would it have worked?"

"Your magic missile feeds off your life-force, which is limited in this place," he answered. "What do you think?"

"I think you lost your damn mind," I said. "Why the theatrics?"

"That choice you just made...it's what every mage in a schism faces," Dex said, gazing into the gate. "Control the power or surrender to it."

"Monty told me once: power isn't good or evil," I said. "He said that it all comes down to how it's wielded."

"My nephew is young, stubborn, and ill-informed," Dex said, his voice low. "Make no mistake about it: some power, some sources, are evil, corrupting influences."

"So you're saying some power is evil?"

"Aye, lad," Dex said with a nod. "Unless you can think like evil, really understand it, then you're defenseless. Evil will go and do things that seem unimaginable. If you can't meet it and stop it...it will win."

"Is that what he's going through right now?" I asked. "That power tugging at him to surrender?"

"On a massive scale—which is why I'm keeping him hidden," Dex said. "He couldn't mask himself now, even if he wanted to."

"Evers would find him if he were out in the open?"

"With ease," Dex said with a nod. "The same way you should be able to."

"Through there?" I asked, pointing at the gate. "This is the doorway?"

"Aye, through that gate you'll find my nephew," Dex said, his expression hard. "He will try to harm you if he crosses over to the dark. He was right about one thing, though."

"What?"

"The power he is facing is not good or evil."

"You just said..."

"We are the sources, boy. Every single one of us has darkness within," Dex answered. "Even him...especially him."

"That sounds about as clear as fog," I answered, exasperated. "How do I bring him back?"

"Right now, he's walking the razor," Dex said, looking at the gate runes. "You need to bring him back the same way you resisted the impulse to attack me."

"Great idea," I said, frustrated and still upset at the deception. Truthfully, I was more upset by the fact that I had fallen for it. The simulacrum had me totally fooled. "How do I do that?"

He looked down at my hand and pointed at Ebonsoul.

"You need to use your weapon."

"What? Are you sure you didn't hit your head somewhere?"

"You are his shieldbearer. That, along with your totem and the siphon, should work."

"Should work?"

"Wielding energy is an...imprecise exercise at the best of times," Dex said. "Mages risk unleashing chaos every time we cast."

"Then why take the risk, if it's so dangerous?"

He gave me a slow smile.

"Because it's bloody fun," he said, growing serious. "That combination you have may be the only thing that works on him at this point."

"Great, I have the tools; that doesn't tell me how to use them to help Monty."

"No one can tell you how to do that," Dex said. "All anyone can do is give you the tools and help you understand how they work. Ultimately, you have to use them to truly understand them."

"I still don't understand how *any* of this works."

"Rubbish, boy," Dex said, waving my words away and walking toward the gate. "If you paid attention, you'd realize you know more than you think. Stop diminishing your ability because"—he wiggled his fingers in the air—"you aren't a mage."

"But I'm not," I said. "I don't do any of those things you and Monty can do."

"So what? You think being a mage just means being able to wield power?"

"No," I said slowly as I recalled the pull, the allure of the power. "It means knowing *when* to use the power as well."

He tapped the center of his forehead and pointed at me.

"You're starting to see...finally. There's some hope for you after all."

"I'm not seeing much clearly," I said slowly, feeling the jumble of thoughts bounce around my head like so many puzzle pieces trying to fit together. "Mages choose to use the power they have. The power that is around us. Its expression depends on the mage."

"Good to see something stuck in that thick skull of yours," Dex said with a nod. "Remember, mages use the power...not the other way around. That is where my nephew is right now. That's what it means to walk the razor of a shift. If he steps into darkness, the power will corrupt and use him. Ultimately..."

"Destroying him."

"Aye," Dex said. "I won't let it get that far. If you fail...I won't."

I didn't have to ask what he meant by that. We stopped in front of the gate.

"What about Peaches?"

"He can't go with you on this one," Dex said, glancing over at my peacefully sleeping hellhound. "I'll keep him safe."

"You said you'd..."

"No," Dex said. "No harm will befall your bondmate. If you fall, I will keep him in stasis and return him to Hades if need be."

"Cerberus will kill him if you do that."

Dex gave me a long stare.

"Then don't fail," Dex said. "I'm not here to paint a pretty picture for you, boy. Tristan *will* try his best to undo you, unless you can get through to him. The Golden Circle is hidden, but not in stasis. My nephew just doesn't know it's hidden."

"How could he not know?"

Dex raised an eyebrow.

"I do have *some* skill," he said. "You thought I was over here, repairing the gate, while I stood next to you. Letting him believe he is at the deserted Golden Circle, while difficult, is not impossible. The fact that he's not in his proper mind helps, but it won't last. As he grows in power, he will see through my deception."

"Was there any moment I was a threat?"

"To whom?"

"To you," I said. "Was there any moment I had a chance against you?"

Dex smiled and then grew serious. He gestured over

my charred arm, causing golden runes to fall on the burned skin. My skin began repairing itself immediately. Once my skin healed, my jacket sleeve reappeared, as if I hadn't tried to barbecue my arm off.

"Thank you," I said, looking at my new sleeve. "I was in real danger here?"

"Mortal, even. Immortality can create a false sense of security," Dex said as he finished gesturing over my arm. "I needed to see how you would act with the knowledge of real death being possible."

"There was no way I could've faced you and won?"

"You weren't here to face me."

"It sure felt like I was facing you, especially when you were bouncing me around this place," I said. "By the way, the insults? Not cool and not appreciated."

"I know the truth stings," Dex said, "It was necessary, but we both know, it's no longer your truth—it's your past. You'll face worse soon. You didn't let me get in your head; don't let anyone else in either."

I nodded at the implication.

"You never answered my question: Was I ever a threat?"

"You mean besides that mouth of yours?" he said with a small smile. "Why bother asking questions you know the answer to?"

"I guess I do know," I said. "Thank you for not smushing me all over the stones."

"There's still hope for you. Not much, but there's a sliver."

"Your compliments need work, old man."

"Just so you know—because my nephew isn't exactly the forthcoming type," Dex said after a pause, "he was never abandoned, even when he was sent away. I always made sure he was cared for, even though his training was rigorous and harsh."

"Maybe he never wanted to be sent away," I said. "Could be all he ever wanted was a normal life."

"For a Montague?" Dex said, with a hint of sadness. "No such thing...ever. Battlemages are trained to stand and die. We've never had a choice in that. It is what we are called to do."

"That calling sucks."

He nodded and gestured, turning the center of the gate into a blur, showing an image of the Sanctuary I remembered from my last visit to the Golden Circle. It shimmered and vibrated with power as the runes in the stone shone with a golden light.

"Ready?"

"Not in a million years."

"Good," Dex said. "I'd be worried if you thought you were. Remember what you learned here. It's the only way you're going to be able to bring him back."

"What did I learn?" I asked, confused. "Besides that you are scary powerful?"

Dex stood next to me and put a hand on my shoulder.

"Take a moment to use that dead sponge you call a brain, and you'll understand," Dex said. "My nephew will be in the center of the complex, beyond the Second Gallery. The defenses are disabled for now. Don't dally; time is not your friend."

"What do you mean?"

"I mean, I can only keep him hidden for so long," Dex said. "As his power shifts, I won't be able to keep him hidden."

"Does that mean...?"

"Aye, lad," Dex said. "Evers and Talin will find him... eventually. At least this way, we control the battlefield."

"Control the battlefield?" I repeated slowly. "What are you saying?"

"That we should limit the amount of collateral damage," Dex said with a glare. "Maybe keep the property damage to a minimum by resolving this somewhere far from a population of eight million?"

"I just want to go on the record here and state that 'damage' can't be spelled without a 'mage.'" I said. "The destruction is not my department."

"Clever," Dex said with a nod, "but irrelevant. You associate with mages, so you're part of the damage. Like it or not."

"Shouldn't we be calling in the cavalry?" I asked, concerned. "Maybe the Dark Council?"

"This is mage business," Dex said. "The Dark Council has, and wants, no part of it in the city. The Director was adamant about distributing large amounts of pain and discomfort, if we failed to comply."

"You spoke to Chi?"

"You haven't?" Dex asked. "I'd arrange that conversation with haste, boy. You don't want a woman like that to come looking for you, trust me."

"What about the Ten?" I asked. "They can handle something like this quietly."

"LD and TK are on it," Dex said. "You do your part, and they will do theirs."

"What happens if I fail?"

"If you fail, you'll die, your hellhound will be placed in harm's way, and Tristan will most likely follow you into death," Dex answered matter-of-factly. "I'd suggest you strongly focus on not failing."

"Great pep talk, thanks," I said, stepping in front of the gate. "Hit me right in the feels. The next time I need—"

"Right then," Dex said, cutting me off and gripping my shoulder tightly. "Off you go."

Dex gently tossed me into the gate before I got to finish the sentence.

TWENTY-SEVEN

I landed in a sprawl worthy of my hellhound. I got to my feet, took in my surroundings, and found myself standing in front of the outer wall of the Sanctuary.

I looked behind me, but there was no Torii gate or Dex to be seen anywhere.

"Cheeky old bastard," I muttered to myself, as I made a mental note to return the shove when I got the chance —, if I ever got the chance.

I dusted myself off and adjusted Grim Whisper, swapping out my ammunition for persuader rounds. If I could incapacitate Monty, I'd have a better chance of knocking some sense into him.

Provided I could shoot him first.

I moved forward carefully. Dex said the defenses were disabled, but I was still approaching this place warily. My memories of the Sanctuary were dark and unpleasant.

The last time I'd been here, Connor Montague had died.

I looked down at my hand and examined the ring. It

gave off slow pulses of power every few seconds. I reabsorbed Ebonsoul, because nothing said, *"Let's stay calm,"* like approaching with a drawn blade in my hand.

I let my senses expand and felt Ebonsoul's presence easily. Whatever Kali had done had made access to my blade easier. I still missed my mala bracelet, though.

"I should've asked Dex for a large steaming pot of tea," I said under my breath, as I approached the inner area of the Sanctuary known as the Second Gallery. "That would've been more effective, knowing Monty."

The massive doors to the Second Gallery were open.

The Sanctuary was a series of rectangles inside of rectangles, inside yet more rectangles, and broken into small squares. The moat around the entire complex was rectangular. Each of the galleries was a rectangle, broken up into four even squares.

The Second Gallery was a large, rectangular courtyard with the temple structure located in the center. Around the Gallery wall, on each corner, stood a tall tower, matching the four towers around the center structure.

The center structure, which looked exactly like Angkor Wat's temple, towered into the air. Realizing that Dex somehow managed to hide this entire complex boggled my brain and gave me a mild headache. To think that I was ever a threat to Dex made me shake my head at my arrogance. It was like an ant asking an elephant if it was a threat.

The little voice in my head answered: Even fire ants can sting.

Until the elephant rolled over and crushed the entire colony without a second thought. Good try, but no.

I really hoped Dex was right about Monty's location as

I took in the Second Gallery complex. Searching the entire complex for one person would take weeks, and that's with them staying in one place. I felt the flush of warmth as my body repaired the damage from Dex's mage-handling of me.

I took stock of my situation. It wasn't looking good. On the downside, I had a shield I didn't know how to use, a gun I didn't want to use, and a blade I needed to use. The upside was, as far as I knew, my curse was in full effect. That would make dying difficult. The associated downside was that if Monty went full Darth on me, he would be putting the strength of my curse to the test.

Not the kind of test I was eager to take part in.

Dex had said Monty would be giving off a massive signature in the midst of a schism. I closed my eyes and focused my breath. All around me, I felt the pervasive, ambient energy of the Golden Circle. The Sanctuary felt dormant, as if waiting for the outcome of this interaction. It felt old, primal, and powerful, magnifying how small I felt in comparison.

It's almost as if the very stones I stepped on said, *You are not a mage,* but it was deeper than that. The very air of sacredness and quiet in such a large expanse of stone and power drove the point home.

You do not belong here.

I crossed the outer gallery as I entered deeper into the space. Each step I took reinforced what a bad idea this was. The immense walls were covered with symbols and runes I had no possibility of understanding.

For all I knew, they could have been words of unthinkable power, describing the secrets of reality and the universe, or the Montague recipe for tea biscuits. There was no way to decipher their meaning. What I did know, was that every symbol was imbued with a palpable power.

Other than the near sensory overload I received from the Sanctuary itself, I picked up no overt runic signatures except for one familiar source of energy...Monty.

Blazing in the center of the temple complex, like some odd runic beacon, I felt Monty's energy signature. I understood what Dex meant about Monty not being able to mask his presence. This energy announced his location easily, almost boldly, daring to be found. For a brief second, I considered turning around and looking for the Torii gate again. Monty had grown stronger since the beginning of his schism at Kali's.

Stronger and darker.

The energy I sensed was not inviting me in for afternoon tea, unless that tea included ample servings of pain... with a dash of death for added flavor. The thought of deadly Earl Grey brought a smile to my lips as I climbed the steps to the main temple of the center complex.

Another set of enormous doors sat open, and led to an inner stone courtyard, similar to the one Dex had recently thrashed me in. I poked my head in the entrance and looked around...empty. I stepped off to the side and followed the stone pathway to another larger courtyard. Whoever designed this place had a thing for courtyards.

The door to this section was closed. I stood next to it and let my senses expand. A force of runic backlash, like a door being slammed shut in my brain, hit me as the door exploded outward, narrowly missing me. It sailed across the courtyard and shattered against a wall. I was fairly certain it was a runed, Buloke Ironwood door that had just been reduced to splinters.

"I told you not to come looking for me," Monty said from inside. I figured the space was cavernous, considering the echo of his voice. "I told you, if you sought me out, I would end your immortal existence."

"Immortality is overrated," I called out without showing my face. "Besides, I was in the neighborhood and felt like dropping by."

"In the neighborhood?" Monty said. "Your attempts at humor only disguise your fear, Simon. Are you so eager to die, that you would come here? Who sent you?"

There was no reason to lie.

"Dex sent me. He's worried about you," I said. "We all are."

"Worried or scared?" Monty answered. "Which are you, Simon?"

"I'm here to help," I said, still remaining to the side of the doorway, and out of the line of fire. I didn't feel like ending up smashed like the door. "You're going through a..."

"A schism," Monty said curtly. "Do not pretend to tell me what I'm going through. What would you know of schisms or of power? You are not a mage."

"Power is dangerous," I said. "I don't think it takes absolute power to corrupt. The power a mage wields, the power you wield...can change you, twist you into something you're not."

"Rubbish," Monty answered. "You've been spending too much time with my uncle."

It was subtle, but I felt the energy spool into the temple where Monty sat. It meant it was only a matter of time before this talk became mage-conversational.

"Actually, I learned that from watching what's happening with you."

"You have no concept of the forces at play here, no reference points, nothing that could inform you as to what a schism entails," Monty said. "You couldn't possibly understand. You're not a mage, and you're completely out of your league."

"You're right, I'm not," I answered, moving away from the wall as I sensed the energy grow inside. "What I am, is your friend."

"My friend?" he asked. "How could I ever befriend someone so weak?"

"I'm stronger than I look?"

I rolled to the side and away, as a black orb punched its way through the wall where I had been standing a moment earlier. He was definitely not in friend mode.

"I see you've gotten better with those dark orbs," I called out. I took a deep breath to calm myself. This was actually scarier than facing Dex, and that realization made this terrifying. "You don't have to do this."

"Do what, exactly?" Monty asked. "What do you think I'm doing?"

"You mean besides trying to squash me with a door, or perforate me with your bloody orbs?" I asked. "You're making a choice."

Silence.

"You're correct," he said after a pause. "Actually, I'm torn, and maybe you can help me. Why don't you come in so we can discuss this like adults?"

In my mind, Admiral Ackbar swiveled around in his command chair and slapped me upside the head, before sliding off to the deeper recesses of my mind.

Don't do it—it's a trap.

I nodded my head and stepped back even farther from the wall. Monty had demonstrated some of his power. I had no intention of turning into a Swiss cheese target from one of his barrage attacks. The hole left by the black orb he'd launched at me held a residue of power. Enough for me to want to make sure nothing he threw at me connected.

"I'm correct?" I answered, surprised. "Why yes...yes, I am. I can help you, but right now, since you're giving me a serious Darth Monty vibe, I'm going to help you from out here, if that's okay with you."

"It doesn't really matter where you are," Monty answered with a low laugh. "You can't escape from me."

"I'm not here to escape. I'm here to bring you back."

"That's exactly what I need you for," Monty said, appearing in the doorway. "You said I was making a choice. Right now, at this moment, I'm trying to choose the best way to erase you from existence."

For a few seconds, the words escaped me.

The last time I had seen him, the sclera of his eyes had become shot through with black veins. Now, they were a solid black. Around him, small arcs of black energy jumped from his body to nearby surfaces, leaving small craters in their wake. If he wasn't dark, he was damn close.

"Easier said than done," I answered, taking a few more steps back. "I see you're really embracing the new look. Do you know what happens if you go full Darth?"

"Power," he said, looking down at the energy arcing from his body. "Infinite power."

"First of all, don't be a dumbass," I said—shocking him, from his expression. "There's no such thing as infinite power. We've faced enough gods to know that's not true. Second, if you go full Sith Lord, you're going to be a permanent guest at Ezra's table sooner than you'd like."

"Fool," Monty said. "You're not here to bring me back. You're here to make sure I never leave...at least not alive."

"What?" I asked, shocked. "Dex said I needed to help you, that I'm the only one, because..."

"You're my shieldbearer?" he answered. "Incredible. How can you not see it?"

"Illuminate me."

"Did you suggest calling the Dark Council?" Monty asked, derisively. "I'm sure you did, it's *so* you. What did my uncle say? 'This is mage business, too dangerous for the Dark Council' or something to that effect?"

"What are you saying?"

"We're bait...Well, I'm bait. You're just a loose end. Evers will find me here soon enough, once my uncle lets her know where I am."

"He would never betray you like that," I said. "He's trying to keep you safe."

"By locking me in some pocket dimension from which I can't escape?" Monty asked. "For someone so observant, you see very little. Who exactly is helping whom?"

"You're not making sense," I said. "He's your uncle, your family. Why would he want you dead? He cares about you."

"You don't know him. I'm becoming stronger, stronger than even him," Monty said. "He feels threatened. If he lets Evers finish me, he can say he tried to help me, but it was too late. I turned dark and had to be eliminated."

"That doesn't explain why I'm here," I said. "I'm not a threat to him."

"How are you supposed to leave this place after you 'rescued' me?" Monty asked. "Where is your creature? The last time I checked, you hadn't mastered teleportation. What were you supposed to do, place a call?" He pointed to my jacket where I kept my phone. "Please, make the call."

I pulled out my phone...no service.

"No service," I said. "That doesn't mean anything."

"It means everything," Monty said. "Once Evers arrives, this place will be untethered and set adrift. We will be lost in time and space. Eventually, we will perish, but not you. *You* will be here for the rest of your days, pondering your stupidity."

Monty was many things, but rude wasn't one of them. All of this was the darkness speaking, creating a scenario where he was betrayed and felt he had to self-preserve, would justify stepping into darkness. Whatever was going on in his head was preying on any insecurities about his family and friends.

"You're not going to take him," I said, letting the menace come through. "He's not yours."

"You're threatening me?" he laughed again. "What could *you* possibly do?"

"I'm threatening whatever is trying to push you over the edge," I said, my voice taking on an edge. "I'm here as your last chance. But the ones coming after me, well... those friendly folks are looking for an excuse to obliterate you. Don't give it to them."

"Now who sounds delusional?" Monty mocked. "This is me, Simon. I know what I'm talking about. You just can't see it."

"All I see is that you're not thinking straight."

"I've never been more lucid," he said. "Can you prove me wrong?"

I had to admit, he was pretty convincing...just not convincing enough. Dex could have killed me before sending me here. The same went for LD and TK. They didn't have to help me or Monty, but they did. Not because they felt threatened, but because they cared. Frankly, after my little sparring session with Dex, I realized I wasn't much of a threat.

"Let's say, hypothetically, that you're right, and this is all a nefarious setup by Dex to eliminate us," I said. "What's *your* plan? You think you can face him alone? What about all the other sects who want you blasted to dust? Can you take them all on?"

"I will kill everyone they send after me," Monty said, his voice hovering around the warmth of an arctic storm. "Every single one of them will die by my hand."

"Even Dex?"

"Dex? Dex will be the first," he scoffed. "That old bastard will pay for doing this to me."

"Doing what? He's trying to help you."

"My uncle trapped me in here," Monty said quietly. "He thinks I don't know, but I do. I'm aware of the energy of this place; after all, it was my home. He thinks he can keep me trapped here"—Monty stared at me with dead eyes—"when all he did was send me the key to my cell."

That look made me feel about as safe as standing blindfolded before a firing squad.

So much for Monty not knowing he was in one of Dex's construct thingies. On a scale from terrifying to nightmarish, Monty took the scale and ripped it apart with his bare hands. If I survived this, Dex and I were going to have some words.

"If you leave here, they *will* kill you."

"No," Monty said, "they will *try*...and fail."

"I can't let you go," I said. "It's my job as your shield-bearer to watch your back and protect you from the attacks you can't see. Even if—especially if—you're putting yourself in danger."

"Let me see if I can tactfully put this in terms your pitifully minuscule brain could comprehend," Monty said, still absorbing energy. "As far as shieldbearers go, you're absolute trash. I know first-year apprentice mages with more runic control in one hand than you will ever possess in your entire body."

Right now I wished I had a squadron of those first years with me to get through this. I pushed my fear back, telling myself that Monty was in there, behind the scary.

"I may be a trash shieldbearer, but I still can't allow you to go all dark side," I shot back. "My job is to protect you."

"Allow me?" Monty scoffed. "Protect me?"

"Yes...protect you," I said. "Even if it's from yourself."

"While you're worrying about protecting me, who is going to protect you?"

"Excuse me?" I asked warily. "Does that mean you're planning to let me help you?"

"Not even remotely," he answered, forming a large, black orb in one hand. "Once I kill you, my uncle will know you failed. He will come here and try to 'stop me in my tracks' before letting Evers know of my location. In so doing, he will need to open a gate. I have a little surprise waiting for him."

Monty had just ratcheted the scary vibe up a few notches.

"In order for this surprise scheme to work, you have to kill me," I said, extending my arms to the side and looking down at myself, before returning my gaze to him. "I'm still here...alive."

"Allow me to rectify that," he said with a chilling smile. "*Dissipare.*"

He released the orb.

It hovered in the air for half a second, rotating slowly as if looking for a target, before racing at me.

TWENTY-EIGHT

Time has a way of being elastic at the strangest moments.

Time is not your friend. Dex's voice echoed in my head.

Three seconds of drinking my favorite javambrosia felt like an instant. Three seconds of watching an orb of death coming at you...that was a lifetime.

I realized a few things in those seconds.

One: Monty was a few steps from Darthness. Thinking his uncle wanted him dead meant he wasn't processing thoughts rationally. Dex loved his nephew. Monty knew this, but whatever was happening to him had inverted his perception of the world to one of persecution.

Two: Monty's awareness that Dex had trapped him meant that his power had grown to the point that Dex wouldn't be able to hide him much longer. Evers would soon find him. This would feed into Monty's betrayal narrative, reinforcing it and possibly launching him off the deep end into embracing the darkness once she appeared.

Three: I seriously needed to consider a career change, or an extended vacation, some place far away from mages and monsters, as immediately as humanly possible. If not, I was the one who was going to lose it.

I drew Grim Whisper and fired.

The persuader rounds did nothing to the incoming orb. I wasn't expecting them to. My real target was standing behind the orb. The rounds punched into Monty with no effect. The orb slammed into me, propelling my body backward at speed.

I hit the courtyard wall with enough force to destroy the stone behind me. The orb spread out and covered my body with black energy as I crumpled to the floor, landing on my rear, sitting against what was left of the wall.

"Goodbye, Simon," Monty said, glancing down at my broken body before turning around to enter the temple. "Even an immortal needs a body...that orb will disintegrate yours. The pain will be excruciating. I warned you. You shouldn't have come after me."

Kali's words blazed in my mind as the orb started to go to work.

You will be the one in the gap, no longer a shieldbearer. You will be my aspis—my shield- warrior. It is not only Tristan that depends on you now.

The orb was powerful. I could feel the effects of the blood magic trying its best to help me shed some unnecessary pounds by melting the skin off my body.

Then it stopped.

The pain came to a crashing halt.

That's when I started laughing.

Monty turned around with a puzzled look on his face.

"I'm not laughing with you," I said, getting to my feet. "I'm laughing at you."

Monty narrowed his eyes at me and slowly reached

behind him, drawing the Sorrows. The soft wails filled the temple as he approached.

"How are you doing this?" he asked. "You should be dust right now."

"I had an appointment at Kali's pain spa earlier," I said, standing as the black energy slid off my body and evaporated. A thin layer of violet energy covered my body, reminding me of Dex's green aura shield. "Your orb hurt, but excruciating? Not even close."

"You've...changed, somehow," Monty said, stepping out of the temple. "You've grown stronger. What did she do?"

"I told you," I said, feeling the center of my forehead burn with power. "Kali gave me a pain makeover. You should try it. It gives you a new perspective on life...and death."

"She marked you," Monty said, keeping his voice low, "*really* marked you."

"You plan on talking all day?" I said, letting the silver mist of Ebonsoul flow into my hand. "Let's get to the killing."

"Indeed," he said with a smile. "Let's."

TWENTY-NINE

Monty wasn't a typical mage.

Most of the mages I met were heavy on the casting and light on the physicality. They spent all of their time becoming runically strong, neglecting the other, just as important, aspects of being a mage.

In a non-magical fight, I could break most of them with a few well-placed strikes. There were a few exceptions to this; Dex was built like a small wall and just as tough. LD and TK were scary strong in every regard, magically and physically. That left Monty.

Monty was a battlemage.

He was the only mage I knew who walked around with a pair of wailing blades—though his uncle, who carried a shrieking battle-axe-and-mace hybrid, was similar.

There was something seriously off about the Montague family.

Monty realized early on that he needed to be strong, both physically and mentally. My training sessions with Master Yat were always torture, and while I understood the significance of the training, Monty reveled in it. He actually enjoyed our training with Yat, pushing it to three, sometimes even four hours of non-stop punishment.

Battlemages are trained to stand and die. Dex's words whispered in my memory.

This fight was going to hurt.

"Can't use your finger wiggles on me," I said, sliding into a defensive stance. "No melting magic for you."

"And you can't use your gun."

"Guess we have to do this the old-fashioned way, slice and dice," I said. "I've always thought the blade a superior weapon. It forces you to get up close and personal."

"You're going to regret coming here, Simon," he said, hefting his swords. "I take no pleasure in ending you."

"Haven't ended me yet," I said, and beckoned him closer with my free hand. "Let me see you try."

The ploy was simple. Monty was an excellent mage, but he was still a mage. They all had fragile egos and identity issues. The buttons were all there, I just needed to know where to push. With Monty, I was going to have to fight dirty.

He slid in with a lightning-fast lunge. I parried the thrust and backpedaled, deflecting the overhead slash from his second weapon. His blades began to intensify, their wailing and take on a blue glow.

I slid in with a front kick to his midsection, causing him to twist his body as I slashed horizontally across his thigh. He brought down his sword before I could connect, but I managed to slice through his pants leg.

I smiled, knowing how much he hated having his suits ruined.

"This will be the last suit you ruin," he said, moving

back and glancing at his leg. "You've cost me a fortune in clothing alone."

The complaint sounded like the Monty I knew, but I wasn't here to be nice. I was here to get my friend back. I needed him off-balance. I needed to create an opening and cut him with Ebonsoul.

"That wailing sound your blades make," I said as we circled, "is that the sound you made when your parents abandoned you at the Golden Circle?"

His expression darkened. Button one pressed.

"You know nothing of my past," he said, closing the distance. "I'd suggest you desist from trying to guess."

"I'm all scared, now," I scoffed. "What happens if I don't? You'll kill me? I think we're past that point in the conversation."

"Unlike you," he said, slashing at my head, forcing me to duck and roll to avoid the thrust from the second blade, "I have friends, a family. What do you have? A hellhound who will eat you out of house and home?"

"Family? You don't have family or friends," I corrected. "Remember? They're all trying to kill you? You have no one...you're alone."

I could feel the anger and confusion roil off him. Button two pressed.

"Which is why I need to eliminate you all," he said, pressing his attack.

Two blades cut across the air as I fell on my back, avoiding the attack. I kicked out, connecting with his shin. I drew Grim Whisper, and managed to shoot one of the Sorrows out of his hand as he fought for balance.

The wails from the remaining sword began to increase in volume. The blue energy around the blade intensified.

Getting cut by that blade looked like a bad idea. He rolled back and into a defensive stance.

He started gesturing.

"I told you, your finger wiggles aren't going to work against—"

I never finished the sentence. A stone from the collapsed wall slammed into my back, knocking the wind out of my lungs and shoving me forward. I managed to raise Ebonsoul in time to parry a thrust, which placed me in the perfect position to block a right cross with my face.

I spun around and took a few steps back, but Monty pressed his advantage. More stones flew at me. I managed to dodge a few as he surgically cut at me. He wasn't smiling now. His expression was cold and hard, harder than the stones hitting me.

The now non-glowing Sorrows managed to cut through my shield, but Kali's curse healed my wounds nearly as fast as he created them.

"I don't need magic to end you," Monty said, slicing across my wrist and flinging Ebonsoul to the side. "You're weak, pathetic, and hopeless."

I slid back away from him and rolled to my feet. I had one last button to press, and I hated myself for it.

"You didn't run away from the Golden Circle, be honest," I jeered, while stepping into the cold lake of energy around me. The ambient energy of the Sanctuary was an explosion of power as I tapped into it. The arctic sensation nearly stole my breath as I aligned with the energy. "Tristan Montague, one-man demolition crew. You destroy everything and everyone you touch. That's why Roxanne wants nothing to do with you. You're toxic. Why don't you surrender to the darkness already, you bloody coward? The world would be better off without you; at the very least, more of it would remain intact."

Rage transformed his expression, and I saw him make the choice. He would use everything and anything to destroy me in that moment. I extended my hand and willed Ebonsoul into mist as I closed the distance, letting the power in the totem flow freely.

The ring began to glow as Monty raced at me, enraged. If this didn't work, I was out of options.

Silver mist raced into my hand as I reformed Ebonsoul. Monty had created a nasty-looking black-and-red orb of energy, but it was too late. I was too close. I buried Ebonsoul in his midsection as the golden light from the ring exploded in my hand, enveloping Monty. He released the orb into my chest and launched me across the courtyard.

I slammed head first into the courtyard wall before the golden light around Monty blinded me.

THIRTY

"Is he dead?" I heard a familiar voice say in the distance. "Where's Farsight? He looks like warm roadkill, that's for sure."

"I'm sure he will wish he was dead, once he comes to."

The second voice was familiar, too.

LD and TK.

"You think that energy surge was Tristan?" LD asked as I opened my eyes and saw his face in my field of vision. "Hey, you're back. Congratulations on not dying, hombre."

"The day is still young," TK said. "Who fired off the beacon?"

"Beacon? What beacon?" I asked, trying to sit up and failing when the ground around me tilted and then flipped. I laid my head on the ground again and closed my eyes. "Stop the ride, I want to get off."

I opened my eyes again and peeked, hoping I was imagining all of this, and that I was back at the Moscow, waking up from a horrible dream. TK looked down at me and raised an eyebrow.

"Do you intend to fight while lying on your back?" she asked.

"Fight? I just fought Monty."

She looked over to where Monty lay, unconscious. LD had gone over to him and was gesturing over his body. Light gray runes, almost white, were descending onto Monty's body.

"That...wasn't a fight," TK said, gesturing as golden runes floated over to me. "That was closer to a clash. One that let everyone know where you were."

"Monty?" I asked, concerned. "Is he...?"

"He'll be fine, but he won't be able to deal with Evers in his current condition," TK said, extending a hand and helping me to my feet. "She is coming."

"What happened?" I asked, still unsettled. "All I remember is stabbing him with Ebonsoul, and then the ring went off."

"You pushed him back from the schism; it was more like a very violent shove," TK said, narrowing her eyes at me. "You, on the other hand, have just stepped into a world of pain. Kali's mark is all over you."

"What does that mean?"

"It means you'd better learn to use whatever newfound abilities you have," TK answered. "Your count of enemies has just increased...exponentially."

"Why would I think her mark would help me?"

"Because you were concerned about Tristan," TK said, almost gently. "But you must always be wary of gifts from gods. There is always a fine print, trust me."

I nodded.

"Evers," I said, thinking about the immediate threat. "Can we stop her?"

"We?" TK asked with a slight smile. "You intend to confront a chronomancer?"

"If she intends to hurt Monty...yes."

"She is a war mage, like Tristan, but deadlier," TK answered. "He was holding back. Some part of him, despite the fact that he was in a schism, didn't want to harm you."

"If that was him holding back, I don't want to see him cut loose," I said, remembering the stone massage he subjected me to while slicing away at me. "He's stronger now. Way stronger."

TK nodded as LD approached.

"I stabilized him, but we can't leave him here. Dex is busy maintaining the gate. I'm taking Tristan to Fordey until this is over. He can't fight anyway; he'll be a liability. Evers will shred him in seconds."

"Wait," I said, looking at TK. "I thought you were tracking Evers. How are you here before her?"

"The energy you released acted like a signal to those strong enough to perceive it," TK answered. "If we sensed it, rest assured that Evers and Talin have sensed it as well."

"Like a bat-signal?" I asked. "I have my own Strong-signal?"

"Well it's good to see you haven't suffered any further brain damage," TK said. "It took considerable energy and weaving to get here. Dex is...creative in his gates, but I've dealt with them in the past. Evers has not. That inexperience will slow her down, but it won't stop her."

"Probably alerted some other heavy hitters, too," LD said, looking at me. "Your life just became more interesting. Erik is having some words with Farsight."

"Jessikah needs training and exposure, or she won't last long on the streets, in her condition."

"Condition?"

"Extreme narrow-mindedness, with a sprinkle of mage elitist attitude."

"That describes most mages," LD said with a nod. "I think the Hellfire will be good for her. She needs to strap in and wake up. Safer for her, too."

"Monty thought Dex was setting him up," I said. "He thought Dex wanted him dead."

LD glanced at TK and shook his head.

"Good thing Dex wasn't here to hear that insanity," LD answered. "Tristan was in a schism. He wasn't thinking properly. The push and pull is hell on the mind. Many mages don't recover."

"Don't recover?"

"They slip into darkness," TK said, "or their mind remains in the state of schism. They grow stronger, but the power is unregulated. It burns bright, then burns out."

"Like a star?"

"Like a collapsed star which then produces a supernova," TK answered. "It never ends well."

"Will Monty make it?" I asked, concerned. "Is his mind okay?"

"He will," LD said, certain. "Many mages don't recover from a schism at his level, but none of those mages were stabbed by your blade, either. You probably saved his life, if not his mind—not that he will ever admit it."

I nodded.

"He is a Montague, after all," I said. "I think he'd drink a mug of Death Wish coffee and eat a pastrami sandwich before admitting I saved him."

LD clapped me on the shoulder and chuckled.

"Got that right," he said. "On my way back to Fordey, I'll let Dex know you're still among the living."

"Wait, what?" I asked, confused. "You're leaving? Evers and Talin are on their way here to erase us."

"I know," LD said. "That's why TK is staying. There is a plan...trust us."

"Are you sure we can't get more of the Ten? No offense, TK, but Evers unleashed some nasty time orb at me, and Talin managed to survive clashing with Grey in his scary sword-goddess form."

"I'm aware," TK said. "Grey was fatigued from a mission with your vampire, and Evers...well, leave Evers to me."

"You're in good, if terrifying, hands, hombre. I trust TK with my life and have on many occasions."

"Because to choose otherwise would be fatal," TK said, with a small, fearsome smile. "You need to get going, before Evers and company arrive."

"You're right, as usual," LD said. "Talin was the first, but Evers has been busy. He won't be the last she recruits to her cause."

"There's more of them out there?" I asked. "How many?"

"You'll be fine, hombre," LD said, reassuring me. "And if not...well, you'll be dead and it won't matter, right?"

"What kind of mage motivational school do all of you go to?" I asked, surprised. "Cheerful nihilism? Every mage pep talk I've gotten sucks."

"Mages don't do cheerful, we do realism," LD answered, as he headed over to where Monty lay. "We see things as they are, not as we want them to be."

He gestured, gave TK a look and a smile, and vanished in a gray teleportation circle with Monty. TK turned to me and nodded.

"Let's get you ready."

THIRTY-ONE

"I'm not a mage."

"And you never will be. Stop stating the obvious," TK answered, narrowing her eyes at me. "What you are, besides mildly irritating, is a dangerous unknown with potential."

"Can you fight Evers?"

"Of course," TK said, and I felt relieved. "Fighting her is not the issue. Beating her is."

My relief evaporated.

"Can you beat her?"

"Given time and preparation," TK said, looking around the Sanctuary. "Yes. Unfortunately, we have neither. This will be...a challenge."

At this point, the little voice in my head, which had been so brave up to this moment, jumped off the balcony of my mind and wished me well.

"What do I need to do?"

"Listen while remaining silent. Are you capable of this?"

"Yes, if it means walking away from this in one piece."

"Good," TK said. "I've had my doubts about your coping mechanism. Sarcasm is a skill best used sparingly."

"Someone has to point out the absurdity of my life."

"Emphasis on, *sparingly*."

"I was shoved into this entire world of mages, runes, magic, and monsters against my will."

"And?" she asked, raising an eyebrow. "Are you looking for pity? Do you suppose your situation is unique, that you are somehow special?"

"No."

"Do you need a moment to weep about your ill-fate at discovering this world by force? Are you harboring regrets?"

"No," I said, after some thought. "I don't regret it at all. My life may be unreal and insane, but I don't regret a second of it."

"Then start acting *and* speaking like it," TK answered. "You're a cursed immortal. A certain amount of *gravitas* is fitting—at least, in this present situation."

"I promise to age," I said, "but I will never grow up."

"You're incorrigible," she said with a sigh, "but it may be that your way of being is exactly what Tristan needs in his life, especially now, while dealing with this schism."

"I inject much needed levity into our dire situations," I said. "Plus, I'm still getting used to all of this." I waved an arm around. "Mages, runes, and gods aren't exactly what I would call a normal day...before I met Monty."

She nodded.

"True, you are still relatively new to this world, barely scratching the surface of the darkness it contains," TK answered. "It's not like you're in service to the most fearsome goddess in creation, who then tasks you with carrying out assassinations in her name, right?"

"You were an assassin?"

"What exactly did *you* do in Shadow Company?"

"Does everyone know about my past?"

"Everyone who matters, yes."

"My background was scrubbed, or so I was told."

"Then humor me, what did you do?" TK asked again. "Were you the designated coffee boy?"

"No," I said, knowing she knew what I was about to say. "I was a dead-eye in the Shadows. I handled personnel retirements...permanent ones."

"We all have a past, Simon," TK said, heading over to the main temple. "The key is to not let the past define you. I worked with Badb Catha. It was equal parts thrilling and horrific. I did it for several lifetimes. I became very good at what I did—so good, in fact, that she allowed me to leave her side...alive. Others were not as fortunate."

"Understood," I said with the realization that TK was even more of a badass than I had previously thought, and sat in a different dimension of fearsome than I had imagined. "That would explain her presence at Monty's reckoning."

"Yes, among other things," TK said. "If I had fallen at the reckoning, she would have made sure it was the last time I fell."

I shook my head and shuddered at the memory of Badb Catha.

"Nothing like having a homicidal support system in place."

"It's complicated," TK said. "In many ways she and I are still entwined. In certain respects, I still represent her.

A failing on my part reflects poorly on her. Badb doesn't do well with failure."

"Or bad PR, it seems."

"She has her pride, brutally earned over millennia."

"Any chance we can call her to deal with Evers?"

"Of course," TK said calmly, which should have clued me in immediately to what a bad idea it was. "Unlike the Morrigan, she will require some years of service from you for her assistance."

"How long?" I asked. "I mean, hypothetically speaking, suppose I agree to her help?"

"Nothing too extensive, just one or two cycles."

"Cycles? What's that? Years, decades?"

"Centuries," TK said, her voice grim. "One or two centuries serving a living nightmare. Do you want that, or do you want to take your chance with Evers?"

"I'll take my chances with Evers, thanks."

"Good choice, because *you* will be the one facing her."

"Excuse...excuse me?" I asked in mild shock. "I could've sworn I heard you say that *I* was facing Evers. What will you be doing? Cheering me on?"

She gave me a glare and I dialed it back immediately. Skating on thin ice is only fun until the ice breaks. Then you're drowning in the dark frozen water. That look was the ice cracking.

"I'm a creative mage," TK answered. "What is Talin?"

"He's a negomancer...Oh. That makes sense. Me facing Evers doesn't make any kind of sense though, unless it's nonsense."

"Evers is a chronomancer, and you're an immortal," TK pointed out. "She will try to kill you how?"

"With extreme prejudice?"

For a brief second, I could sense she wanted to *thwack* me. I saw her take a slow breath and let it out.

"What *method* will she use?"

"Chronomancy? I'm guessing?"

"Her chronomancy works by accelerating the age of anything it impacts."

For a moment, I wanted to ask her how she knew all of this, and then I remembered who I was speaking to. She probably had files on every serious mage on the planet.

"Roxanne said under no circumstances should I get hit by Evers' orbs of death."

"Normally, she would be right. Evers casts instances of frozen time, and then accelerates whatever is caught in the instance."

"I'm guessing that this isn't a normal situation?"

"You aren't facing her the same way you did on the skywalk," TK clarified. "Kali marked you and corrected your tangled mess of bonds. More importantly, it looks like she made some changes I can't figure out right now. In addition, you have that"—she pointed at the ring on my hand—"and you're going to need it. You have one use left."

"One? I only used it against Monty," I said, glancing down at the softly glowing ring. "Kali told me I had three uses."

"Dex informed me you fired a blast of pure energy at him."

"Yes, he was trying to kill me; or at least I thought so at the time."

"Do you find yourself firing blasts of pure energy often?"

"No, I've never fired a blast like that one."

"One use left," TK said. "Save it for Evers."

"So, I'm immune to her ability?"

"Did I say you were?"

"No, but..."

"I said she will try and kill you with chronomancy," TK said. "You can still be hurt by other methods. I don't know what will happen if she decapitates you. Can you survive something that catastrophic? I don't know. Do you?"

"Can we not find out?"

"What I want you to understand is that she will try and use her ability on you," TK continued. "Once she sees it's ineffective, she will resort to other, less magical methods of dispatching you. She's dangerous and deadly, but we will try and even the battlefield, if possible."

"You have an army of mages hiding around here somewhere?" I asked, looking around the columns inside the temple. "Because that would totally make things even."

"There are nullifying runes in here, runes you can activate, but only as a last resort," TK said. "Tell me why."

"Because if I create a null space, my curse stops working, which means she can..."

"Kill you, with ease. She possesses the ability to manipulate energy, but she's also a war mage. They are trained to..."

"Stand and die."

"Precisely," TK said with a hint of approval. "I will try to help you if I can. I will replicate Tristan's energy signature in here and draw Talin away. Negomancers are difficult to face, but not impossible. Once I separate them, you will be on your own for the most part. Can you do this?"

"Do I have a choice?"

"Yes," TK said, surprising me. "You can refuse and run, as long as you are prepared to run for the rest of your extended life. Evers won't be the last to come after you and Tristan, especially now with your...upgrade, Marked of Kali."

"I'm not a big fan of running and dying tired, thanks," I said. "Besides, where would I run? I'm standing in a pocket dimension waiting for a chronomancer bent on revenge. I'd say my travel options are limited."

"Agreed," TK said. "Now pay attention. I will show you the sequence you need to activate the complete null state of this room. The key to this working lies where?"

I looked around the spacious temple room. There was only one large doorway. I saw where Monty had been sitting, and realized he'd been channeling energy to disrupt the null runes in the temple. Part of him must have been fighting the schism using the runes in this room.

"I have to stay in this room, don't I?"

"Correct," TK said. "I will place a simulacrum of Tristan with his energy signature in here with you. The deception won't last long. Once it's dispelled, the room will seal, closing off the only exit."

"With me inside of it? With Evers?"

TK stared at me for a few seconds.

"Sorry, of course, with me inside of it with Evers."

"I'm not asking you to kill her," TK said. "I don't think you can. You need to keep her engaged. Eliminating her would be a pleasant bonus."

"Keep her engaged for how long?" I asked, concerned. "This sounds like me being bait."

"Long enough for Dex to untether this pocket dimension," TK said. "This will trap her inside and..."

"Cast her adrift forever?"

"Yes, how do you know this?"

"Monty mentioned something similar, but he thought Dex was going to do it to him," I said. "Wouldn't it be more merciful to eliminate her outright?"

"When you face her, you are welcome to inquire which option she would prefer," TK said, stepping around several columns, over to a wall of runes and symbols. "Dex wants her trapped for crimes she never paid for during the war. I'm not going to argue with him. Do you want to?"

"Pass," I said. "He bounced me around enough today. If this place is going to be her cell, what's going to happen to the Golden Circle?"

"We can ask him if we survive this."

"Well, now my confidence is really boosted."

"Close your mouth and pay attention as I show you the sequence," TK said, pointing to the wall of symbols. "If you get this wrong, it will be the last thing you do...ever."

THIRTY-TWO

TK was an excellent teacher. Without a word, she was adept at using fear as a motivator to memorize the runes and symbols in front of me. We ran over the sequence until she was satisfied I knew what I was doing.

"What happens if I get this sequence wrong?" I asked, leaning on one of the ornate columns. "Does it have a reset button if I mess it up?"

"No. The null state won't activate," TK said matter-of-factly. "Evers will retain the use of her ability and attempt to escape...after killing you."

"That sounds like the worst-case scenario."

"It isn't," TK said. "The worst-case scenario is her locating Fordey and launching an attack there against LD and an incapacitated Tristan."

"She's a mage," I said. "Yet she wants to destroy magic?"

"Yes," TK said, nodding as she began gesturing. "Her kind usually does."

"What does that mean? She's a *mage*," I repeated. "How can she want to destroy magic?"

"There's usually a condition," TK said, focusing in front of her. "Destroy all magic, except the magic I wield, or destroy all magic, except the magic that serves me."

"She's insane."

"No," TK said sharply. "Do not minimize her mental state. If you do, you will perish. She's not just insane, she's corrupt. Corruption doesn't equal madness any more than power does. Evers has abandoned ideals, morals, and limitations. For her, killing you, Tristan, me, and anyone who obstructs her path is a means to an end. She will lose no sleep over it."

"So, she's insane and pissed?"

"No, she's insane *and* corrupt," TK stressed. "Vengeance will do that to a mind. Twist it, deform it, until there's nothing else left except an all-encompassing, burning hatred that can never be satiated."

I took a step back at the intensity in her voice.

"Whoa, can we dial down the murder vibe a notch?"

"Do not conflate the two, Simon. She is unstable, but she is also corrupt. Remember the distinction. The two states feed on each other like an ouroboros."

"Got it, madness and corruption," I said. "Why is she so angry at Monty and Dex?"

"She was one of the original Black Orchids during the war," TK said. "I'm sure it has something to do with that."

"You don't know?" I asked, surprised. "I thought... Well, you have information on everything."

"I didn't say I didn't know," TK said, focusing on the gesturing again. "Did you do things you regret in your past?"

"We all have."

"Some of us more than others," TK answered as if lost in thought. "The things the Orchid did during the war would be considered unthinkable now. The root of her vengeance lies there."

"But you can't say?"

"I *won't* say," TK answered, with a smile that warned me I was back on that thin ice and the cracks were getting larger. "There is a difference. If you really must know, ask Dex or Tristan. It's not my place to answer for them." She pointed to the wall with the symbols. "Now, practice the sequence again."

I went around the columns, over to the wall, and went over the sequence when I felt the familiar energy signature.

Monty.

I turned to see him sitting on the far side of the floor in a lotus position, eyes closed, and back to the wall.

"Monty?" I said under my breath. "What the hell?"

"Look again," TK said, still gesturing. "This time, *really* look."

I focused on the unmoving figure of Monty and saw the energy racing around his body, interlaced and intertwined with symbols. It was and wasn't Monty at the same time.

"It's him, but it isn't him," I said, pointing at the illusion. "Won't Evers see through that?"

"I'm almost finished. When the cast is complete, it will appear to be him with the flaw of the schism," TK said. "You, on the other hand, need to be under a veil. Explain why."

"If she walks in and sees me and Monty just hanging

out, it will seem off," I said, giving it thought. "If he's in a schism, he would be attacking me, not meditating in here."

"Precisely," TK said and gestured one last time. "It's done."

The simulacrum of Monty was incredible. If I had not known TK was creating an illusion of Monty, I would have been fooled. Even with the knowledge that it wasn't him, it was convincing.

"Is Dex a creative mage like you?"

"Dex is...an anomaly," TK said. "Most mages master one discipline and work to perfect it over the course of their lives. Dex has mastered several disciplines. This makes him powerful, and deadly."

"No kidding," I said, remembering my recent sparring session with him. "He created a simulacrum that had me fooled."

"That sounds like him," TK said, moving to the corner next to the entrance. "He was instrumental in making most of Nana's 'deaths' seem authentic. Over here, please."

She pointed to the corner.

"What do I do when she arrives?" I asked. "It's not like I can invite her to a duel."

"I'm sure you'll think of something," TK answered. "She will sense you once the veil drops."

TK gestured, and the world became hazy. I looked down at my hands and they appeared transparent. I drew Grim Whisper and switched out for entropy rounds before holstering it again.

"Am I invisible?"

"Only if you keep absolutely still," TK said, stepping back and narrowing her eyes in my direction. "That will work. Once the seal closes off the exit, the veil drops."

"How's this for the duel invitation?" I asked. "Hallo, my name is Simon Strong. You tried to kill Monty. Prepare..."

"Finish that sentence and I will blast you myself," TK said, pointing at the simulacrum. "That gets her attention. Then, you keep her attention. She will be homicidally livid when she uncovers the ruse. Be ready."

"I'm really looking forward to an enraged, unhinged chronomancer—thank you."

"Use your wits, abilities, and your strengths," TK said, heading to the exit. "This is one of the few times I would actually suggest speaking. It will unbalance her. You have an uncanny ability to anger everyone when you do."

"Thank you," I said. "It's a gift."

"Don't make it a curse."

I felt the energy shift a second later, and TK nodded.

"She's here, isn't she?"

"Yes," TK said, stopping at the exit and looking out into the distance over the complex. "I will draw out Talin. Are you ready?"

"Nothing in my life has ever prepared me for something like this."

"You only believe that because you're scared. It will pass."

"The fear?"

"The belief. The fear is a constant companion. The sooner you embrace it, the easier it is to overcome."

"You feel fear?"

"Yes, fear for what I could become if I ever lose myself...again."

"Again?"

"Prepare. She's close."

TK vanished from my sight.

A few seconds later, another figure entered the temple.

Evers.

THIRTY-THREE

She was dressed the way I remembered, from the time she tried to melt me on the skywalk at Haven: black Armani power suit, white shirt with a silver pocket kerchief, a silver triquetra pin rested in her short black hair.

The only difference was that this time, she made no effort to hide her energy signature. She radiated power as she stepped into the room. A few steps behind her stood Talin, looking much better than the last time I saw him.

"He's here," Talin said. "I can sense him. He's still in the schism."

"And he will die in it," Evers said. "After I destroy him, we kill the uncle."

"That's...not going to be easy," Talin answered, peering into the dim interior of the temple. "Dex is powerful and dangerous."

"Are you scared of him, Talin?"

"Yes, and you should be too," Talin answered. "Killing Tristan is one thing. Dex will not be an easy matter."

"Where would the pleasure be, if it were easy?" Evers

answered, stepping forward. "It will only be satisfying if it's difficult."

"Difficult, yes; suicidal, no," Talin said. "We will need reinforcements, many of them."

"That is being handled," Evers answered. "In time, we will have all the help we need."

"You contacted them, didn't you?" Talin asked, fear evident in his voice. "There's no stopping them once they begin."

"I never mentioned anything about stopping," Evers answered. "They will help me eradicate magic."

"They will eradicate...everything," Talin said, stepping around one of the columns. "Think hard upon this. Once unleashed, they will not be easily contained."

"Are you questioning me?" Evers answered. Her voice was soft, but held a dangerous edge. "Do you question my judgment, my motives?"

"Never," Talin answered with a slight hesitation. "I just don't think dragons are the solution, nor a good idea in any scenario."

"They are the only ones strong enough to deal with Dexter Montague...unless you would like to face him?"

Talin shook his head at the invitation.

"No," he said. "You're right. They will accomplish what we can't."

"More importantly, he will never expect it," Evers answered. "By the time he realizes what is happening, it will be too late."

"With him gone, we can begin."

Evers gave him a smile that only confirmed that she was near the top of the psycho-batshit mage scale.

The muffled sound of an explosion filled the temple, stopping Evers in her approach to pseudo-Monty.

"Go see what that was," Evers said, looking around the interior. "He may have friends trying to come to his assistance."

"Are you certain?" Talin said, sweeping the room with his gaze. "This seems suspect."

"It's only Tristan in a schism. Whoever is out there is no match for a negomancer of your caliber. Dispatch them, and return to watch me make a Montague beg for his life."

Talin nodded and smiled, sweeping the room with his gaze one more time before leaving.

Evers watched him leave, and then turned back to face pseudo-Monty.

She smiled again, creeping me out.

"It's no use, Tristan," she almost whispered. "No defense you have prepared will protect you from me, from my vengeance."

Pseudo-Monty remained silent, in lotus position with his eyes closed. Evers stepped closer, narrowing her eyes.

"You dare ignore me?" she said, forming one of her silver-black orbs. "Your schism must have you more addled than I thought. Let's begin your suffering."

She unleashed the orb, which crashed into pseudo-Monty. The simulacrum writhed on the floor for a few seconds, before disappearing slowly. I felt the veil lift slowly as the entrance, and only exit, disappeared, replaced by a stone wall.

"A lure?" she yelled, looking around. "Where are you, Montague! Show yourself! Are you too much of a coward to face me?"

I stepped out of the corner, Grim Whisper in hand.

"I'm your huckleberry," I said in my best Val Kilmer drawl. "Are we playing for blood?"

"Simon Strong," she hissed. "You're still alive?"

The arrogance of mages usually contributed to their downfall. She must've thought the orb she released on the skywalk had finished me. Mage egos only came in two sizes: enormous and obnoxious.

"Still," I said, "Monty's not here. He had other, more important matters to attend to. Left me here to deal with the trash. Guess he meant...you?"

Even in the dim light, I could see the rage flit across her face.

"He left...you...to face, me? Alone?" she asked, incredulously. "I thought he was your friend?"

I fired Grim Whisper.

She rolled to the side and unleashed three small orbs at me. Only my reflexes saved me from the attack. I slid behind a column as the small orbs punched holes in the stone. I didn't even see her gesture to create the second set: she was fast and dangerous.

"Step out so I can end your miserable existence," Evers said. "You should have let my orb finish you. It would have been quick. Now, you will suffer."

I peeked around the corner and fired Grim Whisper again, ducking behind the column and rolling as I heard more orbs impact the column.

"Tell me," I said as I reloaded Grim Whisper, "why would a mage want to get rid of all magic?"

"You would never understand," she said. "How could you?"

"I wouldn't understand that you're insane?"

"To some, yes," she answered, as I felt a surge of energy from her direction. "It's simple calculus. Mages and magic users upset the balance. The only way to restore that balance is to—"

"Eradicate magic?"

I shifted to another column, but I didn't want to get too far away from the null wall. The last thing I wanted was to be across the room from my last-resort play. A large, silver-black orb smashed into the wall next to me. The energy of the orb spread out several feet along the surface of the wall, which was reduced to dust in seconds.

I made a mental note to avoid her orbs.

"Not all of it...just some," she answered. "Starting with the magic wielded by those named Montague. It's a simple, elegant equation. Magic without the Montagues equals balance."

She laughed then—it was a small sound, just loud enough to convince me.

She wasn't insane, she was beyond insane.

Her madness held the certainty exhibited by genocidal maniacs who justified their actions because they felt it was necessary, for the greater good. The greater good always included themselves.

"What gives you the right?" I asked, shifting again. At this point, I was going to run out of real estate soon. "Who are you to determine who has magic?"

"I'm the only one willing to do so, to do the hard work. Left unchecked, magic does more harm than good. I am the check. I am the balance."

"You are the judge and jury?"

"And in your case"—she unleashed another orb—"the executioner."

I ran across several columns, but she wasn't aiming for me. I turned in time to see the orb smash into the symbols of the null wall...turning them and the wall to rubble and dust.

That...was bad.

"Dex is going to be pissed if you keep breaking the place. He's not going to appreciate your renovation."

"Dex," she said, the name like a curse, "will be dead when I'm done. Stop hiding, Strong. I recognized the symbols as soon as I saw them. You have no hope of making this room into a null zone. Surrender, and I promise you a mage's death."

"Pass, thanks," I called out, and moved as orbs hit the column where I had been a second earlier. "Not a mage, never will be."

"Then you will die like the dog that you are."

That escalated quickly. I ran down a narrow passage at the edge of the room, as the columns were being blasted to bits behind me. She was getting angry at my expert evasiveness—also known as hiding.

How did I ever think this was a good idea? I was outclassed and outmatched in a closed room, with no way out.

TK's words came back to me: *This is one of the few times I would actually suggest speaking. It will unbalance her. You have an uncanny ability to anger everyone when you do.*

Outclassed and outmatched, but not outwitted.

I needed to get her unbalanced; after all, she was still a mage.

"You sound angry," I said. "Maybe some therapy would help...like a century or two of it."

"You mock me?" she said, gathering more energy. I

noticed the pattern. She needed to restore her energy after every few attacks. I was guessing the temple had something to do with that. "Magic took everything from me."

"Starting with your mind, it seems."

"I will kill you slowly, Strong. You will beg for the mercy of death and I will deny you its release."

"You let it control you," I said, ignoring the threat of a slow, agonizing death...well, not completely ignoring it. "You were weak."

"Magic is corrupt. The world would be better without it."

"Starting with you?"

She was stalking me—even as I moved around and directed my voice at the walls to bounce the sound. She was doing the same, and getting closer.

"Of course. I'm an object lesson in the dangers of power. Watch how I destroy your world."

"You're twisted."

"Am I? Ever since you fell into this world of magic, has your life gotten better?"

"Yes, and I'm happier, too."

"Don't insult me with your lies," she scoffed. "Before, you may have had human enemies, but now? Monsters and gods want you dead...Kali's Chosen."

"I've been promoted, haven't you heard? My new title is Marked of Kali now."

"Frying pan and fire, Strong," she answered. "The world is better off without magic—it stole everything from me, like a brutal thief. It's over."

Her voice was on my right, but she appeared on my left and I knew in that moment, she had outplayed me. If we were playing chess, she'd just executed a checkmate.

Except I wasn't playing chess.

I raised Grim Whisper to fire, only to see it fly across the room, as several orbs impacted my wrist, breaking my grip. Another, larger orb, headed right for me. There was no time to dodge. So I didn't.

I ran forward.

And slid...under the nasty-looking orb. The surprised expression on her face told me everything I needed to know. She recovered fast, but I knew she was off-balance. I formed Ebonsoul as I came out of the slide and thrust the blade forward.

In her hand she held a silver, rune-covered blade about as long as Ebonsoul, parried my thrust to the side and introduced the side of my head to a hammerfist.

"Shit," I said as I stumbled back. I must have been wearing the same expression of surprise she had moments earlier. "Nice blade."

I moved into a defensive stance. This had gotten worse. Much worse.

Dex's words flashed in my mind: *Unless you can think like evil, really understand it, then you're defenseless.*

I was treating her like an enemy mage, not a force of evil. I was going to need to adjust my attitude before she adjusted it for me...permanently.

"You thought you could face me?" Evers asked, circling around me. "I am a war mage. We are trained to stand and die, in any and every circumstance."

"So I keep hearing," I said, recovering from her strike as the familiar warmth flushed my body. "Can we hurry to the part where you die?"

"You first," she said, moving to the side. "Didn't Tristan show you?"

"I must have missed that lesson," I said, reaching for the energy around me. The shocking cold erased any warmth I was feeling. "Why don't you educate me?"

"With pleasure," she said, stepping in with a thrust I barely parried. She was fast. "The energy we wield is a tool; what matters is the will. I don't need orbs to destroy you. With or without magic, you will die by my hand today."

For the first time in my life, I was thankful for the torture sessions with Master Yat. Evers was an accomplished blade fighter. She slashed, feinted, and evaded my counters, cutting me. My body healed, but this was a battle of attrition. She was good—better than me, by orders of magnitude. I was barely holding on.

In scientific language: I was getting my ass kicked.

She and her blade whirled around me. I moved, dodged, and slid away, only to find myself at the end of her blade. The expression 'death by a thousand cuts' suddenly held new meaning.

She slashed diagonally. I pivoted at the last second, causing her to miss, only to encounter one of her silver-black orbs waiting for me as I turned. The orb smashed into my chest with a *whump,* catapulting me into a column, nearly shattering it, as bits of debris exploded around me.

My body flushed hot as I fell to the ground, but I was too banged up, bleeding from too many small wounds, to recover in time. The black energy of the orb covered me and slowly evaporated.

I spit up blood as she approached.

"Have you had enough?" I asked. "Don't make me hurt you."

"My orb did nothing to you," she said, driving a brutal kick into my side and cracking a rib, while stripping Ebonsoul from my hand. It turned to silver mist a second later, reabsorbed into my body. "It seems I will have to end you the old-fashioned way."

I managed to roll out of the way as she slashed down, missing me. My body was dealing with damage overload. I was healing, but the damage she'd caused was so extensive, it seemed to be slowing the process down. I felt like I was running a fever and freezing at the same time. I stood slowly, but the situation was bad.

There was a good chance I would die here.

My curse and the energy around me fought in my body for dominance, until I stopped struggling against both. I fell back, suddenly tired, and leaned against a column, one of the few that remained intact.

"We should take a break," I said, raising a hand. "I'm sure you're exhausted..."

She leapt forward with a thrust aimed at my chest. I moved my hand to deflect the blade, but my reaction time was off, and I miscalculated. She stabbed right through my hand and kept pushing.

"I'll take a break," she said with a twisted grin, "once I see you, Tristan, and his uncle dead. Look around you, Simon. Tristan left you here to die. There is no one here to save you"—she twisted the blade in my hand and I bit back a scream—"and no one is coming. You are forgotten, abandoned...alone."

"He is not alone," a voice said from the other side of the temple. "He is thoroughly irritating and exasperating, but he is a true friend, closer than my brother."

It was Monty.

Which meant I was truly hallucinating, because he was

supposed to be at Fordey Boutique with LD, not here facing off against psychomage Evers.

Evers pulled the blade out of my hand and backhanded me across the floor for good measure. I gently moved my jaw to make sure it was still connected to the rest of my face.

"Stay there, scum," she said, looking down at me. "I'll be right back to put you out of your misery."

That's when I heard the growl...and smiled.

THIRTY-FOUR

My hellhound padded up to my face, dropped Grim Whisper in my lap, and gave me a slobbering of a greeting. I holstered my gun and hugged my hellhound.

<*You were lost in between.*>

<*I was busy trying to find Monty.*>

<*The angry man smells better now. You smell different. Good, but different. Do you have any meat?*>

<*I will take you to the place and get you all the meat you can eat...after we deal with her.*>

<*I like that. She hurt you. Can I bite her?*>

<*No, she's dangerous. I want you to stay away from her. She will try to hurt you.*>

"How quaint. Your beast came to say goodbye," Evers said, looking at Peaches with disgust. "What kind of mutation is that?"

I hugged Peaches to my side, and replied with a one-fingered answer.

"No matter," Evers said, turning to Monty, ignoring me. "I will dispatch that creature along with the both of you.

Thank you for saving me the trouble of finding you, traitor."

"I did what was right," Monty said, his voice low. His body was covered with dark energy that crackled with bursts of violet light as it criss-crossed his body. "It needed to be done."

"You cost me everything, everyone," Evers answered. "I will erase you first, and then you will suffer, like I suffered. You will beg me to kill you, and I will refuse."

Monty drew the Sorrows.

"Evers, how many times must I remind you, that only simpletons spend their time talking when there is killing to be done?"

Evers let out a low growl and raced at Monty, blade in hand. If I ever thought I could take Monty in bladed combat when he was serious, I was mistaken. Evers was dazzling to watch. She moved in a blur, attacking, causing openings only to have them close again. For all her skill, Monty made her look like an amateur.

She was good. He was better.

He wielded the Sorrows as an extension of his body. Every slash, every attack from Evers was met and countered. Then I saw it—he wasn't attacking, but only defending.

"What's the matter, Tristan?" Evers asked. "Can't deliver the killing blow? Seems like the schism affected you more than you anticipated."

She was right. He was doing his best to stop her attacks, but couldn't capitalize on the openings. She was too fast, and he was slowing down.

"You plan on wrapping this up anytime soon?" I asked from where I stood. "Or do I need to lend a hand?"

"I've been told you're keen on helping," Monty answered as he fired a violet orb at Evers, only to have it deflected into a wall. "It seems like there is still power in the one to rule them all. Now would be a good time to use it, I think."

I looked down at the totem.

"You can't beat me," Evers snarled at Monty. "Not you or your uncle. I'm stronger than you, I always have been."

"That has always been your weakness," Monty said. "Your self-reliance."

"I need no one," Evers snapped. "My self-reliance *is* my strength."

"My friends and family are mine."

Monty parried a sword thrust and followed up with one of his own. Evers deflected his thrust, ducked under a slash, and launched a fist at Monty's chest. If it had connected, it would've shattered his ribs.

Monty executed a cross block that absorbed most of the blow and sent him back, sliding across the stone floor for several feet. Evers gestured, and Monty shot me a glance that said, *It's now or never, but now would be preferable.*

Evers unleashed a barrage of black orbs at Monty. Another swarm materialized behind her, and sped at me. I reached for the energy around me again. It felt like dunking my head in a bucket of ice water.

I took a deep breath, as the sensation of cold washed over me.

"*Ignisvitae*," I said, as golden light exploded from the ring. A large, golden orb formed in front of me, like a miniature sun. "What the...?"

I saw the fear in Monty's eyes.

"Release it!" Monty yelled as he dove to the side. "Now!"

I mentally let go of the orb, and it raced at Evers. It devoured her swarm of orbs, cut a trench in the stone, and punched through several of the columns as if they were made of paper.

Evers, figuring I wasn't much of a threat, turned at the last second.

She was too late.

She raised both hands and created a shield of silver energy, but it wasn't enough. The orb slowed for a few seconds, and then, as if revving up, steamrolled through her shield and her, engulfing her in energy.

She screamed for a few seconds, and then suddenly went eerily quiet.

She was gone, but the orb remained.

It didn't stop.

It blasted through the far wall, and started to expand once it was outside the temple. I sensed the energy around the orb grow. The ring went black and crumbled to dust around my finger.

TK peered through the newly created opening, glared at Monty for a second, then looked back out in the direction of the ever-growing orb. She stepped into the temple and examined the destruction.

"Whoever unleashed the runic nova will get to explain to Dex how you obliterated the entirety of the Sanctuary," TK said, gesturing and frowning. "Tristan, I need your assistance. The orb is siphoning the energy faster than I can cast a circle. We are running out of time."

Monty limped over to TK and began gesturing.

Together, the two of them managed to get a faintly

glowing, green circle to materialize under them. I grabbed Peaches and ran over to where they stood. By the time we made it across the floor, they were gone.

I looked down at Peaches.

<*I hope you know how to get home, boy.*>

<*I wasn't lost. You were. I know where I am all the time.*>

<*Is that a yes?*>

<*Only if we can go to the place on the way home. I'm starving.*>

I lacked the energy or will to argue with my bottomless hellhound. Distant rumbling followed by tremors reached the temple. I looked out of the blast hole and saw the orb still growing. It was beautiful and terrifying all at once.

<*I'll make sure we stop by Ezra's. Take us home.*>

<*This place is far. You will have to hold on.*>

I crouched down and grabbed my hellhound by the neck.

He took a deep breath, the runes along his flanks bursting with red light and he barked, nearly bursting my eardrums with the sound.

Everything blurred, and we left the Sanctuary behind.

THIRTY-FIVE

"A runic nova," the familiar female voice said as I rubbed my eyes. "Impressive. That is a cast beyond your level of power."

"I had...help," I said with a groan as my head pounded. "Dex is going to be pissed."

"A fair assessment," she said. "The Sanctuary has been destroyed...by your hand, literally."

"Where...where are we?" I asked as I slowly recovered, lifting my head from the cool, smooth marble floor. "This is..."

"A mandir dedicated to me," Kali said from behind me. "Your companion is very resourceful, and hungry. Does he always eat like this?"

I turned to see Kali sitting on a stone bench while Peaches was busy burying his face in an immense bowl of sausage at her feet. He was oblivious to everything except the meat.

"Only when he's awake," I said with another groan, as I

tried to sit up. "Right now, he's just shamelessly taking advantage of you."

<I like the blue lady. She makes good meat.>

<Make sure you say thank you.>

<I will. When I finish the delicious meat.>

This time, Kali was dressed in a loose-fitting, burnt-sienna robe, finished with white brocade. Like before, indecipherable, orange runes flowed around its surface. Her black hair was pulled back into a tight braid, flowing down her back, and coming to rest in a small coil on the bench beside her. Her blue skin glistened with a deep undercurrent of power.

"He is an excellent bondmate," she said, waving a hand and creating more sausage, "and still so young."

"He is," I said, my voice hoarse. "I'd be lost without him."

"Indeed," she said with a nod. "I will speak to Hades about procuring some hellhounds for my domain. They seem much friendlier than my Rakshasas."

The idea of Kali getting a pack of hellhounds to patrol her domain was a scary thought.

"We're in Jersey?" I asked, looking around and slowly sitting up. "Jersey, really...?"

"We are in my mandir, which at the moment happens to be in New Jersey, yes," Kali said. "I see you have aligned." She pointed to my ring-less finger. "Was it unpleasant?"

"Let's just say, once is enough to last an entire lifetime...maybe two," I said, looking at the scars on my arms. "These are new."

"The blade used against you was a kamikira," she said. "A god-killer. If she had delivered a fatal blow—"

"She would have killed me. Permanently."

She nodded.

"And the scars?"

"Will remind you that even immortals can die," she answered after a pause.

"Immortal doesn't mean death is off the table?"

"Everything dies eventually."

"I'm getting that."

"This alignment will bring you awareness...and attention. Not all of it desired."

"I heard," I answered. "My upgrade from chosen"—she narrowed her eyes—"I mean cursed, to marked, means stronger enemies, too."

"Yes," she said. "My mark will keep them away, initially."

"Initially. And then?"

"Then they will want to prove themselves."

"Why does this sound painful?" I asked. "How do they prove themselves?"

She smiled. It was horrifically enticing. I forced myself to look away.

"By killing you, of course."

"Of course," I said. "Why would I think it would be otherwise?"

"The old ones will look for you now. You will need to prepare."

"Why now? Why not before?"

"Before you were a nuisance, easily removed. Now... now, you pose a significant threat."

"Is there any way I can downgrade to nuisance level again?"

"No," she said. "This power, once obtained, remains.

You are now the Aspis—*my* Aspis—and you will be tested."

"How many of these aphids are out there?"

"Aspis, and you are the current holder of this position."

"Aspis, right," I said. "What happened to the previous holder?"

"There can only be one living Aspis at any one time," Kali said. "Even though you step slightly outside the norm due to my curse, you are technically...living. The previous Aspis departed your plane long ago."

"Oh, I was hoping there was some kind of Aspis Club."

"For camaraderie?"

"I just don't like being the *only* Aspis target."

She smiled again. This time I was ready and looked away early.

"You are not alone," she said. "You have your bond-mate, your vampire, and your mage friend, whom you managed to assist through his ordeal."

"Does that mean he's over this darkness thing?"

"Do you know who I am?"

This had to be a trick question. I opted to answer on the side of survivability.

"Kali, the goddess of destruction?" I answered tentatively. "Is there another Kali I don't know about?"

"Yes, everyone focuses on that part of my aspect, and I must confess I have allowed them to. Being known as the goddess of destruction makes life easier overall."

"Must make it tough in the 'friends coming over to hang out' department."

She gave me a look and smiled.

"You are a peculiar person, Simon Strong, but you are

right," she said. "I do not have friends. I have peers and enemies."

"I'm guessing they're usually the same person most of the time."

She nodded.

"Aside from being the goddess of destruction, I am also a goddess of creation," she answered slowly. "Life and death, destruction and creation, are two sides, inextricably linked."

Elton John's "Circle of Life" blasted in my brain.

If I kept this up, I was going to get myself killed. I got a grip, booted Elton from my brain, and calmed myself. On some level, I understood what she was saying.

"Monty's not over this darkness thing, is he?"

"Nor will he ever be," Kali said, standing. "We all possess dual natures. I can no more be all creation, than I can be all destruction."

"But you seem to favor destruction, or at least that's my impression."

"Do you recall the first time you met me?"

She gazed at me. It was a soft gaze, but it felt like she was looking through me. I was exposed, raw, and vulnerable. Nothing was hidden from that gaze. It was the look a parent gave their child, knowing what the child had done wrong, but asking anyway.

"Do I have to?" I said as she furrowed her brow at me. I realized my typical answers could get me atomized. I quickly reversed course. "Yes, I do. You were saving children. Monty and I thought you were harming them. Turns out we were wrong."

"Then you interfered, and I not only left you alive, but cursed you so."

"Why?" I asked. "Why didn't you just blast me there? That would've been easier for you...and me."

"You resort to violence too easily," Kali said, as the braid of hair wrapped itself around her waist. "Destruction is easy; creation, building when you want to tear down, that is truly difficult."

"Only the strong, can be gentle?" I asked.

"Only the powerful, understand weakness."

"You cursed me as an expression of creation?"

"You're getting there," she said. "Let's just say you've been weak. Now it is time to gain strength. You have much to protect, shield-warrior."

"Thank you," I said. "My life has become exponentially harder, but I have to say it's better."

"You're welcome," she said. "The day will come when you will curse my name, but that is expected. For now, stand in the gap for those near you. One day, you will need to choose between creation and destruction."

Her skin started glowing a deep blue.

"I don't mean to be rude," I said, pointing at her, "but your glow is showing."

She smiled, stepped close to me and gently slapped my face nearly breaking my jaw.

"Your mouth is going to get you killed one day, Aspis," she said. "I will make sure I will be there to witness it when it happens. It's time for you and your bondmate to go."

"I have questions."

"I'm sure you do. What you lack is the capacity for understanding the answers," Kali answered. "Goodbye, Aspis. We will speak again...in time."

The glow of her skin intensified until it blinded me, forcing me to look away.

When I could see again, she was gone.

THIRTY-SIX

I looked around and rubbed my tender jaw. The mandir was empty. Judging from the light pouring in through the skylight, it was early morning.

I looked down at my completely satiated hellhound. He lay on his side, looking like an industrial-sized hell-hound sausage.

"You keep eating like that and you won't fit into the Dark Goat."

He chuffed and gave me a low rumble.

<I can't move. That was some of the best meat I've ever tasted.>

"Don't let Ezra hear you say that," I said, leaving the inner mandir area. "Come on."

<I'm on my way. I almost feel full.>

"I can't believe Kali," I said, looking around and raising my voice. "She's this badass goddess and leaves us stranded in Jersey, of all places. At the very least leave us in the city. This is not a badass move." I glanced down at Peaches. "You think you can blink us home?"

<*No. My stomach is too heavy right now.*>

"Are you saying—I can't believe *I'm* saying this—that you ate too much?"

<*Impossible. There's no such thing. I'm a growing hellhound. I just need some time before taking us home, and maybe a nap.*>

"Fine, let's catch the sunrise," I said. "Then we can find someplace quiet for you to recover from your recent meat-a-thon."

<*That would be nice.*>

I waited by the exit for Peaches to slowly join me.

We walked outside, and there, sitting menacingly in the empty parking lot, I saw the Dark Goat.

"I stand corrected; Kali retains her badass status by delivering my sweet ride for the win."

I placed my hand on the hood, and the Dark Goat clanged unlocked. It rocked to one side as I opened the suicide door and Peaches jumped in. I slid in behind the wheel, feeling the familiar tingle of lethality on my skin. The Dark Goat.

I loved this car.

My phone rang a few minutes later.

It was LD.

"Haven, now."

He hung up.

The urgency in his voice left no room for questions. I stepped on the gas and unleashed the Dark Goat.

THIRTY-SEVEN

The skywalk at Haven was still being repaired when I arrived.

I parked the Dark Goat in front of the building, and raced inside as fast as my still-aching body allowed. Peaches must have digested some of the sausage, since he kept pace with me.

LD was waiting for me at the elevators. He rubbed Peaches' head when we stepped into the lobby.

"What happened?" I asked. "Where's Monty?"

"Slow down," LD said. "Tristan is...well, right now he is under observation."

"Under observation?" I asked, confused. "I just left him a little while ago."

"A little while ago?" LD said, looking at me strangely. "They got back from the Sanctuary last night. We were about to go searching for you, when I sensed your energy signature. What were you doing in Jersey?"

"Last night?" I asked, confused. "What are you talking

about? I just left the Sanctuary not more than twenty minutes ago."

"If you keep talking like that, Roxanne will admit you and put you under observation, too," LD said, keeping his voice low. "You don't want to speak to her right now. She's biting everyone's head off."

"How's Monty?"

"Not in a schism," LD said, leading me away from the elevators and heading into the stairwell. "He came to in Fordey, and then vanished."

"Vanished? In Fordey? I thought you were watching him?"

LD just looked at me and waited for me to get a grip.

"Sorry, I'm not accusing you," I said, raising a hand. "It's just that..."

"Surprised the hell out of me, too," LD said, shaking his head. "He shouldn't have been able to pull off a teleport. Not from within Fordey, not in his condition, but he is Dex's nephew. I should've been more careful."

"He saved my ass."

"I hear it's the other way around," LD said. "You released a runic nova?"

"Not on purpose," I said defensively, "Monty was in trouble, and I was done. Evers would have killed us all. It was about as last resort as you could get."

"You obliterated the entire Sanctuary complex...all of it," LD said with a hint of pride. "I thought you said Tristan was the destructive one?"

"Is Dex pissed?" I asked. "I mean, the Golden Circle is gone."

"The artifacts were all stored safely after Connor died," LD said. "Between you and me, I think Dex is relieved. He never wanted to run a sect. I think he's going to start a school."

The door to the stairwell opened and Dex walked in.

"Your lass is asking for you," Dex said. "Apparently my nephew created an irregularity at Fordey in his hurry to escape?"

"That's my cue," LD said. "Come by Fordey when you can. I think I have some things that can assist you."

"I will," I said. "Thank you. Please let TK know..."

"Family. That's what we do, hombre," LD said, casting a gray circle around him. "I'll let TK know you're still kicking. See you soon."

LD nodded to Dex and vanished.

Dex turned without saying a word and climbed the stairs. He reached the next level and paused before the door.

"Ach, are you just going to admire me from down there?" he asked. "Come on, boy."

Peaches bounded up the stairs. I followed, just not as energetically. How he managed to move so fast after ingesting a cow's worth of sausage, was astounding.

Dex grabbed the handle and whispered something under his breath. Green light raced along the frame of the door. He opened the door which led to a small stone path sitting in a grassy area.

It was Central Park, but not the one I was familiar with.

"Where are we?" I asked as I followed him in. "This looks like Central Park, but I don't remember the two suns. Is this Tatooine?"

"Don't be daft," Dex said, walking over to a small bench. "This is Central Park, just not your Central Park. I didn't want Roxanne to find us in a stairwell—she's on a tear."

I looked around. Aside from the extra light and double shadows, I could easily confuse this place for my city. There was an engraved stone bench surrounded by a small grove of five trees. The bench radiated power. Behind me, the door remained, standing free in the middle of the grass.

"Does this place exist in my park?"

"This here is Green Hill," Dex said, sitting on the bench. The runes in the stone shone a little brighter for a few seconds, then dimmed. "It's named after Andrew Haswell Green. On your plane, he is somewhat obscure, but influential in the formation of the city. On this plane, he is venerated. Each tree symbolizes a discipline he founded. Have a seat."

I sat on the bench, but the runes remained dormant. I guess I wasn't quite at the power level where objects would react to my presence.

"Is Monty okay?" I asked, sliding to the other end of the bench. Peaches plopped down on the grass with a contented rumble. "LD was light on specifics. Just that he's 'under observation,' whatever that means."

"You destroyed the Sanctuary," Dex started. As I prepared for another thrashing, he continued, "But you saved my nephew. For that, I am in your debt."

"It wasn't intentional," I said. "Evers was going to end us."

"You didn't intend to save Tristan?"

"The Sanctuary...I meant the Sanctuary," I said quickly. "I didn't mean to destroy it."

"Aye, it needed a renovation in any case," Dex said. "You and my nephew just sped up the process."

"What about Talin?" I asked. "I know Evers is gone. I saw TK, but no Talin."

"You just answered your question, boy."

"Talin managed to survive facing Scary Grey," I said. "He was beyond dangerous."

"Not to her."

"Remind me to never piss TK off."

Dex nodded.

"The Black Orchid has placed you on their watch list," Dex said with a chuckle. "Mr. 'I'm not a mage' is now on a dangerous mage watch list."

"Wait, what?" I asked, concerned. "How is that funny? This is serious."

"It is," Dex said with a wicked smile. "I explained how seriously Kali would react if she happened to discover Black Orchid agents trying to apprehend you. The Marked of Kali."

"Wonderful," I said. "Can you speak to them about Jessikah?"

"It's been done," Dex said. "They won't accept her. Seems to be some bad blood there, but they will leave her be. I explained how distressed I'd become if I found out different."

I was glad to hear Jessikah would be left alone by the Black Orchid. She was still pretty clueless about life outside the sect. The last thing she needed was a group of BO agents hunting her down while she got her bearings.

"You realize the threat is just going to make them act 'unofficially' against me."

"Yes, but it will give you some breathing room," Dex

said, looking off to the side. "At least for a short time. Enough time to get you ready, I think."

"What will you do now?" I asked. "Move in with the Morrigan?"

"Are you insane? No man on this earth can handle that much Morrigan at once. I am, of course, a superb specimen of manliness, but even I'm not *that* insane."

"Don't forget modest."

"Aye, and humble," he said with another smile. "No, I think what I'll focus on is preparing the next generation of mages. With the Golden Circle gone, there will be a lack of battlemages. Truth be told, we haven't taught battlemages in over a century. I think we need fresh blood."

"LD was right?" I asked. "You're going to open a school?"

Dex nodded.

"A school of battle magic, aye," Dex said. "It's past time we had one."

"Can I feel sorry for the students now?"

"Aye," he said. "The training will be brutal, as it should be."

He narrowed his eyes at me.

"You've grown, boy," Dex said. "But you still have a long road ahead. The enemies that will face you now... You must prepare."

We sat in a comfortable silence for close to half a minute.

"How bad is it?" I asked finally. "Will he still be Monty?"

"Yes, I think so—thanks to you—but a schism leaves a scar, always," Dex said with a nod. "His sorceress won't release him until she is absolutely certain he can cast without danger."

"I don't think he's going to argue with Roxanne," I said with a smile of my own. "Not if he ever wants to leave Haven."

"He will try, and he will fail," Dex said. "It will be good for him."

"I overheard Evers mention she wanted to take you out, too," I said tentatively. "Why does she hate you?"

"She only hated me by extension," Dex said. "She wanted Tristan dead. Ask him when he's well. I'm certain he will tell you. He owes you that much. It's his story to tell, not mine."

"That's what TK said."

"She was right to do so," Dex said. "If I were you, I'd catch up on much-needed shuteye. This all feels like the lull before a storm. Best to snatch it when you can."

"Evers said something about...dragons."

"Aye," Dex said, his expression hard. "Enemies are moving. Powerful and old."

"Are you going to swing by the office?"

"Not for a spell," Dex said. "We'll speak soon, and I'll make sure Yat pays you a visit."

I winced.

"Does he have to?" I asked. "He can just email. I'd be okay with that."

"Evers cut you plenty," Dex said, looking at my scars. "More than she should have. You need more training... more Yat."

"More pain and more agony," I said. "Thanks."

"You're welcome," Dex said. "Visit Tristan in a few

days. By then, his lass should've calmed down enough to allow visitors."

"You think?"

"I'd call first, just to be safe," Dex said. "She barely let me in."

I stood and stretched out my sore parts. They were diminishing, but I wondered why I still felt sore. Normally, my curse would remove all traces of pain. I made a mental note to avoid all kamikiras in the future.

Dex gestured and another door formed on the opposite side of the bench.

"Where does that lead?"

"For you, home," Dex said, standing. "Take it and get your rest."

"You know what I'm going to do?" I said, heading for the new door. "I'm going to sleep for about a week. Then I'm going on a staycation away from anything runically enhanced."

"Aye," Dex said, stretching out on the bench, before standing and stepping to the first door we used. "Sounds like a grand fantasy. Enjoy it while it lasts. I'll be returning to Haven for the next few days."

I opened the door, and Peaches nudged me in the leg... an actual, gentle nudge which didn't dislocate my hip.

<*We can go to the place later. Can we go home now?*>

<*That's the plan, boy. Let's go.*>

We stepped through the door and into the familiarity of the Moscow.

THIRTY-EIGHT

ONE DAY LATER

I stepped into the temporary NYTF HQ.

It was a squat, nondescript building, located downtown near the recent crater created by Chi and Grey. I walked past reception and headed up the stairs to the office at the rear of the floor.

I knocked on the door out of courtesy, not formality. Ramirez and I went way back. He called me in, and I sat in the oversized chair opposite his desk. Peaches rumbled and *thumped* to the ground near my feet.

Most of the furniture in the office looked straight out of the about-to-fall-apart discount store.

"Did you feed your animal?" Ramirez asked as I looked around.

"He's good," I said, rubbing my hellhound's head. "He ate about an hour ago."

"Just making sure," Ramirez said. "Last thing I need is your "dog" chewing up my officers."

"Well, he could always use a snack. Is anyone on your staff getting on your nerves?"

"Not funny," Ramirez said, looking past me. "They're out there soiling their underwear because of him."

I turned to see some of the NYTF staff quickly leaving the office.

"Wow, when the NYTF says temporary, they aren't joking," I said, looking around again. "Where did you find this stuff? In the city dump?"

"Hilarious as a heart attack," Ramirez answered. "I got a call."

"Congratulations? Sounds impressive," I said. Ramirez wasn't smiling. "Don't tell me you just upgraded to a new cell? I told you it was about time you got rid of that old flip-phone."

"You know, most of the time, you being a smartass is an effective shield," Ramirez said. "I chalk it up to you being scared or nervous—which is understandable, considering some of the things you and the mage have faced."

"Most of the time?" I asked. "What about the other times?"

"Your idea of humor can be just like you."

"Suave and charming?"

"A royal pain in my ass. This call I received—"

"We didn't blow up or destroy it, whatever it was."

"You're right," he said with a nod. "It wasn't a call about your hobby of destruction."

"I'm right? I mean, yes, I'm right."

"Do you recall a group by the name of Shadow Company? Crazy black ops stuff?"

It took conscious effort to keep my face impassive.

"Never heard of them," I lied. "I thought that was the stuff of myth."

"You know that's surprising, because I spoke to one of those myths today," Ramirez answered. "A certain Peter 'Pitbull' Douglas. He has clearance so high up on the food chain it gave me a nose bleed."

"I don't see how this has anything to do with—"

"I'm getting to that," Ramirez said. "See, this 'myth,' this Douglas, sure knows you. He says you were an operator with the Shadows. Imagine that."

"He must have me confused with someone else," I said, keeping my voice even. "Shadow Company is a myth. Someone is pranking you."

Pitbull Douglas and George 'Rottweiler' Rott were better known as the Mad Dogs of Shadow Company. It was a memory best left buried.

"Myth?" Ramirez continued, snapping me out of my thoughts. "Apparently not. I've been doing some digging."

"Don't."

"Don't what?"

"Don't do any digging into this, Angel. I'm serious."

"I noticed. I thought it was a myth?"

"Considering my life as of late," I said, rubbing a temple, "I've learned some myths are best left alone."

"You know him...this Pitbull Douglas."

"I know of him," I said, trying to maintain some distance. "Shadow Company doesn't officially exist for a reason."

"He asked for you by name, Strong. Why would he do that?"

"I don't know."

To show me he could reach out and find me...if he wanted to.

"He left a number and said you should call him within the hour. That it's urgent."

It was always urgent at the Shadow Company.

Ramirez handed me a slip of paper. I looked down at the unfamiliar number and memorized it. It was almost certainly untraceable. In an hour, the number would become inactive, rendered useless.

"Did he say anything else?"

"He said they're on the hunt and need your special skill," Ramirez answered. "What special skill do you have? Annoying the hell out of people? Advanced smartassery?"

"Those are gifts, by the way," I said with a tight smile. "I don't have any skills aside from those."

"Bullshit. I managed to unseal some of your records."

"Angel, you're stepping into a minefield way above your pay grade."

"I know," Ramirez answered with a lopsided grin. "It's pissing off all sorts of people, especially the brass."

"I know you're the Director now..."

"Which means I have clearance in the NYTF, but this took some favors, Strong."

"You're playing with fire while being doused in gasoline," I said, my voice a blade slicing through the air. "What else did you uncover?"

"You're a dead-eye?"

"I have good aim," I admitted. "Above average."

"Good, my ass. You were one of the best," Ramirez answered. "What happened?"

"I missed. Drop this, Angel."

"Consider it dropped," he said—a clear lie. "I won't push anymore."

"Do not 'uncover' anything else," I said. "For your safety, leave this alone."

"For my safety?"

"These people don't believe in loose ends. Do you understand? This is not the NYTF."

"Are you in trouble?" Angel asked, concerned. "If you need help..."

"No," I said with finality. "Not with this, not ever."

I left the NYTF HQ and stood outside the building. There was no way this could be a coincidence. I learned early on in my life, that no such thing existed. I scanned the street and headed uptown to the Moscow with Peaches by my side.

<*Can we go the place?*>

<*We need to go see Monty first.*>

<*Then we can get meat?*>

<*Yes, try not to smile at anyone on the way there.*>

<*You said I should be more friendly.*>

<*If you smile you'll scare everyone. Don't smile.*>

Peaches chuffed and gave off a low rumble, forcing some pedestrians to cross the street. I smiled in spite of myself, before my thoughts turned to Ramirez's words.

There was only one thing Shadow Company would need me for. Either Pitbull was offering me a chance at redemption, or he wanted one last opportunity to end me himself. Word was, after Cassandra, the only thing Shadow Company "hunted" these days—which was just another way of saying "exterminated"—were lethal creatures capable of destroying you in a split second.

Ancient things, filled with magic, malice, and hatred.

A hatred so old it defied explanation or reason.

They were hunting dragons.

I needed to make a call.

THE END

AUTHOR NOTES

Thank you for reading this story and jumping back into the Monty & Strong World.

First off, I want to say THANK YOU.

Thank you for your patience in waiting for this book to be written. I know after DARK GLASS, there were rumors of hunting me down, and sharing the PAIN. You were able to ride the tsunami waves of that ending into this story. I truly hope WALKING THE RAZOR was worth the wait. I had a great time writing it. I hope you'll have a great time reading it.

If DARK GLASS was us reaching the the first crest of the rollercoaster, WALKING THE RAZOR is us, on top of that crest, just before the drop, when you get those butterflies in your stomach and you can see out over the park. That moment when you realize just how high up you are, and if you could, you would get off. We're about to head into the drop, and I promise, you need to strap in.

We explored some interesting themes in this story, most important was family. Simon is growing, as is Monty.

That growth will come with pain, danger, and laughter. Very much like what we all have to go through. In order for us to grow, we must reconcile with our past, which is what the next story, REQUIEM will deal with.

In it, we get to see where Simon comes from, at least some of his past. Most of it is redacted. He will realize, like Monty, that no matter how fast you run, there are times your past will catch up to you, and force you to confront certain issues.

That is also a very relevant theme with Jessikah (I can hear the cringe from here) who has to outgrow her past and indoctrination. It won't be easy for her. Her future is a road paved with pain, LARGE doses of pain. Both physical and psychological, but she will learn and grow. On occasion she will make appearances in the main storyline, but she will eventually have her own series, she just needs to have some enlightening moments with Master Yat, first.

The actions Evers set in motion will now take on a life of their own. She may be gone, but what she did will have repercussions in the next books. I look forward to sharing more of that, as the M&S World gears up for what's coming.

Since I get many questions after each book let me try and address some of them here:

Yes, Dex will be starting a school called the Montague School of Battlemagic. It will eventually be his own series. I can't say more on it, because...spoilers.

There are more Night Warden books coming. I really enjoy writing Grey, Koda and his part of the M&S World. He has had appearances in the last few books, but it's time we dive back into what's going on with him, Koda, Izanami, and Frank. I can't wait.

The next series I'm focusing on is SEPIA BLUE and the next book for her is NAMELESS. If you haven't read her stories, please pick up RISE OF THE NIGHT. It's one of the first stories I wrote, and as I read it, I have my moments of wanting to edit and revise(I haven't been in Sepia's world in over four years), but overall, I'm really proud of those books. There would be no M&S without a Sepia Blue.

Everything happens for a reason.

In each story I have the privilege of writing, I try to reveal more about the character backgrounds and lives. This time, even though we touched on Monty's past, our next direction is Simon's life. This will definitely create more questions than answers. The answers will arrive slowly over the next ten books. Its a long ride, but I promise I will get to all of the questions...eventually.

Thank you again for taking the time to read this story and your incredible patience. I wrote it for you and I hope you enjoyed spending some time with Simon as he unraveled Monty's situation, and did his best to be a good friend and brother to the angry mage, while being a worthy bondmate to his ever-ravenous hellhound, Peaches—who we all love.

If you enjoyed this story—please leave a review. It's really important and helps the book (and me).

Thank you again for jumping into this adventure with me!

SPECIAL MENTIONS

Dolly Sanchez: for magealphabet, because Mages need to spell, too.

Reyhan Sanchez: For being an amazing first and fervent reader of all my stories. Your question of "When in the next book coming out?" followed by that great smile, inspires me to keep creating.

Zoya Sanchez, Official MoB TV greeter and closer: For "I don't want to kill you, I'm inviting you to death." This was truly an inspired line of dialogue, little Valkyrie. Thank you, Z.

Larry & Tammy—The WOUF: Because even when you aren't there...you're there.

Larry & Tammy: Because if Karma is going to have an animal companion, it should be large and named Justice.

Larry: One should never be a self-entitled rectal nugget...ever.

Steffon Carlson: for Sid Rat's time focal Patek Philippe.

Ayrton Noble: You are a special being in and out of this book. Also, everyone (yes, everyone) likes to go fast.

Craig 'The Dragon' Zimick: Because you can't spell DAMAGE without a Mage.

Malcolm Robertson: Because you should always fear an old man in a profession where people die young.

Orlando A. Sanchez
www.orlandoasanchez.com

Orlando has been writing ever since his teens when he was immersed in creating scenarios for playing Dungeons and Dragons with his friends every weekend.

The worlds of his books are urban settings with a twist of the paranormal lurking just behind the scenes and with generous doses of magic, martial arts, and mayhem.

He currently resides in Queens, NY with his wife and children.

BITTEN PEACHES PUBLISHING

Thanks for Reading

If you enjoyed this book, would you please **leave a review** at the site you purchased it from? It doesn't have to be long... just a line or two would be fantastic and it would really help me out.

Bitten Peaches Publishing offers more books by this author. From science fiction & fantasy to adventure & mystery, we bring the best stories for adults and kids alike.

www.BittenPeachesPublishing.com

More books by Orlando A. Sanchez

The Warriors of the Way

The Karashihan*•The Spiritual Warriors•The Ascendants•The Fallen Warrior•The Warrior Ascendant•The Master Warrior

John Kane

The Deepest Cut*•Blur

Sepia Blue

The Last Dance*•Rise of the Night•Sisters•Nightmare

Chronicles of the Modern Mystics

The Dark Flame•A Dream of Ashes

Montague & Strong Detective Agency Novels

Tombyards & Butterflies•Full Moon Howl•Blood is Thicker•Silver Clouds Dirty Sky•Homecoming•Dragons & Demigods•Bullets & Blades•Hell Hath No Fury•Reaping Wind•The Golem•Dark Glass•Walking the Razor

Montague & Strong Detective Agency Stories

No God is Safe•The Date•The War Mage•A Proper Hellhound•The Perfect Cup•Saving Mr. K

Brew & Chew Adventures

Hellhound Blues

Night Warden Novels

Wander•ShadowStrut

Division 13

The Operative•The Magekiller

Blackjack Chronicles

The Dread Warlock

The Assassin's Apprentice

The Birth of Death

Gideon Shepherd Thrillers

Sheepdog

DAMNED

Aftermath

RULE OF THE COUNCIL

Blood Ascension•Blood Betrayal•Blood Rule

*Books denoted with an asterisk are **FREE** via my website—www.orlandoasanchez.com

ACKNOWLEDEGEMENTS

With each book, I realize that every time I learn something about this craft, it highlights so many things I still have to learn. Each book, each creative expression, has a large group of people behind it.

This book is no different.

Even though you see one name on the cover, it is with the knowledge that I am standing on the shoulders of the literary giants that informed my youth, and am supported by my generous readers who give of their time to jump into the adventures of my overactive imagination.

I would like to take a moment to express my most sincere thanks:

To Dolly: My wife and greatest support. You make all this possible each and every day. You keep me grounded when I get lost in the forest of ideas. Thank you for asking the right questions when needed, and listening intently when I go off on tangents. Thank you for who you are and the space you create—I love you.

To my Tribe: You are the reason I have stories to tell. You cannot possibly fathom how much and how deeply I love you all.

To Lee: Because you were the first audience I ever had. I love you, sis.

To the Logsdon Family: The words *thank you* are insufficient to describe the gratitude in my heart for each of you. JL, your support always demands I bring my best, my A-game, and produce the best story I can. Both you and Lorelei (my Uber Jeditor) and now, Audrey, are the reason I am where I am today. My thank you for the notes, challenges, corrections, advice, and laughter. Your patience is truly infinite. *Arigatogozaimasu.*

To The Montague & Strong Case Files Group—AKA The MoB (Mages of Badassery): When I wrote T&B there were fifty-five members in The MoB. As of this release, there are over one thousand three hundred members in the MoB. I am honored to be able to call you my MoB Family. Thank you for being part of this group and M&S.

You make this possible. **THANK YOU.**

To the ever-vigilant PACK: You help make the MoB... the MoB. Keeping it a safe place for us to share and just...

be. Thank you for your selfless vigilance. You truly are the Sentries of Sanity.

Chris Christman II: A real-life technomancer who makes the **MoBTV LIVEvents +Kaffeeklatsch** on YouTube amazing. Thank you for your tireless work and wisdom. Everything is connected...you totally rock!

To the WTA—The Incorrigibles: JL, Ben Z. Eric QK., S.S., and Noah.

They sound like a bunch of badass misfits, because they are. My exposure to the deranged and deviant brain trust you all represent helped me be the author I am today. I have officially gone to the *dark side* thanks to all of you. I humbly give you my thanks, and...it's all your fault.

To my fellow Indie Authors, specifically the tribe at 20books to 50k: Thank you for creating a space where authors can feel listened to, and encouraged to continue on this path. A rising tide lifts all the ships indeed.

To The English Advisory: Aaron, Penny, Carrie, Davina, and all of the UK MoB. For all things English...thank you.

To DEATH WISH COFFEE: This book (and every book I write) has been fueled by generous amounts of the only coffee on the planet (and in space) strong enough to power my very twisted imagination. Is there any other coffee that can compare? I think not. DEATHWISH —thank you!

To Deranged Doctor Design: Kim, Darja, Tanja, Jovana, and Milo (Designer Extraordinaire).

If you've seen the covers of my books and been amazed, you can thank the very talented and gifted creative team at DDD. They take the rough ideas I give them, and produce incredible covers that continue to surprise and amaze me. Each time, I find myself striving to write a story worthy of the covers they produce. DDD, you embody professionalism and creativity. Thank you for the great service and spectacular covers. **YOU GUYS RULE!**

To you, the reader: I was always taught to save the best for last. I write these stories for **you**. Thank you for jumping down the rabbit holes of ***what if?*** with me. You are the reason I write the stories I do.

You keep reading...I'll keep writing.

Thank you for your support and encouragement.

CONTACT ME

I really do appreciate your feedback. You can let me know what you thought of the story by emailing me at:
orlando@orlandoasanchez.com

To get **FREE** stories please visit my page at:
www.orlandoasanchez.com

For more information on the M&S World...come join the MoB Family on Facebook!
You can find us at:
Montague & Strong Case Files

Visit our online M&S World Swag Store located at:
Emandes

If you enjoyed the book, **please leave a review**. Reviews help the book, and also help other readers find good stories to read.

THANK YOU!

ART SHREDDERS

I want to take a moment to extend a special thanks to the ART SHREDDERS.

No book is the work of one person. I am fortunate enough to have an amazing team of advance readers and shredders.

Thank you for giving of your time and keen eyes to provide notes, insights, answers to the questions, and corrections (dealing wonderfully with my extreme dreaded comma allergy). You help make every book and story go from good to great. Each and every one of you helped make this book fantastic, and I couldn't do this without each of you.

THANK YOU

ART SHREDDERS

Amber, Anne Morando, Audra Vroman Meyers, Audrey Cienki

Bethany Showell, Beverly Collie

Cam Skaggs, Carrie Anne O'Leary, Cat, Chris Christman II, Colleen Taylor, Corinne Loder

Daniel Parr, Darren Musson, Davina 'the Tao of the Comma' Noble, Dawn McQueen Mortimer, Denise King, Diana Gray, Diane Craig, Diane Kassmann, Dolly Sanchez, Donna Young Hatridge, Douglas Dix

Hal Bass

Jasmine Breeden, Jeanette Auer, Jen Cooper, Joy Kiili, Joy Ollier, Julie Peckett

Karen Hollyhead

Larry Diaz Tushman, Laura Tallman I, Leslie Watts, Luann Zipp

Malcolm Robertson, Marcia Campbell, Mary Anne Petruska, Maryelaine Eckerle-Foster, Melissa Miller

Paige Guido, Pat (the silly sister), Peggy Benson

RC Battels, Rene Corrie

Sara Mason Branson, Sean Trout, Shannon Owens Bainbridge, Sondra Massey, Stacey Stein, Stephanie Claypoole, Stephen Bassett, Susan Brouillette, Susie Johnson

Tami Cowles, Tanya Anderson, Ted Camer, Terri Adkisson, Tina Jonhson, Tommy Owens

Vikki Brannagan

Wanda Corder-Jones, Wendy Schindler

Thanks for Reading

If you enjoyed this book, would you **please leave a review** at the site you purchased it from? It doesn't have to be a book report...just a line or two would be fantastic and it would really help us out!

Made in the USA
Middletown, DE
07 January 2021